Revealing

you

OTHER BOOKS BY S.T. HELLER

THE DOCK SERIES

Enduring You

Revealing You

Regarding You (Coming 2018)

WWW.SHELLERAUTHOR.COM

Revealing *you*

S.T. Heller

ISBN-13: 978-0-9972630-3-9

Dedicated to the loves of my life—
my family.

Prologue

The Past
Eighteen Years Ago
Jack

All I can think of during my drive home after finishing my twenty-four-hour shift this morning at the fire station are my bed and girl, Chelsey, which are both waiting for me at my condo. I'm tired, and my body aches from working a multiple-alarm warehouse fire all night. Although I took a quick shower when we returned to the station a couple of hours ago, a lingering trace of smoke from the night still hangs on me. Another long, hot shower with Chelsey is what I need before hopping into bed with her.

Inseparable since the day we met during our last semester at the local community college, Chelsey and I moved in together after graduation. Neither of us had any problems landing jobs in the county's fire service—me, as a firefighter, and Chelsey, as a paramedic. The only problem is, our new careers have us working at different stations on opposing twenty-four-hour shifts. Our new routine of passing each other, coming and going to work with only a moment for a quick kiss, has put a strain on our relationship. We continue to keep an eye out for opportunities for one of us to transfer to another shift within our stations to give us more time together.

Today is one of those rare times when we're both off because of our coinciding two-day breaks with Chelsey's starting yesterday and mine this morning. My plan is to spend as much of it as possible in bed, making up for lost time with her.

I notice an eerie stillness when I enter the condo. Something seems off as I walk into the living room to go back to the bedroom. As I enter our bedroom, I pull my uniform shirt out of my pants, expecting to find Chelsey curled up under the covers, waiting for me. I am surprised to find the bed not only empty, but also made.

Someone must have called in sick, so she went in to cover the shift and to earn a little overtime. But she always texts me when this happens.

I pull out my phone to double check if I recently missed any messages, but none are there.

I check the bathroom, only to find it as empty as the bedroom. It's then I notice the sparkling clean vanity counter. Chelsey's stuff is always strewed all over the place, and this morning, there's nothing. An uneasiness settles in the pit of my stomach as I start to tour the condo.

It's then I discover that Chelsey's clothes from our closet are gone. Her favorite quilt, gone. Her photos of us, gone. A cherished wooden rocker from the living room, gone.

No warning.

No discussion.

No note.

Nothing.

I waste no time in calling her.

"Hi, Jack. I've been expecting your call."

I can hear in her voice that she's upset.

I speak in a measured, low tone, trying hard not to lose it, "What's going on, Chelsey? Where in the hell are you?"

"I need some space to figure out what I want."

"What? What do you mean, space? Is there someone else?"

"No, there's no one else. I'm staying at my parents' until I can find a place of my own."

"A place of your own? What do you mean? You have a place here with me, damn it!" Anger slowly seeps into the forced calm of my voice.

Chelsey begins to cry as she begs, "Jack, please don't do this. Just let me go."

"Let you go? What the hell is going on? Is this about us getting married? Damn it! I'll marry you if that's what you want. I love you, Chelsey. Please don't leave me!" My emotions take over, and I'm soon in tears, pleading for her to come home.

Chelsey is also crying, and between her sobs, she says, "Jack, it's over. I'm not coming back. Good-bye."

She hangs up, ending both the call and us.

Nine Years Later
Keegan

I walk into the bedroom and hear Alex singing in the shower. I laugh out loud because he is belting out a song that he doesn't know all the lyrics to, replacing them with words of his own.

At times, it's hard to accept that, at the ripe old age of thirty-one, I've been married, had a child, and gotten divorced, and now, I'm living with another man.

I married my college sweetheart, Will Henderson, right out of college after graduation, and we lived a charmed life in the suburbs of Maryland. Both Will and I were busy with our careers—he, as an investigator with the state police, and me, working up the financial corporate ladder. I gave birth to our son, Kyle, the following year after we married. I thought I was living the perfect life until it all fell apart. As in all divorces, there have been a few tumultuous moments, especially when I told Will I was moving in with Alex.

While separated from Will, I'd met Alex Parker during a function at work. Alex had been doing research for an article he was writing about the financial world. He'd told me once that my long auburn hair and sass were too much for him to resist. Our attraction had been undeniable with us falling head over heels in love with each other. Since Kyle was an impressionable eight-year-old, Alex and I'd decided not to move in together until my divorce was final.

Even after ten months of living with Alex, both my family and friends still have no problems with expressing their opinions on my current living arrangements. My parents question my moral turpitude for living with a man out of wedlock with their grandson. Ryan, my older brother, continues to claim the only reason I moved in with Alex was to get out of our parents' house. My two best friends since elementary school are unhappy with me. Marcy thinks I'm rushing too fast into another serious relationship, and to this day, Seth continues to preach about the virtues of playing the field.

I notice that Alex left his clothes lying in a crumpled heap on the floor before hopping into the shower. *Why is it so hard for him just to walk across the room and throw them in the hamper?*

While picking up after Alex, I see his cell phone on top of the dresser, buzzing with a message flashing across it. I take a look to see if it's the magazine, knowing he's been frantically writing to meet an upcoming deadline. I stand frozen, trying hard not to jump to the wrong conclusion from the message I'm reading.

Ashley: Hey, sweets. What time are we hooking up tonight? Call me.

Since their breakup, Ashley, Alex's ex-girlfriend, always finds reasons to contact him. If it's not to send messages on special occasions like his birthday, then it's to congratulate him on an article. Each contact causes me to question Alex, followed by him swearing that nothing is going on between them. This message seems to only give credence to my suspicions that past texts weren't as innocent as he argued.

I sit on the bed, holding his cell in my hand, with the foot of my crossed leg wiggling nervously in the air as I wait for him to finish in the bathroom.

Alex walks out with a towel hanging low on his hips, exposing not only his well-defined chest, but also that sexy V of his.

"Hey, hon. Why didn't you come in and join me?" he asks, smiling at me.

I toss his phone over at him, and his quick reflexes allow him to catch it.

"I thought you might want to save your energy for your hook-up with Ashley later tonight. She needs you to call her back." I get up and walk out of the room without saying another word.

Ten minutes later, Alex casually comes down the stairs, dressed in jeans and a black T, as if my confrontation with him upstairs never happened. He walks into the kitchen where I'm cleaning up from lunch and gets a bottled water from the fridge. I continue to go about my business while giving him the silent treatment.

"Come on, Ginger, it's not that kind of a hook-up." He tries to sweet-talk his way out of this by using his pet name for me, derived from my auburn hair color. "Ashley just wants to talk about something."

I turn to face him, crossing my arms. "So, call her back. Go ahead. I don't have a problem with you talking to her in front of me."

"Where's Kyle?" He asks, looking around, trying to change the subject.

"My parents picked him up while you were in the shower. I thought we could go out tonight, but I see you have other plans."

"Stop it, Ginger."

"Stop what? Calling you out on your bullshit? So, are you going to call her back?"

"No."

"Liar."

Alex pulls his keys out of his pocket. "I'm going for a drive to give you some time to cool off. We'll talk when I get back."

Knowing full well that he is leaving to call Ashley in private, I say to him, "Don't bother coming back. You two deserve each other."

My cell phone rings as he walks out the back door. I see Will's name flash across the screen. For the past few weeks, I've only been getting random texts from him about seeing Kyle, but he picks now to call.

My first thought is to ignore the call, but I decide to answer since Will only calls when it's necessary. "Yeah?"

My less than pleasant greeting causes Will to be suspicious, and he asks, "Everything okay?"

I choose to ignore his question. "What do you want, Will?"

"Is Kyle there?"

"No, he's over at my parents'."

"Keegan, what's wrong? I can hear it in your voice."

It's at that moment I can no longer control my emotions as they wash over me, and I tearfully answer, "I just caught Alex cheating on me."

"That son of a bitch! Are you by yourself?"

"Yeah."

"I'm coming over."

Before I can tell him not to, he disconnects.

In less than twenty minutes, Will is ringing the doorbell. I open the front door, and as soon as he enters, he takes me into a warm embrace.

"How are you holding up?"

"Okay. Terrible."

Once inside, he takes a seat at the kitchen island and asks, "What are you going to do?"

"I don't know. Find a place of my own?"

"Are you sure he's cheating?"

"All I know is, I don't trust him anymore. I can't live with someone I don't trust."

"What can I do to help?"

"Nothing. I've got this. You need to leave."

"Okay. Keep me posted."

I nod as he leaves.

Two weeks later, Kyle and I move out of the duplex and into a place of our own.

1

Present Day
Keegan

As my eyes slowly open, I'm facing an empty side of the bed with a sheet of paper lying on the pillow next to me. I pick it up and read it.

> *Good morning.*
>
> *I thought I'd take advantage of the great weather and go for a run. Hot coffee is waiting for you downstairs. I'll be back soon.*
>
> *Jack*

Smiling at the note, I lay it down beside me on the bed and then roll onto my back. I raise my arms in the air, stretching, as I yawn.

The diamond embedded in the middle of the Celtic love knot design of my engagement ring sparkles as the morning light peeking through the pulled drapes catches it. Every time I look at my ring, it takes me back to the day Jack proposed. Some might think my future husband's choice of a tattoo parlor a strange place to ask someone to get married but not me. He knew my history of getting inked there with Celtic symbols that symbolized the infinite love I had for my Irish ancestry.

A short time later, I'm in the shower with hot water cascading down my body as the steam from it fills the room.

I think back to the sweet note Jack left me this morning and realize how lucky I am to have found my way back to him. I begin to reflect on the past craziness that I call my life.

Psychologists would agree that my childhood spent in a traditional home with two loving parents and a brother on a lake in Maryland was the perfect environment to raise a child to be a responsible adult. Instead, I grew up to be an impetuous adolescent who never takes the time to think things through. I blame this character flaw on my father. Before his retirement in the fire department, he made a career out of running into burning buildings without giving a second thought to the possible danger.

Often, there is a price to pay for my recklessness, but my parents, Sandy and Mitch Fitzgerald, are there for my teenage son, Kyle, and me, no matter how bad things get.

My older brother, Ryan, is the quintessential example of the perfect son who has never given my parents a sleepless night. Growing up under Ryan's shadow of perfection was hard for me. I was determined to march to the beat of a different drummer and not follow in my brother's footsteps. Unfortunately, this mindset led me to marry and divorce my college sweetheart twice.

After our first divorce, Will was there for me following my breakup with Alex. Slowly, his time with Kyle usually turned into the three of us hanging out together, as if we never divorced. During that time, Will persuaded me that he was a changed man. He charmed me into remarrying him, only for us to divorce again in two short years.

I feel my face redden with embarrassment, thinking back on it. Sadly, I recognize that this is only the tip of the craziness of my past.

After the end of my second marriage to Will, I thought I had hit rock bottom when I moved back home to my parents' because of the threat of being laid off from a job I loved, and that eventually happened. I didn't think things could get worse until my car accident and the discovery of a benign brain tumor.

The only good that came out during that period of time in my life was that I met Jack Grady.

After I'd had a bad breakup with a guy named Cameron, Marcy had taken it upon herself to set up a page for me on a dating site. I had been furious with her until my eyes landed on a picture of Jack, who, according to his bio, was a career firefighter like my dad.

As I squirt shampoo in my hand and carefully start massaging it into my scalp, I vividly remember our first meeting at the coffee shop. Marcy was out of town, and she had arranged Seth to be there as my wingman in her absence. I can still see the expression on Jack's face when he saw Seth sitting there. I can remember *every* detail of that date, right down to our first kiss when he walked me to my car.

Our second date didn't quite go according to Jack's plan.

When I arrived at his house, his ex-girlfriend, Annie—whom he used to live with and who is also the mother of his son, Sean—answered the door for him. At first, I thought I had the wrong house. Jack quickly appeared to introduce Annie to me and give an explanation for her being there.

Although it was an uncomfortable first encounter with his ex, Jack has never hidden anything from me about his relationship with her and their shared custody of Sean. Ever since that morning, Annie tried her best to tear Jack and me apart. Annie almost succeeded once when she cruelly misled me to think that Jack had died in a fire instead of receiving only minor injuries. As corny as it might sound, our love along with the trust we had built between us got us through all of that nonsense with Annie.

As I tilt my head back to rinse the shampoo out of my hair, my thoughts skip to the night that ultimately changed my life forever. I was clueless when I saw the light at the end of the tunnel because it was actually an oncoming train traveling at warp speed.

I was on a picnic with Jack, celebrating my recovery from my car accident and the removal of my brain tumor. It was such a wonderful evening until Dad called with news that Will was taken to the Shock Trauma Center in Baltimore. By the time we got back to my parents', Dad had already received word that Will had died from a gunshot wound. We found out that he had been working undercover when a shooting occurred between him and a local drug dealer, Troy Martin, who died at the scene.

It was only six weeks after my surgery when this occurred, and I was still having problems with processing information. Although Will and I were divorced, we had developed a close friendship through the co-parenting of our son, Kyle. This devastating news set in motion a series of events that I was unable to handle.

After Will's funeral, I learned at the reading of the will that he had left the majority of his estate to Kyle and me. He'd also left two letters with his lawyer to give to me in the event of his death. In the letters, he confessed all the secrets and lies of his life along with an apology and declaration of love for me.

His death and letters were the proverbial straw that broke the camel's back, and they sent me spiraling down a dark hole. In a matter of days, my mental breakdown cost me everything, including Jack. My dad took me to a local psychiatric facility where I was admitted and spent almost three weeks. Feeling lost and disconnected, I didn't want Jack to feel obligated to stay. I ended it with him while I was in the hospital, leaving me to fight my way out of the darkness alone.

One of my saving graces during my hospitalization was talking with my therapist about opening up a pottery studio. Growing up, I had always dreamed of having a career in art. One of the few times that I'd chosen to think things through responsibly, I'd decided to pursue an MBA instead of an art degree because of the income potential. More simply put, I had done it out of greed. My thinking had seemed to be sound until the financial company I worked for as a manager decided to reorganize the corporate offices, leaving me unemployed.

One day, my therapist had asked, "If you could do anything in the world, what would it be?"

It was then that the idea of opening the pottery studio had emerged.

Once back on my feet, my inheritance from Will allowed me to open both a studio and a small shop selling art and furnishings. I hired Marcy to help me oversee the day-to-day operations of both businesses. I was also able to purchase a townhouse close to my shops and a weekend getaway home at a nearby lake in Pennsylvania.

For years, my hours were filled with getting the pieces of my life back together. Getting the studio and store operating in the black and setting up two homes for Kyle and me occupied all my time. I found out all too soon that the distractions I had created in my life could not protect me forever from the heartache of losing Jack.

In her job as an interior designer, Annie became a customer at my shop along with signing up for pottery classes at my studio on a regular basis. I always made myself scarce when she was around. One day, while working in the back room, I overheard her talking to a friend, saying that she was back with Jack. If that wasn't bad enough, she'd also found an engagement ring in the nightstand in his bedroom. Although I no longer had any claim to Jack, I was hurt and angered by this news. After all she had done to us while he and I were together, I couldn't understand how he could have gone back to her.

As fate would have it, around eight months ago, I ran into Jack by chance one evening at my favorite local Irish bar called Donnelly's. I stood there and lied through my teeth, telling him how great things were going for me.

Watching him leave the bar that night spurred me on to find out why he had gone back to Annie. I went to his townhouse and confronted him on his front doorstep, only to find that Annie was there, witnessing my meltdown firsthand. When I saw Annie standing behind Jack with her blouse half-unbuttoned and him shirtless, it no longer mattered why he had gone back to her. Immediately, I left for my house at the lake to nurse my broken heart.

Jack showed up on my doorstep the next day to set things straight with me.

Goose bumps spread over my body as I reach out to the faucet to increase the temperature of the water to warm me up as I think about that weekend at the lake. It was the start of our journey to where we are today, living together, engaged, and getting ready to run errands for our wedding this weekend.

As I rinse the body wash off me, I look at the matching Celtic love knot tattoo that Jack and I each got on our wrists the day he proposed to me. I trace the endless design of the tattoo with my finger, knowing in my heart that my upcoming marriage is not another hasty misstep in my life.

I look up into the water's spray beating down on me, as if trying to wash away the ugliness from my past and to keep only the good. But I know it is of no use. My past, both good and bad, is an indelible piece of who I am and who I will be until the day I take my last breath.

2

Jack

It's a crisp spring morning in May, perfect weather for an early run before the day becomes too hot. My feet hit the pavement in time to the beat of the music I'm listening to through my earbuds. The song's lyrics are a warning not to squander second chances at love. The artist could be singing about Keegan and me.

Each morning I wake up next to Keegan, I thank God for my second chance with her. The years we were apart were a living hell that I never want to go through again.

I'd thought I knew what hurt was when Chelsey left me without any explanation eighteen years ago. That pain pales in comparison to what I experienced the day I left the hospital after Keegan told me not to come back. She was the paradigm shift in my point of view that allowed me to fall in love and want to get married.

I planned on proposing to Keegan during a picnic I took her on to celebrate her release from her doctor's care. Just when I was beginning to propose, her father called with the news of Will's shooting. It was then that my life took a drastic change in a direction that I hadn't seen coming.

Witnessing Keegan's breakdown and not being able to comfort her tore me to shreds. I didn't see her for days after her admittance to a nearby psychiatric facility. When Keegan called, asking me to visit, I thought she was starting to get better. Instead, she ended it with me, causing me more pain than I could have ever imagined.

During that time apart from Keegan, I felt an awful emptiness with no sense of direction in my life. To take my mind off of her, I slipped into the old habit of spending my free time over at Annie's with Sean. It was understandable that Annie would mistake my actions as a sign of me wanting to get back together with her. Things between Annie and me got even more complicated the night we both got drunk, and we ended up sleeping together, which I regret doing to this day.

It took three long years for Keegan and me to find our way back to each other. The first time I saw her was the night my crew from the fire department took me out to celebrate my promotion to battalion chief. Listening to Keegan going about her great life pissed me off, and I couldn't get out of there fast enough. As I was leaving, Keegan came running out to apologize for the way she'd ended things with me when she was in the hospital. She had nothing else to offer, except for her pathetic apology. It was as if she had put the final nail in the coffin of our relationship.

Hurt and angry, I drove home, only to have Annie show up, looking hotter than hell. She started to seduce me the moment she stepped into my house with me being more than willing to oblige. Luckily, before things got too far along, we were interrupted by Keegan's persistent ringing of the doorbell. There I stood, shirtless, in the doorway with Keegan on my front step, unleashing years of pent-up anger, when Annie decided to make her presence known. After taking one look at Annie, Keegan stopped her rant and left.

As I watched Keegan walk away that night, I couldn't believe I was losing her again. The next day, with the help of Mitch Fitzgerald and Marcy, I tracked down Keegan at her lake house, determined to get her back.

After we spent the weekend making up for lost time, I got a ring on her finger, and we started planning a small wedding on her parents' dock.

The dock has become a special place for us. It's there where Keegan often goes to sort out her thoughts when life gets complicated. I remember our first fight and finding her there, smoking a cigarette. It was then I told her to come to me when she was stressed instead of lighting up a cigarette. That was when our catch phrase of, *I need a cigarette break*, became code for us needing to take a time-out.

I slow my jogging until I'm walking to cool down as I round the corner of our street. Drenched in sweat, I head inside to take a quick shower.

I enter our master bath and see the silhouette of Keegan's body through the steamed glass shower door.

God, she's beautiful.

I waste no time in stripping out of my clothes to join her. As I open the door to the shower, she turns toward me and watches me enter.

At first, Keegan is quiet as she pulls me under the spray with her.

She wraps her arms around me and says, "I missed you this morning. Please make love to me."

Without hesitation, I respond back to her, "Yes, ma'am."

3

Keegan

While Jack and I catch our breaths from making love, we continue to hold on to each other as my legs slowly slide down from around him until reaching the tiled shower floor. My head rests against his chest as the water continues to beat down on us. Jack reaches for the faucet and turns off the water while I still hold on to him, afraid to move because my legs feel like jelly. The shower stall becomes deathly quiet, except for our breathing and a few random drops of water hitting the floor.

I speak just loud enough for Jack to hear, "Thank you for loving me."

I hear his soft chuckle reverberate in his chest.

"I keep telling you, babe, it's easy to love you. I just thank God we found our way back to each other."

"Me, too."

When I look up at Jack, he leans down and gives me the sweetest kiss.

"We'd better get out of here, or we'll never get anything on your list done today," he tells me.

As we leave the stall, Jack hands me a towel and then grabs one for himself, wrapping it low around his waist. It's hard to focus on our busy day of wedding errands with him looking like this.

Running his fingers through his wet hair, Jack asks, "So, what's on the agenda today?"

"We have to drop off and pick up Kirby at the dog groomer, stop by the jeweler for our rings, pick up my dress from the seamstress, and get some things for the reception. Also, I need to stop by the studio and see Marcy about some maid-of-honor things."

"Well, I guess we'd better get dressed and get out of here. Hey, I didn't see the hairball stretched out on the bed when I came in. Where is he?"

Hairball is Jack's favorite term of endearment for our dog, Kirby. He is a small mixed terrier that I rescued from the animal shelter when Jack and I were separated. It took Jack a little while to warm up to Kirby, but now, they're best buds.

"Hiding under the bed. I made the mistake of asking him if he wanted to get a haircut today."

Jack starts laughing as he leaves the bathroom to get dressed.

We've just checked off the last item on the wedding to-do list, and we decide to celebrate by getting a bite to eat at one of our favorite restaurants before going home.

"What will it be tonight for the future Mrs. Keegan Grady? Steak or crab cakes?" Jack asks with a grin as we look over our menus.

"Excuse me?" my inner bitch snaps back over the assumption of my new name, which I never thought was an issue until I heard it said out loud to me.

"Steak or crab cakes?" He asks again with a questioning look.

"Maybe I want something else."

"Sure, get whatever looks good."

"Okay, how about Keegan Henderson-Grady?"

"What?"

The waitress interrupts our conversation, returning with our drinks, ready to take our orders.

"Could we have a few more minutes, please?" Jack politely asks her.

"Sure." She walks away without further comment.

Once she is out of hearing range, Jack asks, "What are you trying to tell me, Keegan? That you want to keep Will's name and tack mine on at the end?"

"Maybe. After all, Will and I did have a son together."

"Seriously? Well, at the rate you're going, it'll take hours for you to sign your name!" he sarcastically retorts back.

I throw my napkin down on the table. "You know what? I'm a little tired and cranky. I see where this conversation is heading, and it might be best if I call it a day. Please stay. Enjoy your dinner. I'll catch a cab home."

"No, you won't. We're going to have this conversation either here or at home, but trust me, we are going to have it tonight!" Jack throws some bills on the table as he gets up from his chair. Then, he storms out of the restaurant with me following.

During the drive home, there is an uncomfortable silence between us. I'm lost in thought, trying to think of a way to make him understand what my name means to me. In marriage, I don't want it to signify that I'm some man's piece of property but who I am as a woman. One of those things is Kyle Henderson's mother, and I want my name to reflect that.

Once home, I take care of Kirby and go upstairs to say good night to Kyle. I tap on his bedroom door a couple of times, and I hear, "Come in."

I find him at his computer, doing what I assume is homework. I shut the door behind me and say, "I just wanted to say good night."

Without looking up, Kyle answers back, "Night."

I hesitate for a moment and then ask, "You have a minute to talk?"

He turns in his chair toward me and answers, "Sure. What's up?"

"Jack and I were talking tonight about my married name. What do you think I should go by?"

Kyle gets a puzzled look on his face. "I guess Keegan Grady. Why?"

"What about Keegan Henderson-Grady?"

"Why would you do that?"

"It wouldn't be weird to you for me to drop Henderson since that's your last name?"

"I think it's dumb for you to keep it," Kyle says matter-of-factly. "I mean, I don't see the point in doing that since you and Dad were divorced way before he died."

I nod. "Okay. I was just checking to see how you felt about it."

"Mom, it's your name. I'm good with whatever you decide to do."

I smile. "Thanks, bud. Well, good night. Love you."

"Love you, too. Night."

Kyle turns back toward the computer screen as I leave, and then I head down the hall to my bedroom. When I enter, Jack is already in bed, reading a book. I walk into the bathroom to begin my evening ritual of getting ready for bed.

I take a deep breath before turning off the bathroom light to go crawl into bed because I know it's time to clear the air between Jack and me.

Once I'm in bed, he pulls me into his arms. "Okay, explain to me why you want to keep the name Henderson."

Now regretting my earlier behavior at the restaurant, I say, "I'm sorry for being such a bitch earlier. I was afraid Kyle would be hurt if I dropped Will's name. I didn't want him to feel as if his dad was forgotten or never existed in our lives."

"Have you talked to Kyle about this?"

"Yeah, I just did before coming to bed."

"And he said?"

"Kyle thinks it would be dumb for me to keep Henderson."

"So, what's the problem?"

"I guess nothing."

With a worried expression, Jack asks, "Keegan, are you having doubts about getting married?"

Wrapping my arms around him, I look him straight in the eyes so that there is no misunderstanding with what I'm about to say. "The one thing that is absolute in my life is my need to marry you. Living without you is not an option."

Jack softly kisses me. "That's good to hear because I feel the same way. Now, try to understand my feelings about your name. Call it being a Neanderthal, but it's important to me for your name to reflect that you belong to no one else but me. Sticking my name on after Henderson…well, quite frankly, it makes me feel like an afterthought." He heaves out a heavy sigh. "But it's your decision."

I realize my words have hurt him. "You could never be an afterthought. I'm sorry."

"So, what's it going to be?"

"Keegan Grady," I answer quietly.

"Good. I'm glad that's settled." He smiles at me.

"Jack, something else has been bothering me."

"What?"

I shake my head. "It feels like something is out there, lurking in the shadows, waiting to ruin everything for us."

"Continue," Jack says.

"That's the problem. I don't know how to continue or to explain it."

"Are you afraid Annie is going to do something?"

"No. I don't give her a second thought anymore. Maybe it's because of all the stuff that came out when Will died. When I was married to him, I had no idea what was going on and that he was working undercover with a drug dealer. What if there's more to it than that?"

"Like what?"

"Someone could be out there, planning some sort of sick revenge. What if they—"

Jack interrupts, "Babe, that was years ago. All of those guys are locked up in prison."

"I just don't know how to shake this feeling."

"We'll figure it out," Jack answers back.

"We?"

"Babe, we're a team. It's no longer your problem but ours. It's been a long day. Let's get some sleep." Jack tenderly kisses me and then reaches over me to turn off the light that sits on the bedside stand next to our bed.

The day before the wedding, I have this strange impulse to visit Will's grave. It has become customary for Kyle and me to go to the gravesite to pay our respect on Will's birthday, the anniversary of his death, and holidays. I make those trips to the cemetery more for Kyle's benefit than mine. I have no idea why it's so important for me to go today.

I pull up close to where Will is buried and see a woman with short blonde hair standing over his grave. I have no idea who she is.

I decide to stay inside the car and not intrude since she doesn't seem to be aware of my presence. After a few more minutes, she brushes her fingertips across her cheeks, as if wiping tears away. Then, she turns and sees me. She stops in her tracks as I get out of the car with flowers and a water jug.

I walk up to her. "Good morning. I'm sorry. I didn't mean to startle you. Did you know Will?"

"I knew him in college."

Although the woman looks familiar, I can't seem to remember how I know her. She is wearing just enough makeup to freshen her look. I notice a tattoo on her wrist of a date that I can't quite make out. Then, it dawns on me; I know who she is.

"Brittany?" I ask.

"Hi, Keegan."

I don't know why I'm shocked to find Brittany here. She was Will's girlfriend in college, up to their senior year when I started dating him. I found out in one of his letters that they had hooked up again after each of our divorces. Brittany also served as an informant for Will during his undercover assignment.

"How long has it been? College?" I ask her.

"No. I was at Will's funeral. You were in pretty bad shape and probably didn't even notice me."

"You're right. I was sort of out of it. I'm sorry."

"There's no need to apologize."

"So, how are you? I understand you were helping Will with his work."

"How did you know that?"

"By a letter that Will left me."

"You have a letter from Will? What did it say?" she asks with tears welling up in her eyes.

"I'm sorry. I don't feel...I really," I stammer, searching for the words to tell Brittany in a nice way that the letter was personal and none of her business.

"Never mind. It doesn't matter. Um, I need to get going." She looks off into the distance. "I was visiting my grandmother's grave over there." She points in the direction of a grave with fresh flowers a few feet away. "I bring flowers on her birthday and on the anniversary of her death."

I sense it's important to her for me to know this information. Our conversation is an uncomfortable, odd exchange.

"Well, it was nice seeing you," are Brittany's parting words before she hurries away to a car parked a little further down the road.

With flowers in one hand and the water jug in the other, I stop in front of Will's headstone and begin talking, "I have no idea why I'm here this morning. I'm getting married to Jack tomorrow, and I had an overpowering urge to come here. I brought some flowers from Mom's flowerbeds."

Momentarily, I tilt my head up toward the sky, as if looking for some divine inspiration.

I drop my head back down as I continue, "You said to me more than once that no man would ever take your place as Kyle's dad. I want you to know, even though I'm getting married tomorrow, you will always be Kyle's father, no matter what. I promise."

I wipe away the tears running down my face. Even after all this time, it seems odd to speak to a headstone instead of the man I shared a special connection with, who I miss to this day.

Will's mother, Joyce Henderson, had an inverted-style bronze vase installed at the foot of the headstone that disappears into the ground whenever it's not in use. She took all the trouble to do this but has yet been able to visit Will's grave since his funeral. My ex-mother-in-law and I have never been the best of friends, but that doesn't stop me from offering to come with her to the cemetery. Joyce politely declines each time I ask, so I bring flowers on her behalf when I come here.

As I lift the vase up from its case and turn it right side up, I see an envelope jammed inside it. I stand there, staring, almost too afraid to touch it. The two letters left for me after Will's death taught me how something so innocent can have a profound impact on a person's life.

Conflicted as to what to do, I pull out the envelope and see that it's blank on the front with no name indicating the intended recipient. Since the deed for the gravesite was among the paperwork given to me after Will's death, I decide to take the envelope home.

I couldn't have asked for a more picturesque spring day for our wedding at my parents' dock. The spring blossoms in full bloom along the lake's banks were the perfect backdrop as Jack and I exchanged our vows in front of family and friends.

Standing on the dock after the ceremony, I sway to the Irish music playing at the wedding luncheon that is taking place behind me.

My solitude is interrupted as my new husband comes up from behind and takes me into the safe haven of his embrace. "Wife, are you taking a cigarette break without me?"

I laugh, resting my head against his chest. "Maybe. I was thinking back to our conversation the other night about the way I've been feeling lately."

"And?"

"I could see someone writing a book about Will's undercover work. What if I told you I wanted to be the one to write it?"

I turn in Jack's arms, facing him, fearing I will see disapproval in his eyes.

"Wow, I didn't see that one coming." He goes quiet for a moment as he processes what I just said.

"Well?" I ask again.

"I think you're going to end up writing one hell of a book," he says with a kiss.

We say nothing, standing there, looking over the lake in each other's arms, watching the ducks flying over us.

Jack breaks the silence. "Over there is a party going on in honor of us. How about we join them for a few more minutes before leaving?"

With him giving me no clues as to the destination of our honeymoon, I ask, "Now, can you tell me where we're going?"

"Nope." He reaches in his back pocket to pull out the green scarf that he had me wear the day he proposed. "Are you up to wearing this again?"

"Um, okay. For how long?"

In a seductive tone that makes me melt, he says, "I haven't decided yet. Maybe all night if you're lucky."

"Okay, but you need to know, with or without the scarf, I know where we're going," I say in a cocky know-it-all manner as we walk arm in arm back to our guests.

"And where would that be?"

"Ireland."

"Funny. I don't remember telling you to pack your passport."

I stop walking, realizing I forgot about that one little detail.

"Are you disappointed?" he asks.

I smile and wink at him. "Nah. I'm good as long as you and the green scarf are coming with me."

We say our good-byes and give hugs to our sons, Kyle and Sean, along with our parents before running through a shower of birdseed while making our way to Jack's Jeep.

Once out on the main road, he drives the short distance to the parking lot of the strip mall where my pottery studio and shop are located along with our favorite coffee shop and tattoo parlor.

He pulls out the infamous green scarf, saying, "I didn't want to blindfold you in front of our parents or sons."

I laugh. "Thank you for not doing that."

Jack sits, looking at the stores in front of us. "The coffee shop is where we met for the first time, and a couple of months ago, I proposed to you at the tattoo parlor." He grins at me. "I thought this would be the perfect place to put the scarf on you. Turn around."

I eagerly turn my back to Jack for him to blindfold me. "Can you see anything?"

"Nope. Nothing."

"Good. Let's get going."

It seems as if we are driving forever as the warm breeze blows through my hair from the Jeep's windows being rolled down. With the scarf on, I find it's true that, when one of our senses is taken away, the others become sharper. For instance, although I've lost my sight, I can tell from the swooshing sounds of the cars passing on both sides that we're on a highway. At one point, I hear planes overhead. Instantly, I come to the conclusion that we're close to the airport.

Finally, we slow down and stop.

Jack instructs me, "Don't take off the scarf yet. I'll come around and help you out."

I hear someone greeting him, and I jump in my seat when the rear hatch slams shut after our luggage is unloaded. Jack guides me out of his Jeep and inside a building. It seems as if we walk for the longest time before stopping at, what I assume, is a counter of some sort.

"Mr. and Mrs. John Grady," Jack states proudly.

A girl giggles to my right as I hear someone else whispering nearby, making it clear to me that others are watching us.

God, what they must be thinking!

A man responds back, "Congratulations to the both of you. We have your room ready."

With his arm around me, Jack walks us to another location where we stand, waiting for what I assume is the elevator. My guess is confirmed when I hear a ding, and then doors open.

We step inside, and after the doors shut, I lean in close to Jack and whisper, "Are we the only ones in here?"

He laughs. "Yeah. Why?"

"I feel like everyone is staring at me. Is it okay to take the scarf off now?"

"Sure, if you don't care about missing out on some fun."

I start to reach up to pull the scarf off, but then I stop midair when I change my mind, dropping my hand back to my side.

"I promise, you won't regret it," he assures me.

We exit the elevator and walk a few feet before stopping. I feel Jack's movement and hear the door open to our room. He then leads me to a spot inside the room that I believe is the bed from the way it feels against the back of my legs.

He then says, "Here, sit down on the bed while I take care of a few things."

For the next few minutes, I hear movement around the room.

There is a knock at the door, and Jack says to someone, "Thanks. I've got it."

He then rolls something by me that I guess is probably a room service cart.

A few minutes later, he comes back over to the bed and pulls me up to stand. "You've been very patient, Mrs. Grady, while I got things ready. Have you guessed where we are?"

I shake my head. "No, other than a hotel room."

"Do you like not being able to see what's going on around you?" he whispers in my ear.

I quiver at the sensation of his breath against my ear. "It's frustrating."

"Do you want to keep the blindfold on or take it off?" he asks.

"On."

"Good. I'll clue you in along the way, so you're not totally in the dark. Pun intended." He laughs.

I giggle at his little quip.

"First, I'm going to get you out of these clothes. Tonight is all about me giving you mind-blowing pleasure."

"Mind-blowing? Aren't we a little cocky? Pun intended."

Jack lets out a small chuckle as he kisses my neck. "You know there's nothing little about it. Answer the question. Do you want to play?"

I nod, fully trusting him and knowing he would never do anything to make me feel uncomfortable.

Anticipation shoots through my body as each piece of my clothing is removed, followed by sweet kisses. Once naked, I hear him unzipping his khakis, indicating to me that he's getting undressed, too. A deafening silence then fills the room for what feels like an eternity.

Nervously, I ask, "Jack, what's going on?"

He comes up to me to reassure me that everything is okay. "Shh…I was just admiring your body. Do you have any idea how much I love looking at you naked? I love it when you walk around with no clothes on when we're home alone."

I feel myself blush from his compliment as I reach out to him, but he stops me.

"No, this is all about you tonight. Here, let me help you lie down on the bed on your stomach. I want to give you a massage."

Jack assists me as I lie facedown on the bed, and then he places my arms on the sides of my body with my palms facing up. I hear soft music begin to play in the background as the most heavenly scent fills the air. A moment later, I feel Jack's oiled hands on my back. I moan as he starts kneading the muscles in my neck and then shoulders before slowly working out the kinks down along my spine.

As he works the tension out of my muscles, Jack begins to talk in a low, seductive voice, "Tonight is all about me showing you through my touch and words what you mean to me."

He applies more oil to his hands and then continues my rubdown, starting at my arms and then my legs before reaching my feet. I'm becoming so relaxed, it's hard not to doze off.

He tells me, "Roll over onto your back." Once I'm on my back, Jack says to me, "Keegan, hold on to your pillow, and keep your hands there."

As I reach to grab ahold of each side of my pillow, I feel him push my legs apart, exposing all of me to him to do as he wishes.

"God, you're beautiful," he mutters under his breath.

Jack begins to repeat the process that he did on my back, but this time, it is more about arousal than relaxation. He gently takes each arm and massages them down to my fingertips. He places each back in place on the pillow and says again, "Don't move them."

Jack then draws his oiled hands down to my chest, paying particular attention to my breasts. He gently massages each one until I start moaning softly. I feel one of his hands travel down my body to the apex of my thighs as he kisses me.

Jack is right. This is mind-blowing pleasure.

When he leaves me for a moment, with my body alive with sensation, I find myself missing his touch and craving more.

From across the room, I hear the clatter of metal, as if a lid is being removed and then set down on a table.

Jack instructs me, "Don't open your mouth until I tell you."

I feel something smooth and warm on my lips.

He then commands, "Open your mouth."

I obey, being a little fearful of the unknown.

"Bite down."

I bite into a sweet chocolate-covered strawberry and start giggling as its juice tickles me, running down my chin.

Quietly, I hear Jack say, "God, I love to hear your laughter, but your tears shred me."

I feel him playfully catching the juice with his tongue before he starts kissing me, deep and hard.

I feel the bed sink with his weight.

I'm desperate to touch him, and my hands come off the pillow to hold him. "Jack, I need you."

He takes my wrists and places them back on the pillow. "You have me, baby. I'm right here."

I'm acutely aware the moment Jack enters me, and our bodies become one. Our lovemaking is passionate as we create a rhythm that culminates in an orgasm that causes me to cry out his name.

As we lie in bed, spent, neither of us capable of moving, I feel him rest his forehead on my shoulder.

"God, I love you." He lifts his head and removes the scarf.

Jack chuckles at my constant blinking as I slowly adjust to the soft candlelight that fills the room.

"So, Mrs. Grady, did you enjoy that?" He laughs.

I nod, smiling back at him. "You can blindfold me anytime you want. By the way, where are we?"

Jack rolls over to the side, enabling me to prop myself up onto my elbows to look around the room. He gets out of bed to walk over to a chair that has two hotel spa robes draped over it. He slips one on while handing the other to me. "Here, put this on, and I'll show you."

Once I have my robe on, he opens the drawn drapes, and I see a balcony outside our sliding glass door. It overlooks the interior of a massive atrium filled below with beautiful flora, shops, restaurants, and fountains. At one end of the atrium is a wall of glass that spans from the ground up to the ceiling that is several stories above us. There is a spectacular water view beyond the glass with the vibrant hues of the sunset painting the sky. I notice an enormous Ferris wheel off to the side down at a marina.

"My dearest wife, we are at the National Harbor on the Potomac River."

"It's beautiful," I tell him as I take in the scenery and activity below.

"So, here are our choices for this evening. We can shower and eat what I've ordered from room service." He nods over to the cart filled with an assortment of goodies. "Or we can dine at one of the restaurants here in the hotel. Your choice."

Closing the drapes, I turn to face Jack. I undo his robe and tenderly feather kisses up his chest to the nape of his neck. "Why don't we take a very long, hot shower and stay in for the night?"

He answers by lifting me in his arms and carrying me off to the bathroom.

The next morning, I wake up to find Jack asleep on his back. The bedsheet is draped across him just below his waist, barely revealing the start of the V of his hips. His well-defined abs are in full view. He looks like a sexy advertisement for bed linens with his toned arm lying on the pillow above his head. I become mesmerized, watching him sleep.

I smile as he starts to snore softly. My imagination begins conjuring up wicked ways of debauchery to thank him for yesterday's fun. Then, I spot one of our spa robes along with its belt lying at the foot of the bed.

Since we fell asleep, naked, in each other's arms, all I have to do is pull back the cover to have full access to him. Kneeling on the bed beside Jack, I carefully place the arm lying on the bed alongside his body with the other one above his head on the pillow. I take the robe's belt and gingerly bind his wrists together in a manner so as not to wake him. Spotting the massage oil from last night sitting on the nightstand, I pour some on my palms and warm it by rubbing my hands together before straddling him.

Jack is startled awake when I place my hands just above his hips and slide them up his chest.

I wink and then whisper, "Good morning. Payback time."

When I lean forward to continue up his arms, he watches as my breasts come teasingly close to his face. I do this repeatedly as his chest begins to glisten from the oil. I can see my foreplay is starting to drive him crazy with want. I sense the time is right to make my move and place my body in a position to sink down on him.

Looking straight into his eyes, I rock my hips in a way that makes him crave more. "Let me make something clear to you, husband of mine. You are the center of my universe and the love of my life."

I want him to experience the same degree of frustration from not being able to touch that I did yesterday.

Just as we are both reaching the point of losing ourselves, he growls at me, "Untie my fucking wrists *now*!"

The intensity of his tone and expression tells me that he means business. Wasting no time, I stop what I'm doing to him and free his hands. He grabs me by my hips, flips me onto my back, and takes control as our climaxes surge through us.

Best damn honeymoon sex ever!

As we lie in bed afterward, Jack breaks the news to me that it's almost time to check out of the hotel.

This time, as we walk to our SUV parked in the hotel's parking deck, I simply hold my hand out to Jack for my blindfold, as I'm now anxious to put it back on. He just laughs, saying nothing, as he reaches into his pocket for it.

During the drive, I hear a lot of traffic and airplanes.

Once Jack parks the car, he asks, "Do you know where we are?"

"Airport?" I ask.

"Yes, we are, and I'm sad to say, this is where the blindfold comes off for good because I don't want you to miss a moment of our trip." He removes the scarf and then reaches over to pull our passports out of the glove compartment. He hands mine to me. "You might need this because we're going to Ireland."

I smack his shoulder, squealing at the same time, "Oh my God! For real? I knew it!"

When we moved in together, my sneaky husband convinced me to put my passport in his lockbox, making it easy for him to retrieve it before our wedding yesterday.

Soon, we are going through the check-in for overseas flights, and then we board a plane, Ireland-bound.

Once on the plane, he tells me our itinerary, and I find out that we will be landing in Dublin, home of the Fitzgerald clan. We'll stay there for a couple of days, and then we'll take a train to Galway, the home of Jack's ancestors. We will return to Dublin the day before departing for home.

We get settled in for the long flight above the clouds of the Atlantic, and soon, Jack and I are drifting off to sleep.

I'm woken up by Jack stretching next to me.

"Sorry. Go back to sleep…unless you care to join me in the restroom and become a member of the mile-high club," he says, raising his eyebrows up and down.

"Um, no, thank you. I can see me now, trying to explain the ugly blue stain on my clothes."

Laughing out loud, he gets up, and I—along with half of the other women on the plane—watch his sexy ass walk down the aisle.

He soon returns to his seat, puts his arm around me, and kisses the top of my head. "How are you doing, Mrs. Grady?"

With all the wedding excitement during the past couple of days, I haven't found the right time to tell Jack about my encounter with Brittany. I figure now is as good of a time as any since we're sitting on a side aisle of the plane where there are only two seats per row, giving us plenty of privacy to talk.

"I'm doing okay. Um, there's something I need to tell you."

"Yeah? What's that?"

"I went to Will's grave the day before our wedding."

"Why?"

"I have no idea why. I just had this need to go. Maybe it was a way of closing that chapter of my life so that I could start a new one with you."

"Continue."

"Brittany was there."

His eyebrows rise, as this news has taken him by surprise. "Did you talk to her?"

"Yeah, we spoke to each other. After Brittany left, I found an envelope in the vase Joyce had installed at the grave."

"Who put it there?" he asks.

"I don't know."

"What did you do with it?"

"There was no name on the envelope, so I brought it home with me since I have the deed to the grave. I want you with me when I open it." I look at Jack and see a small smile spread across his face.

"Good thinking. Thank you."

"Why are you thanking me?"

He shrugs. "For letting me be there for you."

"I wouldn't have it any other way," I tell him as I lean over to kiss him.

4

Jack

Our honeymoon went off without a hitch. I'd planned the trip, so there would be plenty of time to leisurely explore each of our ancestral homes in Dublin and Galway. We toured the areas during the day and made love at night. Who could ask for any more than that?

When our return flight takes off from Dublin Airport, Keegan is animated as we reminisce about the places that we visited during our honeymoon. So, I can't help but notice her changing demeanor, the closer we get to landing back home.

"You seem a little preoccupied," I casually mention to her.

"I forgot about the letter from the cemetery while we were in Ireland. Now, it's the only thing I can think about, no matter how hard I try not to worry about it. I can't help but compare it to Will's letters, and we both know how well that went when I read them."

I do my best to give Keegan the reassurance she needs. "You and I are at a different place now. No matter what's inside that envelope, I'm not going anywhere."

Once our flight lands, we go through customs and claim our bags.

Walking out of the airport to the parking deck, I ask, "Ready to go home, Mrs. Grady?"

Keegan smiles. "I sure am, Mr. Grady! Can we make a stop at the studio on the way? I need to check in with Marcy before going home."

"Sure, as long as you promise not to stay too long because I'm beat."

"What? Did I wear you out this week?" she asks with a sexy grin.

I chuckle at her innuendo. "*You* wearing *me* out? I don't think so."

From the back alley, we walk into the studio to find Seth talking to Marcy in the back office. He looks up at us like a deer caught in the headlights and stops mid sentence.

Before we can say hello, Annie walks in from the studio through another door across the room and says to Seth, "Okay, honey, I found all my pieces. Let's go." She then sees Keegan and me standing on the other side of the room. "Oh, shit!" are the next words out of Annie's mouth.

Awkward does not begin to describe the silence that fills the room as the five of us just stare back and forth at each other.

I bring an end to it by asking, "*Honey?* Is that what I heard you call him?"

"I can explain," says Seth, trying to come to Annie's rescue.

I hold my hand up to him. "Save it, Seth. I want Annie to tell me why she's calling the man-whore of the century *honey*."

"Hey, wait a second," Seth protests as he takes a step toward me in reaction to my comment.

Annie grabs ahold of Seth's arm to keep him from going any further. "Jack, Seth and I are dating. We've been together for over a month. I was planning on telling you this week. I'm sorry you found out this way, but now, you know. I'm going to tell Sean about Seth and me, so the three of us can start spending time together."

"Over my dead body," I respond in a cold tone.

"What?" Keegan and Annie both say in unison.

I flash a dirty look in Keegan's direction before saying to Annie, "No way in hell is that happening."

Keegan mutters under her breath while shaking her head, "You have got to be kidding me."

Annie says, "So, let me get this straight. You're the only one around here who's allowed to be happy?"

"What I'm saying is, Sean's my son, and no one else is going to take my place with him. I'll be damned if you're bringing another man into his life, especially Seth with his track record of here today, gone tomorrow."

Trying his best to maintain his cool, Seth responds back, "Jack, I'm not going anywhere. I'm here to stay. I love Annie, and I want to have a future with her. I would never do anything to hurt Sean. You're his dad, and you will always be his dad."

"Fuck off, Seth."

"That's enough!" Keegan shouts at all of us. "Jack, I think it's time we say our good-byes. Everyone just needs to take a step back and calm down. Marcy, we'll talk later. Jack? Jack!" Keegan grabs my arm to break my death stare at Seth. "Jack, let's go. Now!"

During the drive home, all I do is mumble to myself, "There's no way in hell I'm letting that fucker hang around my son." This is followed by similar sentiments while Keegan sits, looking out the window, being unusually quiet.

By the time we walk into our townhouse, Keegan has grown tired of my tirade. "Jack, will you please just stop? That is one of my best friends you're trashing. I happen to love him, and he has been by my side through some pretty shitty times during my life. Now, grow up, and accept the fact that Annie is with him."

"Are you kidding me? Thanks for being there for me. Yeah, I'm supposed to be in your corner when it comes to all things Annie, but you're nowhere in sight when I need you!"

"Seriously? You don't think I'm here for you? Nice to know," she replies back in disbelief. "I think this might be a good time for me to go pick up Kirby from my parents' house. I want to ask you something before I leave. Is it fair to expect Annie to be lonely for the rest of her life because she had the misfortune of getting knocked up by you? Annie gave you a son, and what did you give her in return? Years of misleading her to think marriage might be in the cards while you knew all along that there wasn't a snowball's chance in hell of it ever happening. Annie has finally moved on with someone who makes her happy, and you have the audacity to shoot it down. I suggest you suck it up, buttercup!

"One more thing. You might not think I'm in your corner, but I'm the only one here, telling you the cold, hard truth." She then walks out the back door to get hairball, leaving me with my jaw hanging open, stunned by her words.

How did our day go to hell in a matter of hours?

The doorbell rings, snapping me out of my thoughts. I open the front door to find Seth standing on our doorstep.

How can this day get any worse?

"Hey, man. Can we talk? I mean, talk—no name-calling or yelling. Just talk this out. Please?" He asks uneasily.

I walk away from the door, leaving it hanging open, indicating for him to come in.

Once we reach the TV room, begrudgingly, I ask, "You want a beer?"

"Yeah. I think a beer would be good."

After I get our beers, we have a seat in the TV room—me, in my recliner, and Seth, on the couch. Each of us drinks our beers, not saying anything for several uncomfortable minutes.

I give him my best death stare before taking a long draw. "So, talk."

He begins, "I'm in love with Annie. It's that simple.

"There was one other time when I thought I was in love, and that was back in college. I fell hard for a girl named Cassidy, just to find out she was using me. I swore never to let another person hurt me like that again, and my man-whore days began.

"A little over a month ago, I saw a woman sitting in a booth at the coffee shop, wiping a tear from the corner of her eye. All that time Keegan and you were together, I had never met or seen Annie. I had no idea who she was when I slid into the booth across from her to see if she was okay. You can imagine my shock when we introduced ourselves. Annie was looking at the picture of Keegan and you at the tattoo parlor when you got engaged. We spent hours talking that day. One thing led to another, and here we are now.

"Jack, I don't want to take your place as Sean's dad. He idolizes you. I could never fill those huge shoes of yours. I do want to be his friend and be with Annie. Is there some way we can both be in their lives?" he asks.

Seth's words cause me to remember a past relationship that altered my feelings about marriage. The name of my albatross was Chelsey. I knew all too well about the pain he described and how it could alter your perception about relationships. Keegan was my saving grace, and now, Annie is his.

Heaving out a heavy sigh, I say to him, "I'm going to tell you the same thing Will said the day I met him."

"What's that?"

"If you ever hurt Sean or Annie, I will track down your sorry ass and become your worst fucking nightmare. I'm not joking!"

"I get it," he says, standing to shake my hand. "Are we okay?"

"Yeah, I guess so."

"Um, since Keegan and I've been tight since we were kids, Annie is worried that this is going to mess up my friendship with her."

"Listen, why don't we take this one day at a time, okay?"

"Sounds good to me."

After Seth leaves, I decide it's time to find my wife.

When I arrive at my in-laws', Kirby meets me at the door with Sandy and Mitch close behind him.

My new father-in-law informs me, "Keegan is taking a nap in her old bedroom downstairs."

I waste little time with small talk, and I go to her. I stand in the doorway for several minutes, watching my beautiful wife sleep, thinking how lucky we were to find our way back to each other.

I quietly shut and lock the door, kick off my shoes, and slide under the covers behind Keegan, pulling her close to me. I can feel my body respond as I take in her heavenly scent. *God, I love this woman.*

"So, are you here to grovel or fight with me some more?" she asks.

"I thought you were sleeping," I answer while my fingertip traces the Celtic love knot tattoo on her wrist.

"I'm just dozing. Now, answer my question," she insists.

"Grovel."

"Continue."

"I'm sorry for being such an ass today."

"It's Annie you should be apologizing to, not me."

"I know. I'll call her later."

"What made you come to your senses?"

"Seth came over to talk. We got squared away, and in the process, he made me take a good, hard look at myself. I didn't like what I saw."

"By all means, please continue," Keegan says as she turns to face me.

"Do you remember when I told you about living with another woman named Chelsey before I lived with Annie?"

"Yeah. You didn't say anything other than you lived with Chelsey, and it was good and then bad before you guys broke up."

"Chelsey is the one responsible for my whole screwed up perception about marriage. I used my job as an excuse, but the real reason is because of how things ended with her.

"We met in college while working toward our fire science degrees and started to date. Later, we moved in together. After graduation, Chelsey became a paramedic in one station, and I was a firefighter in another, working opposite shifts. Our days off together were few and far between. It was never a question of if we would get married but when. We agreed to wait until we got settled in our jobs, and we could afford to buy a house.

"Then, one morning, I came home from work to find she'd moved out. All she could tell me was she needed space—whatever the hell that meant. I swore, I was never going to allow another woman to hurt me like that again."

"So, you never found out why she left?"

"Nope. I guess it was because we never saw each other. She eventually transferred out of the county's fire service. Later, I heard she met another guy and got married. When Annie got pregnant, I used what had happened with Chelsey as an excuse to not get married. Instead, I asked Annie to move in with me—not out of love, but out of my guilt for getting her pregnant.

"Annie was right for calling me out on my bullshit today. She deserves to find happiness with someone else, especially after what I did to her."

"Then, you met me, and I put you through a whole different type of hell," Keegan says with a distant look on her face.

I remind her, "But, in spite of everything we've been through, here we are, lying in bed together, married."

"We certainly do make a pair, don't we?" Keegan halfheartedly laughs.

"I think we make the perfect pair." I kiss the top of her head.

Keegan grabs the hem of my tee and lifts it over my head. "Did you lock the door?"

"Yes, ma'am, I did."

"You know we have to be very, very quiet. Mom hears everything! Can you do this without making a sound?"

"I can if you can. Is it time for makeup sex?"

"It sure is. I'm going to show you just how perfect we are, babe."

5

Keegan

The next night, Jack is waiting for me in bed as I get Brittany's letter out of the nightstand drawer. I climb under the duvet and cuddle up to him with the envelope in hand. Kirby nestles himself on the other side of me, as if protecting me.

"I'm scared to see what's in this envelope."

"Then, don't open it. Bury it at the gravesite where no one will ever find it."

"No. I'm convinced whoever put the envelope in the vase wanted someone to find it."

"Go ahead. Kirby and I are here for you, babe."

I open the envelope to find a handwritten letter along with a photo.

Dear Will,

I miss you. I feel lost without you in my life.

The night you died haunts me to this day. I felt helpless, holding you in my arms and not being able to do anything to save you.

I can still hear your last words when you said you loved me.

You left, not knowing that I was carrying our child. Yes, we have a son. His name is Jace William Peters.

Jace reminds me so much of you. I promise to keep him safe and to have him grow up to be someone you would have been proud to call your son.

Know that Aiden continues to be a good friend, and he takes care of Jace and me in your absence.

I will always love you.

Brittany

I lie next to Jack in shock with tears streaming down my face.

"Babe, are you all right? I'm right here. Talk to me," Jack says as he holds me close to his chest and nuzzles his nose into my hair.

"Brittany was there the night of the shooting, and then she had Will's son?" I ask out loud to give credence to what I just read.

From over my shoulder, Jack looks at the enclosed picture of Jace. There is no way to deny that he is Will's son. It's as if I am looking at a picture of Kyle when he was that age.

Jack takes the letter along with the picture from me and puts them on the nightstand. Placing his arms back around me, he asks, "Do you think Brittany left the letter for you?"

"No. Brittany wanted Joyce to find it, not me."

Realizing that the letter didn't have the power to destroy Jack and me, as I once feared, a sense of peace comes over me.

I gently place my head against Jack's chest. "Thank you."

"For what?"

"Everything."

"Come on. Let's get some sleep."

We snuggle further under the covers. With my head on his chest, I say a silent prayer of thanks to God for bringing this man into my life, and then I fall asleep, listening to the beat of his heart.

The following morning, I wake up alone in bed. Reaching over for the letter and picture, I discover they are gone. I jump up from the bed and tear downstairs to find Jack standing at the coffee pot.

Thankfully, Kyle is still at Ryan and Liz's, where he stayed while we were in Ireland. The last thing I need is for him to find out about his brother by stumbling across Brittany's letter.

"Good morning," Jack greets me.

"Where is the letter and picture?" I ask in a panic.

"Relax. I put everything in the lockbox in my study. I think it would be a good idea for you to get a safe deposit box. You might end up discovering other things while researching the book, and it would be best to keep them locked away."

"You're probably right," I say, agreeing with Jack.

"While we're on the subject of your book, how much detail are you going to get into with Will's undercover work? Do I need to hire a bodyguard for you?" Jack asks with a look of concern.

"No, I'm only going to use what is already public knowledge. I'll need to talk to Joyce about Will's arrest as a teenager and find out more about that time in his life."

Breaking the news to Joyce Henderson about my plans to write a book and asking her for information is not my idea of a fun time. There is no love lost between us. The only reason she gives me the time of day is because I'm the mother of her grandson. I've always found her to be a little coldhearted, except for her overindulgence with Will and Kyle.

Joyce's husband, whom I've always referred to as Mr. Henderson, had already passed away by the time Will and I started dating in college. From Will's stories, his love for his father was a complicated one.

After Will's death, I found out that, at the age of fifteen, he and his older best friend, Troy Martin, were arrested for running drugs for a dealer. This is the same Troy Martin who Will was trying to bring down in his undercover work that cost both of them their lives. It was Mr. Henderson's powerful connections within the community that got the charges dropped against Will and allowed him to walk away with a clean record.

"Are you going to show Joyce the letter from Brittany?"

I shake my head. "No, not until I get a chance to talk to Brittany again. I need to know more before giving the letter to Joyce. It pisses me off a little bit that I couldn't get any details about the night of the shooting because I was no longer Will's wife. Now, I find out that Brittany was at the shooting, which was never in any of the news coverage."

"Didn't they tell Joyce?" Jack asks.

"They only told her what was in the news."

"Is there anyone else you could ask other than Brittany?"

"Not that I can think—wait a second. There's that federal agent. I delivered an envelope to him the day after the reading of the will. His name was on the envelope. What was it?"

I think hard, trying to visualize the name in Will's handwriting.

It suddenly comes to me. "Aiden. Aiden Collins. I wonder if that's the same Aiden whom Brittany talks about in her letter."

I start to recall in detail that afternoon when Will's lawyer, Mr. Shrewbridge, gave me three envelopes. Two of them had my name, and the other was addressed to Aiden Collins with a phone number to call to make arrangements for delivery. *Why was I even involved with this envelope since Mr. Shrewbridge could have just as easily called the number himself? Unless Will had a reason for me to meet Aiden.*

The next day, I invite Will's mother over to the townhouse for lunch. Knowing how much she values her privacy, this will probably be my one and only chance to gain any personal information from her.

Homemade vegetable soup is simmering on the stove with crusty bread warming in the oven. It's my hope that the soup will have a soothing effect and help Joyce open up to me about Will's childhood.

I jump when the doorbell rings.

Once we exchange niceties, I invite her to have a seat at the dining room table as I serve lunch.

We chat for a couple of minutes about everyday things when she blurts out, "What's going on, Keegan? We both know that doing lunch like this is not our thing."

Suddenly, I'm at a loss for words. "It's-it's…I don't know where to begin. It's…"

"Stop your stammering, and just tell me."

After taking a deep breath, I confess to the ulterior motive behind my lunch invitation, "I'm writing a book about Will because I want everyone to know the real man and the sacrifices he made to bring down the drug cartel. I don't know very much about Will's childhood, and I need you to tell me about it, including his drug addiction and arrest."

I brace myself, waiting for her to get up and storm out of my house.

She gazes at me for a moment and then says, "Thank God! With all the media during the trials, I was afraid somebody would eventually write a tell-all book full of half-truths, but now, I'm glad it'll be you. What do you need from me?"

"Everything and anything you can think of up to the time I met Will in college."

Through her laughter and sometimes tears, Joyce tells stories of Will as a little boy. He had a fearless, thrill-seeker personality, causing his mother to make numerous trips to the emergency room for his stitches and a couple of broken bones throughout his childhood. Then, she shares her feelings of helplessness while watching her son hit rock bottom as his habitual drug use spiraled out of control.

My curiosity gets the best of me, and I ask, "Why was Will's drug abuse and his arrest kept from me?"

I can see the pain my question causes in her eyes.

"Will's pride. When I saw the two of you getting serious, I told him to tell you."

"And?"

"Will said to stay out of his business. He was ashamed of it and didn't want to bring you down into the dirt of his life. He wasn't going to take the chance of losing you."

Now, it is all beginning to make sense to me. Will's letters were his way of being honest with me without seeing my possible disappointment in him.

"Did you know Troy Martin and his family?" I ask her.

"Yes. Troy's mother and I were members of many of the same clubs. She was a lovely lady, and I encouraged Will's association with Troy. God, I feel so guilty for not finding out more about that young man," she berates herself.

"Do you remember anyone by the name of Aiden Collins?"

"Yes, Aiden was Will's roommate in college for a few years. Why?" she asks, looking at me with furrowed brows.

This information is unexpected since I had no knowledge of this man until after Will's death.

"I remember some of Will's college buddies at the viewing, reminiscing about their past fun, and they mentioned Aiden. It sounded like he and Will were close, but I couldn't remember ever meeting him; that's all." I've never been good at lying, and I hope my face doesn't give away that I just told Joyce a whopper.

"Aiden and Will hung out together all the time up until Aiden moved in with his girlfriend at the beginning of Will's senior year. I guess they just lost contact with each other after that."

"Do you know how I can get in touch with him?"

"I have no idea. I never really knew him all that well. Sorry."

"That's okay. It's no biggie. From the stories I heard, I thought Aiden might be able to tell me more about Will before I met him in college."

I decide to move on to a new topic before I get too far into the lie and trip myself up.

Surprisingly, somehow, our conversation takes a turn, and Joyce starts talking about her marriage with extreme candor. I discover that it wasn't Will's addiction that was at the heart of the Hendersons' marital issues but her husband's philandering. By the time Will's drug arrest occurred, their marriage was unsalvageable. It sounded as if their primary concern was not to become a part of the gossip of their upper-class social circle of friends. They made the conscious choice to live separately under the same roof instead of getting a divorce. As a result, Joyce became devoted to her son to ease her pain for remaining in a loveless marriage.

I get her a tissue as she finishes saying, "It was nothing but a big sham. I tried my best to hide it from Will. So many times, I wanted to be strong enough to do the right thing and tell him the truth about his father and me. I was just too embarrassed to admit to my son what a weak woman he had for a mother because I'd allowed his father to disrespect me like that."

"Did you ever meet Brittany, the girl Will dated before me?"

"Yes, I did. Our first meeting was disastrous. While Will went to the bathroom, my husband told Brittany she wasn't good enough for him. After that, my husband didn't even bother to hide his disapproval of her."

"When we met, what was your first impression of me?"

"Keegan, I was so torn over you. On the one hand, I was thrilled Will had found someone with a good head on her shoulders, who came from a respectable family. But, on the other, my son was my life. I saw you as competition for his love. Yes, I know; it's a little sad, isn't it? I'm sorry for my behavior after your divorces. Will seemed so lost during each time, and it was too easy to blame you for everything. I hope you can find it somewhere in your heart to forgive me."

Her candidness not only shocks me, but also offers a new perspective of my marriages to Will. I also have a new appreciation of the dynamics of his family now that Joyce has revealed the skeletons that were hiding in her family's closet.

An afternoon I dreaded flies by way too fast.

As I walk Joyce to the front door, I tell her, "Thank you for talking to me this afternoon. I know it wasn't easy for you."

Giving me a comforting hug, she says, "I should be thanking you. I feel like the weight of the world has been lifted from my shoulders. Show everyone that my son was a good and decent man. I'm a phone call away if you need anything else."

I nod. "I will."

From my doorway, as I wave and watch her get into the car, I begin to feel guilty for not telling her about Brittany's letter.

6

Jack

Occasionally, I find myself missing being on the front line, fighting fires. I especially miss it at times like this when I'm dealing with the day-to-day minutia of administrative paperwork for the battalion.

I notice an email in my inbox from county headquarters with the subject line, *Announcement: New Admin Chief Chelsey Hamilton.*

I almost fall out of my chair when I discover that my ex-girlfriend is the county's new administrative chief. *What are the odds of that happening?* Especially since several of my stations are due for new equipment, and I will need to work closely with her on the specifications along with the budget for each piece.

As I continue to read further, I see an invite for all the county's fire service administrators to attend a meet-and-greet at a local bar to welcome Chelsey to the department. I could just not attend, but I know the county's fire chief expects all staff to be there, and my absence would cause a lot of questions.

Our home is full of activity when I walk in the back door after work this evening. I forgot that it's prom night. Keegan is scurrying around the house, making sure her phone is charged to take pictures. Minutes later, Kyle walks in the front door from picking up his date, so we can take photos of them before they leave for the big event. Keegan's eyes glisten, admiring her son, as the handsome couple poses for us in their formalwear.

As she watches Kyle drive away, Keegan says, "Time is going by too fast for me. I wish there were a way to slow it down."

She stares off into the distance, becoming lost in her thoughts.

She turns to me and changes the subject by asking, "Any excitement at work today?"

I chuckle and say, "Funny you ask. I would say it was more interesting than exciting."

"Yeah? What happened?"

"I got an email announcing the county's new administrative chief position."

"Anyone you know?"

"Intimately."

Keegan looks at me, confused by my response.

I continue, "Chelsey Hamilton."

It takes a moment for the name to register with Keegan.

"Oh, really?"

"Yep, and to make matters worse, there's a happy hour for everyone to meet her."

She eagerly asks, "Are spouses invited, too?"

"Well, yeah, I guess so. Why? You wouldn't want to go, would you?"

"Hell yeah, I want to go!" she answers a little too enthusiastically for my liking.

"Why would you?"

"If I told you that there was a happy hour in honor of Alex Parker, wouldn't you want to go with me to check out the competition?" Keegan asks with an evil grin.

"She's not competition," I say defensively.

Keegan just stands, staring at me with raised eyebrows.

"Okay, I get it. It's just going to be weird for me to have you there since I haven't seen Chelsey since she left the county's department."

"That's all the more reason for me to go. I can be your wingman for the evening. Plus, I could ease your stress if things got to be too much for you to handle." Again, Keegan gives me a smile that leaves no doubt as to what she means.

"Oh, I bet you could. Seriously, it's going to be a night full of shoptalk between a bunch of firefighters."

"Babe, I wouldn't miss it for the world." she turns from me and sashays her way to our bedroom upstairs.

The next day at work, I receive an email from Chelsey saying that she would like to meet me in my office later in the afternoon to discuss preliminary plans for my battalion's new equipment. The tone of her message is all business. By reading it, no one would ever guess we had a shared past. My guess is, Chelsey's intent is to get our first meeting behind us before the upcoming happy hour.

The day flies by, and before I know it, there's a light tapping on my office door.

"Come in!" I shout without giving a thought to the time.

As Chelsey walks into my office, I notice that she's still the stunning woman I remember from years ago.

Unsure of how to greet her, I clumsily stand as she steps forward with her hand extended out to shake mine, setting the tone for our meeting.

"Hi, Chelsey. It's been a long time."

"Yes, it has. How are you?"

"I'm doing well. And you?"

"I'm good. Are you ready to discuss the specs?"

"Sure. I've got everything set up for us over there at the conference table."

We get down to business, and soon, we have a wish list composed for the new apparatuses.

As Chelsey begins to pack up, she glances over at the framed photos of Keegan and the kids on my desk. "You have quite a collection of pictures on your desk. Is that the happy family?"

"Yes, it is."

"I see you have two good-looking boys."

"One is my son, Sean, and the other is my stepson, Kyle."

She snaps her head to look at me and asks, "This is your second marriage?"

"No."

I'm beginning to feel a little uneasy as to where this conversation is heading. "After you and I broke up, I met Sean's mother. She got pregnant, and we lived together for a while."

At first, Chelsey says nothing, and then she abruptly stands up. "Well, I guess I should get going. It was nice seeing you again. I'll go over the specs and get some figures to you as to the cost, and we'll go from there. I'm looking forward to working with you, Jack."

As I watch her leave, I think to myself, *Chelsey might look like the same beautiful woman, but something is different about her.*

Annie asked me to stop by on the way home this evening to discuss the best way to tell Sean about Seth. I agreed because I still owe her an apology for my behavior the other day at the studio.

After my meeting with Chelsey today, the last thing I want to do is talk about how to introduce my son to his mother's new boyfriend.

Annie wastes no time in getting to the heart of the matter. "Jack, I'm sorry you found out about Seth and me like that, but I will not apologize for falling in love with him. Seth made me realize that what you and I shared wasn't love."

Sometimes, I just can't resist being a jerk. "Is that so? Like Seth is an expert on the subject. Wait a second. I guess he is with all of his past experiences with women. Just how many has he been with, Annie?"

"I know all about Seth's history with women, and I'm not discussing it with you. All I want is for us to agree on Seth meeting Sean and how to handle it."

"Annie, I've had a real shitty day. Whatever way you think is best is fine with me."

"Thank you. But what about us, Jack? The worst and best night of my life was when you so eloquently told me we only fucked and never made love. You forced me to open my eyes and see that I deserved better than what you ever offered me."

I cringe as I remember saying that to her the evening Keegan confronted me on my front doorstep and then left after seeing Annie was there with me.

She continues, "I'm in love with Seth, and I will not tolerate any more of your condescending bullshit about my relationship with him."

I sigh. "You're right. I'm sorry."

She then adds, "That night you told me Keegan completed you, I didn't get what you meant until Seth came into my life. I guess Keegan's not too happy about Seth and me either."

"Believe it or not, after we left the studio, she gave me hell for the way I'd acted."

"Do you think Keegan and I could ever get beyond what happened between us? I don't want things to be strange between her and Seth because of me."

"I don't know. We'll just have to wait and see."

When I arrive home later that evening, Kirby greets me at the door with his tail wagging, but Keegan is nowhere to be found.

I shout out, "Wife? Where are you?"

"Upstairs."

Taking a couple of steps at a time, I stop at our open bedroom doorway to find Keegan in some sexy lingerie consisting of a black see-through lace corset and thong. I tilt my head back into the hallway to look over at Kyle's room, finding it dark. "Um, I hope Kyle isn't home with you waltzing around the house in that get-up."

"You like?" Keegan asks as she twirls and strikes a pose.

"I like very much. What's the occasion?"

"I thought you might need a little de-stressing after meeting with Annie tonight."

Walking up to her, I pull her into my arms. "Where's Kyle?"

"He's out with friends, and he won't be home until later tonight. How are things with you and Annie?"

"She is the last thing I want to talk about right now."

"What do you want to talk about?"

"How about my raging hard-on? I'm finding it very stressful. You know of anything that can take care of it?"

Keegan makes fast work of stripping me out of my shirt. She then drops her hands down to my waist to unbuckle my belt.

I then comment, "Babe, I'm sorry, but my stress level is getting worse instead of better."

She smiles up at me. "That's the plan."

I chuckle as she helps me out of my pants along with my boxers. Then, she tosses them over onto a nearby chair.

I return the favor by stripping the few pieces of lingerie that Keegan's wearing off of her.

Our teasing and foreplay quickly turn into an intense session of lovemaking that allows us to enjoy every inch of each other's bodies, ending too soon as our orgasms wash over us like an ocean wave.

Afterward, I play with Keegan's hair as we lie in bed, holding each other.

She asks, "How's that for stress relief after an evening with Annie?"

"If only it were just Annie. I also had a meeting today with Chelsey about some new equipment."

"And how did that go?"

"It was weird. Even though Chelsey is as beautiful as ever, something has changed about her. She seems cold and distant."

"Beautiful, huh? And just how beautiful is she?" Keegan asks with a bit of snippiness in her tone.

"You can see for yourself tomorrow night. Chelsey has long blonde hair and green eyes. She must still be running marathons because her body is in great shape."

"Really? I'm not sure how to react to you going on about your ex-girlfriend while in bed with me."

I shrug. "Hey, you're the one who asked."

Saying nothing, Keegan gets out of bed, puts on a robe, and leaves our bedroom. After slipping on some sweats, I find her downstairs in the kitchen, pulling a casserole out of the oven.

I watch her for a few minutes. "Talk to me."

"I've got nothing to say," she answers back.

"Don't shut down. Tell me what you're thinking."

"Not sure if you want to hear what I'm thinking right now. Here is your dinner. I'm going upstairs to get dressed, and then I'm going to run down to the studio to make sure the kiln was taken care of after today's firing. It shouldn't take me very long. Please be sure to clean up after yourself."

She leaves me standing in the kitchen, unsure of what to do next. I glance over to the dining room table and see place settings for an intimate dinner for two.

Shit! I feel like a heel for going on about Chelsey.

What the hell was I thinking?

When Keegan comes back downstairs to leave, I try to apologize. "Sweetheart, I'm sorry. Please stay," I plead.

Keegan looks at me straight in the eyes and says, "Why? You have your memories of Chelsey with her long blonde hair, green eyes, and great body to keep you company tonight."

I flinch at Keegan's words as I watch her leave through the back door.

With my appetite now gone, I decide to take Kirby for a walk, thinking she will be home by the time we get back. I'm wrong. An hour later, Keegan still hasn't returned, and she isn't answering my phone calls or texts, but I know where to look for her.

As I pull up next to Keegan's car parked in the driveway, her parents' home is dark. No one is home, so I head straight to the dock.

I stop a few feet away from the dock, watching Keegan, as she sits on the edge of it with her feet in the water and a lit cigarette in her hand. If that isn't bad enough, I hear her sniffling, and it looks like she is wiping away tears with the back of her free hand.

I start repeating my wedding vows loud enough for her to hear, "I, John Patrick Grady, take you, Keegan Brigid Fitzpatrick Henderson, to be my wife. From this day forward, know I will always remain true and honest to you. I promise that you and our sons will always be my first priority in life. I will be by your and our children's sides through both the good and bad times. And, above all, I will always respect, love, and cherish you until we are parted by death."

She looks around at me, stands, and answers back, "I, Keegan Brigid Fitzpatrick Henderson, am honored to have you as my husband, John Patrick Grady, to have and to hold from this day forward. I will share in the joy of our good times together and be your beacon of light when you are struggling to find your way out of the fog. I promise to build our marriage on a foundation of honesty, respect, and trust. But, above all, I will love and cherish you until death."

Still standing in the same spot, a few feet away, I beg, "Please forgive me."

I notice she remains standing on the dock without making a move toward me.

"Jack, do you still have feelings for her?"

"Jesus Christ, no! I love you and no one else."

I catch her as she runs up and throws her arms around me.

As we hold on to each other, I tell her, "I fell in love with you the day that picture of you on the dating website popped up on my computer at work. God, it took my breath away. No other woman has ever done that to me. Never forget that, okay?"

"I'll try not to."

I pull back a little, and she lifts her head to kiss me.

"Babe, I'm sorry, but you need to ditch those damn cigarettes!"

She giggles and says, "Think of it as your punishment."

"How about us heading home for a little de-stressing in the shower?"

"The first one home and naked gets a full-body massage!" she yells over her shoulder as she takes off running for her car.

7

Keegan

I lie in bed, awake, thinking about the day facing me, as Jack gets ready for work. He sees me as a confident woman and is sometimes clueless of how often I doubt myself. Today is one of those times.

Scheduling a meeting with Agent Aiden Collins on the same day as Chelsey's happy hour is not the smartest thing I've ever done. Maybe I should reschedule with Aiden or come up with an excuse to miss happy hour, but I know that neither option is going to happen.

Jack walks out of the bathroom and asks, "Are you worried about your meeting this morning? You know, it's okay for you to miss Chelsey's happy hour tonight."

Not believing my ears, I sit up in bed and confront him, "You don't want me to go to this evening, do you? Why? Come on, out with it."

"I told you it's okay for you to go."

Jack's words are telling me one thing, but his body language is sending an entirely different message.

"Liar. Come on, tell me. Why don't you want me to meet Chelsey?"

He shrugs. "I don't know. No reason, I guess. It's just that a lot of guys from back in the day when Chelsey and I were together will be there. It would be easy to misunderstand some joking around about those days."

"Okay then, I won't go." I show my irritation with Jack and this conversation by crossing my arms in a huff.

"Well, if you think it's for the best," he answers back.

Now angry, I get out of bed to head to the shower and say in passing, "Yeah, Jack, I feel it's for the best. Heaven forbid I put you in a situation where I meet Chelsey and might hear something about your past. Wouldn't want the old ball and chain cramping your style while you're hanging out with the beautiful ex-girlfriend! Excuse me while I take my shower. Oh, one more thing, go ahead and put your wedding band in the jewelry box before leaving today. I would hate to see you lose it because it fell out of your pocket tonight." I slam and lock the bathroom door behind me.

While in the bathroom, I hear Jack leave the bedroom to go to work without saying good-bye. I adjust the showerhead to let the hot water beat down on me in a feeble attempt to try to wash my hurt feelings away.

Once out of the shower, I get dressed and go downstairs to let Kirby out. I'm startled when I walk into the kitchen and see Jack reading the morning paper at the kitchen island.

My hand flies to my chest as I exclaim, "God, you scared me! Where's Kyle? Why are you still here? You are way beyond late for work."

"Kyle had to get to school early to help set up for some program. I called in to let them know I'd be late, so we could hash this thing out." He then points his finger at me. "First, don't you ever accuse me or even suggest that I would take my wedding band off to try to hide our marriage. I thought I had made it clear to you how I felt about taking off our rings."

"Yeah, I know. I'm sorry," I say with my head hanging down.

I remember the night of our argument over Annie's meltdown about us getting engaged. I gave my ring back to Jack after finding out he was running over to Annie's to talk to her. He told me that night that we were never to use the removal of our rings as threats to each other.

"Don't let it happen again," he warns.

I nod and wait for him to go on.

"As for me not wanting you to go this evening, let me ask you something. Why haven't you asked me to go with you to meet Aiden today?"

Now, it's me shrugging. "I don't know. I guess because you have to go to work, and some of the stuff we'll talk about happened before we knew each other."

"Exactly! My past with Chelsey happened before we met. After all the crap we went through with Annie, I don't want a repeat of history."

"Okay, I understand. I'll stay home tonight."

"No, you won't."

"Huh? I get it. It's not a problem. I'll stay home," I repeat.

"And I said, you won't. If I were off today, would there be a problem with me going to your meeting today?"

"No. In fact, it might help to get your perspective on things if you were there with me. Maybe I'm too close to be objective, and I might not ask the right questions."

"Once again, you've hit the nail on the head. That's why I took off this morning to go with you, and tonight, you'll accompany me to happy hour. Come on, let's get out of here, so we have time to swing by the coffee shop to get you a chai latte before the meeting."

Jack and I sit in the same conference room where, years ago, I waited for Aiden, so I could deliver Will's envelope to him. As we look out a huge window at the magnificent cityscape and harbor view, Aiden enters, and to my surprise, Brittany is with him.

Aiden greets me with his right hand extended, "Good morning, Keegan. It's been a while since we last met."

"Yes, it's been a few years," I politely reply back as we shake hands.

I look over to Brittany as Aiden offers us an explanation for her attendance, "I hope it's okay that I've asked Miss Peters to join us."

"That's fine. I'm glad Brittany is here because I have some questions for her as well." I see Aiden give Jack a questionable look. "This is my husband, Jack Grady."

Aiden reaches out to shake Jack's hand. "Mr. Grady. May I call you Jack?"

"Yeah, sure, Aiden," Jack answers in a guarded tone.

The atmosphere changes into an almost adversarial one as we take seats on opposite sides of the table with Aiden and Brittany facing Jack and me.

Aiden wastes no time and asks me, "Now, how can I help you?"

"I am writing a book about Will's undercover work. Since I don't know much about the shooting, I was wondering if you could tell me more about it."

Delivering a well-rehearsed line, Aiden replies, "Well, as you know, this is all considered sensitive information with some of it still being classified. I'm not at liberty to discuss much with you."

I look over to Jack sitting beside me and then back at Aiden and Brittany. "Brittany, why are you even here?"

Taken aback by my bluntness, she starts to stammer, "I'm here—Aiden thought—"

Aiden interrupts and answers on her behalf, "Because she has a personal vested interest in this meeting."

"What does he mean, personal vested interest, Brittany?" I ask, looking directly at her.

Again, Aiden answers, "That's irrelevant at this time."

Looking back over at Aiden, I say with irritation, "The last time I checked, your name wasn't Brittany, so why don't you let her answer? I know Brittany was Will's informant. I know she was at the shooting and with Will when he died. Oh, one more thing, I also know she had Will's baby, so she must have been a hell of a lot more than just a damn informant."

"You read the letter I left at the cemetery? It wasn't for you to read. It was for Will," Brittany says just above a whisper.

"And I call bullshit! You saw the flowers in my hand. You knew I would be using the vase, and you never once tried to stop me. Also, I'm sure you know, dead people can't read. You put it there for Joyce to find out that she had another grandson. You figured that, no matter who found the letter, they would tell Joyce. Why?" I confront her.

Brittany says nothing.

"I need some answers for the book. There are two choices here. Either you answer my questions or I come up with a theory of my own to fill in the blanks."

Aiden chuckles as he shakes his head. "Will warned me about you. I remember when you two met back in college. I knew he was in for one hell of a ride."

"That's another thing. Why haven't we ever met?" I ask, annoyed at his amusement over my last comment.

I see Aiden exchange a look with Brittany, as if they share a secret about those days.

He then answers, "We never met because I moved in with my girlfriend during my senior year and was never around. That's why you and Will always had the dorm room to yourselves with no interruptions." He smirks, looking over at Jack.

"There's more to it than that. We invited all our friends from college to the wedding. You never even made the guest list. Why?"

Shifting uneasily in his chair, Aiden says, "Let's put it this way; Will and I had a disagreement back in college, and we came to blows over it. I moved out of our dorm and never heard from him again until he contacted me about Operation Skater."

"Operation Skater. That was the name for his undercover work with Troy Martin."

"Yeah. How did you know?" he asks.

"Will left me a letter explaining his dealings with Troy and how he was working undercover to put him away. A news report said that there was a connection to Will's work and all the drug arrests that happened after his death. Is that right?"

"I can only confirm the news releases issued by the FBI," Aiden reiterates.

"Since Brittany was his informant, was she connected to the cartel?"

"No, Brittany had no connection to the cartel," Aiden explains to me.

"If you didn't have anything to do with the cartel, Will would have protected you from ever meeting Troy, like he did with me. Why were you there the night of the shooting?" I ask her.

Both Aiden and Brittany freeze, not knowing how to respond.

Aiden starts, "Um, that's something—"

Brittany stops Aiden's attempt at blocking my question and says, "After graduating from college, I landed a job as a social worker in the county's Department of Social Services. For a short time, Troy became my lover and drug dealer."

"Your drug dealer?" I ask, astonished by this news.

"I'm a recovering prescription drug addict, and I've been clean for twelve years. Troy had been carrying a grudge against Will ever since he got off scot-free when the two of them got arrested for delivering drugs for a dealer. Troy said the only thing he could think about while serving his time was getting even with Will.

"Troy persuaded Will to run interference with the police on anything dealing with his drug business by threatening harm to you and Kyle. Troy's plan was to make Will look like a crooked cop to get him arrested and sent to prison.

"Troy knew Will and I had dated in college and wanted me to find a reason through work to reconnect with him, so I could keep an eye on him. One of the kids I was working with had joined a gang, and I used him as my excuse to contact Will. When I started sharing more information about my clients with Will, he told me about his undercover work and to let him know if I heard anything about Troy's operation. I made sure Troy never found out that Will was working undercover. I also convinced Troy that Will was too valuable to be framed and sent to jail."

"You still haven't answered my question. Why were you there the night of the shooting? What happened? There's more to this than what you're telling me," I fire back at her.

It's Aiden who speaks this time, "Do you remember when Will visited you in the hospital after your car accident, and you said the only thing you could recall was the a black motorcycle and the color red?"

"Yes."

"Troy drove a black motorcycle with the gas tank covered in bold red flames. Will thought Troy had purposely caused the accident with his motorcycle. Will planted a bug in his office, and that was how he got the information on the cartel."

Brittany then says, "Troy found the bug. He thought Will and I were trying to take over his business and forced me with a gun to go over to Will's condo with him. Troy gave Will a choice to hand over the recordings or watch him shoot me. Once Will told Troy where the recordings were, I was told to get them. That was when Troy saw Will reaching for a gun hidden in the chair where he was sitting. They ended up shooting each other at the same time."

Jack holds my hand under the table during Brittany's account of the night. I'm visibly shaken by this news and thankful that he's here with me.

I look over to Aiden. "The envelope I gave you had something flat and hard in it, like a key. What was it?"

"You're right. It was a key."

"To what?"

"A safe deposit box."

"What was in it?"

"That's information I'm not at liberty to share with you at this time," Aiden tells me.

"You know, it occurred to me that Will's lawyer, Mr. Shrewbridge, could have handled getting your envelope to you. Why was I involved with it?"

Aiden is quiet for a second and then says, "Our fight in college was a pretty bad one. A lot of things were said that we both later regretted. Operation Skater allowed us to put it behind us. The only thing I can think of is that he wanted you and I to know each other, and this was a way for it to happen."

By the time the meeting ends, my head is reeling from all the information. After finally getting the details of the night Will died, I find little comfort in knowing them. It only ends up raising a new question that I'm not sure I'll ever be able to ask out loud.

It's decided that the only way I can write about any of the information from today's meeting is by using aliases. Also, Aiden and Brittany want to read the book's manuscript to approve before I publish it. Although Jack finds their conditions questionable, I agree to them.

When we get back in the car, Jack turns to me and asks, "Are you okay?"

Finding the courage to ask the question that has been nagging me, I ask, "Did I cause Will's death?"

"No, you did not cause Will's death. He made a choice to take risks that caused his death."

"But if I hadn't told him about remembering the color red and a black motorcycle, he would have never planted the bug in Troy's office."

"Keegan, you never said the bike had red on it. Will used what you told him to justify planting what was probably an illegal bug."

With tears welling up in my eyes, I ask, "Then, why do I feel like it's my fault?"

Jack takes me in his arms to comfort me. Then, he pulls his phone out to make a call to take the rest of the day off.

When we get home, Jack heads upstairs to draw us a fragrant bubble bath with soft music playing in the background. We strip out of our clothes. I climb in first, and then he follows, pulling me back into his arms.

"You're awfully quiet," he says, massaging my neck and shoulders.

"Just thinking."

"About?" he prods.

"When reading the letters, I remember thinking how strange Will's wording was when he talked about being this badass runner for a dealer and getting arrested. It almost came across as if he were grieving a loss of some sort. At the time, I took it as regret for his actions, but now, I'm not so sure."

"Continue."

"It was all about how his dad made him take the plea bargain. His dad forced him into rehab. His dad moved his family to the suburbs, and then there was the strain on his parents' marriage."

"And?"

"Will said he received a picture from Troy. It was of Kyle and me with what, at first glance, looked like blood.

God, that must have scared him. Will told me that, when he received the picture, he came up with the idea of leaving me. His thinking was, if we were no longer together, Troy couldn't use Kyle and me as blackmail. We were happily married up to that point. Don't you think the whole thing of going undercover and ending our marriage was a bit drastic? He had other options. I think I know why he reacted the way he did."

"Why?"

"Coming up with this whole undercover thing allowed him to return to the place that felt like home to him—the inner city. He was able to go back to the world he missed. If his dad hadn't stepped in, who knows where Will would have ended up?"

"It's hard to say," Jack agrees with me.

"Will's earlier life was such a contradiction of his principles as a state trooper, and on some subconscious level, I think he missed the life he'd lived when he was a kid."

"Well, I don't know about that," Jack says with a tone of doubt in his voice.

"Think about it for a minute. Will's father made him testify against Troy, go to rehab, and walk the straight and narrow. It was all about his father saving face in the community."

"Did you know his dad?"

"No. Will's father died the year before we started dating."

"Did Brittany know him?"

"Yeah. According to Joyce, Brittany didn't rise to their high standards."

"And you did?" Jack laughs a little.

I jerk my head around at him.

He quickly apologizes, "Sorry. Bad joke. It was just too easy."

I playfully jab him with my elbow and continue, "Seriously, our marriage was just another way to make up for the shame he put his parents through."

"All I know is Will loved you. I saw it every time he looked at you, and it drove me nuts," Jack comments.

"Will told Joyce once how he never wanted to bring me down into the dirt of his life. After today's meeting, I'm not sure what my reaction would have been if Will had told me all the sordid details of his youth. Maybe Will sensed that on some level, and that's why he came up with the scheme to go undercover. It created a legitimate way to return to a world that he missed," I explain.

Jack begins to lather up some soap in his hand. "Or Will just wanted to get Troy off the streets. I guess we'll never know for sure."

I play with the slowly disappearing bubbles floating in the water. "Don't you see, Jack? When he found Brittany immersed in the same subculture in her job as a social worker, it was the perfect environment for the two of them to get back together. Brittany's love for Will was unconditional, even after he left her to marry me for a second time. Brittany accepted Will for who he was, warts and all. He could stop pretending to be something he wasn't, which created an unbreakable bond between them."

"Like us?" Jack asks.

I grin. "Yeah, like us. Thank you for taking off work and being there with me today."

"I'll always be there for you," Jack tells me, kissing the side of my head.

"And I, you." I lean my head back against his chest.

I grow silent, lost in thought, as we soak in the tub together.

"Keegan, stop it now," Jack softly scolds into my ear.

"Stop what?" I ask innocently.

"I know how your mind works. The book is to answer your questions, not to create doubt."

"What do you mean?"

"Somehow, in that brain of yours, you've made a connection between Will and Brittany getting back together through her job to Chelsey and me working together. I'm not Will, and Chelsey is not Brittany. The love you and I have is the real deal, and it will get us through whatever life throws at us. Understand?"

Knowing deep down inside that all of that is true, I nod.

"Hey, let's cancel tonight and just stay in for the evening," he suggests.

Splashing water out of the tub as I turn toward him, I say, "No way in hell, bud! We're going! Oh my God, look at the time! I can't believe we've been soaking in this tub for this long. I need to swing by the studio before going to the bar. Why don't you go to happy hour, and I'll meet you there?"

"It's dumb to drive two cars. I'll just go to the studio with you, and we can go from there."

"And what if Seth and Annie are there? Do you want to get into all of that tonight after the day we've had? Marcy wants me to take a look at a shipment of clay that she thinks needs to be returned. I won't be long. You can hang with Chelsey, and when I get there, we'll grab a bite to eat and then come home."

"Okay, maybe it would be better to go by myself for a little bit before you roll in," he agrees.

Little does he know, I have no intention of going to the studio. I just want to give him an opportunity to talk to Chelsey. They need closure, and it will never happen if I'm hanging around. Hopefully, they can find a quiet corner to talk and to say the things that need to be said.

8

Jack

As soon as I enter the bar, I see the guys from headquarters around some tables off to the side of the room. Chelsey is the center of attention, and she's enjoying every minute of it. Her laughter brings back memories of the girl I thought I once loved.

She sees me and walks over. "Hey, I got the figures done on your equipment and would like to meet with you sometime this week to discuss them."

"Great! I'll check my calendar and let you know when I have some free time," I shout over the noise of the crowded bar.

Chelsey then asks, "Hey, can we go someplace quieter to talk for a couple of minutes?"

"Sure, where do you want to go?"

"Let's slip out back."

"Lead the way."

After entering the alley through the bar's back exit by the restrooms, Chelsey turns toward me and says, "So, you got married and now have kids."

"I heard you got married, too. Any kids?"

"Um, no. I got divorced last year."

"I'm sorry to hear that."

She stares off into the distance with a tentative look. "So much has changed. I always thought you and I would end up married with children. What happened?"

"You're the one who left. You tell me."

"I guess we wanted different things," Chelsey says dismissively.

"How would you know? I was never given a chance to tell you what I wanted."

She takes a step closer to me. "We had turned into being two roomies who occasionally hooked up."

I take a step back from her. "Is that how you saw us? As roomies?"

"That's the way it felt back then. I mean, how does a couple build a future together when they only get to spend a day here or there together?"

"There are a lot of couples who see less of each other than we did, and they make it. I'm sorry. I just don't buy that that's the reason we didn't make it."

"Well, it doesn't matter. You seem happy."

"Very," I respond, crossing my arms, as I slowly find myself becoming irritated with this whole conversation.

She says nothing at first and then quietly sighs. "I just don't want our history to get in the way of working together. It felt a little awkward during our meeting the other day."

I see no purpose in rehashing the past with her any further because what matters to me is my future with Keegan. "I'm good with things if you are."

A tight smile comes across her face. "Me, too. We'd better get back in there to stop God only knows what they're thinking is going on back here."

"You go ahead. I'll catch up with you inside," I tell Chelsey as my phone makes a pinging sound, signaling an incoming text.

Keegan: The talk of the bar is that you're out back with Chelsey. Want to have some fun with these jokers?

Me: Hell yeah!

Keegan: Ignore me, and follow my lead. BTW, I'm the hot-looking chick sitting at the bar. ☺

When I walk back in, I notice Keegan sitting at the bar, talking to Phil, a fellow battalion chief. She's wearing her little red dress that drives me insane. It's hard to ignore her when she looks so good.

I have no idea what Keegan is planning, but I'm sure whatever it is, Phil is never going to forget it.

9

Keegan

Unable to locate Jack in the crowd, I decided to take a seat at the bar. There are two guys to my right who are in mid conversation, pausing long enough to check me out. From their expressions, I see my decision to wear my short red bandage dress was a good one. They then return to the topic at hand, which apparently is my husband and Chelsey.

"Yeah, I saw them go out back. I can't believe Jack is sniffing around her again, especially with him just getting married."

"Chelsey is about as hot as they come, and I wouldn't blame him for tapping that one more time. What the old ball and chain doesn't know won't hurt her."

I chuckle to myself, hearing them use the same term I did at home during my argument with Jack about coming here this evening. These two need a little schooling, and I think I'm just the person to do it.

After sending Jack a couple of texts, I see a stunningly beautiful woman who fits his description of Chelsey walking into the bar from the back.

The guy closest to me confirms my suspicions. "Well, there's Chelsey but no Jack. He's probably putting his Johnson back in his pants."

Seriously? Did he just say Johnson? I haven't heard that expression since before Dad retired.

"Excuse me. I'm sorry, but I couldn't help but overhear. Who's this guy you're talking about?" I ask innocently.

They see Jack returning and nod in his direction.

"That guy there. Back in the day, he and that chick over there had a hot thing going on. Jack just got married about the same time Chelsey returned to the department. Trust me, it's only going to be a matter of time before they hook up again."

"Really? Is his wife here?" I ask while looking around the bar.

"Nah. There's no way Jack would take Chelsey out back if she were here. Hey, can I buy you a drink?"

"Sure."

Turning his back toward his buddy to give me his undivided attention, he asks, "What are you drinking?"

"Whatever is on tap is good with me."

He catches the bartender's attention and orders me a beer.

"Thank you."

I get the distinct feeling that this guy thinks he's about to get lucky tonight. If only he knew what was about to happen to him.

I continue, "Hey, I'll bet you twenty bucks I can get that guy—what's his name again?"

"Jack."

"I'll bet you twenty bucks that I can get Jack to go home with me tonight."

"Nah, not Jack. He's married now. It's never been his style to pick up women at bars. Not even you. And I've got to say, you are one hot-looking babe, darling," he says while winking at me.

First, Johnson. Now, this? Ew.

Trying to keep a straight face, I ask, "As hot as what's her name over there with your friend?"

"Chelsey?"

"Yeah, am I as hot as Chelsey?" I ask, pouting.

"Hell yeah! Chelsey isn't even in the same league as you."

"Aw, you're sweet. Come on, the worst thing that could happen is, you'd be twenty bucks richer. Go ahead. Call him over here." I give him my best pretty-please look.

He yells across the room, "Hey, Jack. Can you come over here for a sec?"

Not only does Jack start to walk toward me, but for some odd reason, Chelsey also follows behind him. Funny, I didn't hear her name being called over.

Once Jack reaches the bar, he asks my new friend, "Yeah? What's up?"

Before the guy can answer, I tap his shoulder. "Excuse me, but he called you over because I wanted to meet you."

He turns to look at me and grins. "Is that so?" He then pulls up a stool to sit down beside me. "And why did you want to meet me?"

I lean in close to him and wink. "I'm bored and looking for some fun."

"What do you have in mind?" he asks, winking back at me.

I get down from my stool to stand and rub up against him. I put my right arm around him, hiding my rings on my left hand. Then, I nibble on his ear and start whispering any naughty thing that comes to mind. The smile now spreading across Jack's face is indescribable. The guys can't believe the scene unfolding in front of them.

Chelsey is not happy and tries to interrupt by saying, "Um, Jack, I see the chief over there. I think we should go over and say hi."

I whine to him, "Baby, don't go."

He chuckles. "There is no way in hell I'm leaving this little piece of heaven right here."

I pull my arm back from around his neck and seductively run the back of my right hand down the side of his face. Then, I lay the biggest kiss on Jack's lips. He takes my kiss to the next level; it's to the point that people might start making comments about us needing to get a room. By now, everyone is standing there, gawking at us.

When we break off the kiss, we look over at everyone and start cracking up, laughing.

I lean over, extending my hand out to the guy who bought me a beer. "Hi, I'm the ball and chain, Keegan Grady. Now, pay up."

Chelsey stomps away while my buddy pulls out a twenty-dollar bill, claiming he knew all along what was going down. I take his money and add to it before instructing the bartender to put it toward the tab for Chelsey's party.

Jack says to me, "You know these guys will never stop talking about this. I think you're about to become a firehouse legend."

I laugh and then look over at Chelsey glaring at me, making sure I know she doesn't approve of my bit of fun.

Looking back at Jack, I say, "I don't think your girlfriend is very happy with me."

"Girlfriend? That's not even funny."

"According to the guys, you're eventually going to tap that again."

"Nope, never going to happen."

"Maybe we should go over and make nice with her. I think she feels like my little joke was at her expense."

"Yeah, you're probably right."

When we approach Chelsey, she doesn't waste any time in telling me her opinion of my little game. "I can't believe you pulled a stunt like that in front of Jack's bosses."

"That's enough, Chelsey. You can just—"

I put my hand on Jack's chest to interrupt. I then address Chelsey, "I'm sorry if you thought what I did was inappropriate. My dad is a retired fire chief, and early on, I learned the limits for a good joke with the guys. Can we start over?" I then say to her, "Hi, I'm Keegan. It's nice to meet you, Chelsey."

She begrudgingly replies back, "It's nice to meet you, too."

After talking with her for a few moments, I know we will never be friends. I remember my first meetings with Annie and how uneasy she made me feel. It isn't like that at all with Chelsey. I don't feel threatened or bothered that I don't measure up in her eyes.

I jump when two arms come around me from behind, and an all-too-familiar voice says, "How about you and me run away together?"

The voice belongs to Cameron, who was someone I dated for a few months after leaving Will for the second time. We were perfect together until, through social media, I discovered he was seeing someone else behind my back. Since then, Cameron has apologized, and we've been able to become friends. The last time I saw him was at Donnelly's the weekend Jack and I got back together. It was Cameron who convinced me to apologize to Jack that evening.

Before I can turn around, Jack shoves Cameron's shoulder, and a few other guys take note of what is going down. They take a stance behind Jack, as if daring Cameron to make a move.

In an attempt to defuse the situation, I pull out of Cameron's hold and go to Jack. "It's okay, babe. Cameron was just clowning around."

Cameron steps back, holding his hands up. "Hey, man, sorry. I didn't know she was with you. I was just messing around."

Jack, still pissed off, says, "Go mess around with someone else's wife."

"Wife? Did you two end up getting married? Christ, that sure must have been one hell of an apology!"

I hold my left hand up to him. "Yeah, we got married a few weeks ago."

Cameron pulls me back into his arms for a hug and says, "Congratulations!"

Jack steps up to him. "Get your damn hands off her!"

We break our hug, and Cameron steps back, extending his hand out to Jack. "Sorry. No harm. Hey, congratulations!"

I can't figure out why Jack is acting like this and barely acknowledging Cameron's well wishes. Then, I remember the conversation Jack and I had up at the lake house when he told me he had fucked Annie during our breakup because she was a sure thing.

My childish response to him plays back in my head. *"You know Cameron, the guy I was with last night? He has one hot, rock-hard body. Guess you could call him a sure thing, too. God, sex with him is awesome."*

Shit! How am I going to explain this to them without looking like an idiot?

"Um, guys, we need to find a table where I can explain some things," I say uncomfortably.

"I don't need to hear anything else about this asshole that you haven't already told me," Jack says to me.

Cameron can't help but chime in, "You know, I've been trying real hard to be nice, but you're slowly getting on my last nerve. I haven't done a damn thing to you, so why don't you just cool it with the attitude and back off?"

Of course, Jack can't let it go and now announces to the bar—or at least to those standing within hearing range— "You call fucking my wife nothing?"

God, please just let the floor open and drop me into hell where I belong.

Utterly humiliated by Jack's outburst, I say in a deliberate voice through clenched teeth, "Stop it! Outside. Now!"

I march the two of them out of the bar to the parking lot, feeling the eyes of everyone on us as we leave.

Once outside, I turn to Jack and Cameron, "No one speaks until I finish talking. Do you understand?"

Both nod with a touch of fear in their eyes.

"Okay. Cam, I apologized to Jack after leaving Donnelly's. We spent that weekend together, and I might have misrepresented some stuff about you and me to piss him off."

Jack and Cameron both have stunned looks on their faces for two entirely different reasons.

"Jack, the stuff I told you about Cameron and me happened when we were dating way back before I even knew you."

"So, what did you say to him, Keegan? It must have been pretty good for him to go off like that," Cameron says with a smirk.

Frowning back at him, I snap back, "Don't flatter yourself. I used you as payback for something Jack said, and I might have enhanced the truth a bit."

This time, it is Jack snickering. "So, all of that was a bunch of bullshit? You weren't with each other after we broke up?"

By now, my head is hanging low, and I squeak out, "No. The night you saw us at Donnelly's wasn't a date. We just ran into each other. I'm sorry if I made you think it was more than that."

Cameron claps his hands together. "Well, it's been fun catching up with you, but it's time for me to leave this little party. Again, congratulations, and I hope you two get your shit sorted out. Just keep me the hell out of it." He exits to go back to the bar, leaving Jack and me in the parking lot.

Jack just stares at me, saying nothing. Then, he turns and goes back to the bar. I stand there, not knowing what to do. I'm too embarrassed to go back in, especially after Chelsey witnessed everything.

I see my car parked a few spaces away from where I'm standing. Fortunately, I have my purse with me, making it easy for me to make a fast getaway.

I text Jack before leaving.

> *Me: I'm wiped out. Think I'm going home. Take your time, and enjoy hanging out with your friends.*

>> *Jack: You want me to take you home? We can come back for your car tomorrow.*

> *Me: No, I'm good.*

>> *Jack: Okay.*

My parents are away at the beach this week. I promised them that I'd check on the house while they were gone. I'm in need of a cigarette break, so instead of going home, I decide to head to the dock and have a pity party for myself.

Once reaching the dock, I kick off my sandals before sitting down. I lean back on its wooden boards while propping myself up onto my elbows to take in my surroundings. The lapping of the water against the lake's bank has a calming effect on me. The things I love about this time of year are the long, warm days and the late sunsets that occur well after eight o'clock in the evening. Tonight, the sky is putting on a show with the most incredible colors as the sun begins to sink behind the horizon.

I start mulling over the day. I can't help but wonder if there will ever come a time when there won't be so much drama in my life.

I sense Jack before he reaches the dock.

He plops down beside me. "Talk to me," he says.

"How did you know I was here?" I ask.

"I knew you would be here when I found you weren't at home. Now, talk to me."

I lie down on the dock, looking up at the sky. "I've got nothing for you. Absolutely nothing."

Jack lies down beside me and takes my hand in his.

He looks over at me and apologizes, "I'm sorry for losing my cool back at the bar and for embarrassing you like that."

He gives me a soft kiss.

"I had it coming. I'm sorry everybody thinks you're married to a slut," I reply back.

"No, they don't. I explained everything and ended up having a drink with Cameron. He's a pretty cool guy," Jack says to me.

My pity party ends abruptly. "What? The two of you had a beer along with a good laugh while I've been here, beating myself up? Well, isn't that just peachy?" I quickly get up and start stomping across the yard, barefooted.

Jack comes running up behind me and swoops me up into his arms. "Someone needs to cool off." He takes off running toward the pool with me screaming in his arms before he jumps into it.

"Damn it! This dress cost me a fortune!"

Jack stops my protest with slow, deep kisses.

As he pushes me up against the side of the pool, he says, "Do you have any idea how much I love you, Keegan Grady? You are my beginning and end. Tonight was amazing. Life with you will never be dull."

Under the surface of the water, Jack inches my dress up, and then he slides his hand under my thong. I start to respond to his touch by moving my hips against his hand.

His other hand starts fondling my breast through my dress as he kisses my neck.

"That's it, baby. Let me watch you fall apart against my hand," Jack says in a low, husky voice.

"Jack, we shouldn't…" I get lost in what he's doing to me.

"Shh…relax and enjoy. You whispered some things in my ear at the bar tonight, and I expect you to keep your end of the bargain."

I look up at him. "You don't play fair."

"Nope. Never promised to play fair. Only promised that I would respect, love, and cherish you until we are parted by death," he says.

10

Jack

After grabbing a cup of coffee, I head to my desk to check emails and the schedule for today. I have a block of time late this morning when I can meet with Chelsey about the new apparatuses; otherwise, it will have to wait until sometime on Friday. I shoot her a quick email. She responds, saying that today's time works best for her but asks for us to meet at headquarters.

Arriving in Chelsey's office just a few minutes before eleven o'clock, I find she still has unpacked boxes stacked in the corner. On her desk are pictures of her time in the fire service. One of them includes me with my arm around her in the center of a group of friends, celebrating our graduation from the fire academy. The picture was taken moments after I asked her to move in with me. Even though it's an innocent picture of friends having fun, it brings back memories that I've tried to keep in the past where they belong.

Chelsey catches me looking at the picture and picks it up. "I think this is my favorite one. We were all so young and happy that night, not knowing what was coming down the road for any of us."

I nod in agreement. "Yeah, that night was a long time ago."

It's almost as if she can read my mind as I wonder, of all the pictures, why this one is on display.

"I keep it out as a reminder of what rookies deal with in their new careers. It's easy to forget what it's like, starting out while quoting the regulations by chapter and verse."

Chelsey quickly changes the subject by inviting me to have a seat at her conference table, and she begins to go over the figures for the new pieces of equipment. As I feared, the rest of the time is spent haggling over what could be cut to bring the costs more in line with the budget. Eventually, we find mutual ground and reach a consensus on the final specifications.

I'm packing up my paperwork to head out when Chelsey notices it's noon. "Hey, it's lunchtime. There's a diner down the street that has some great food. You have time to get a bite to eat?"

"Yeah, sounds good. Let me check in at the station. I'll only be a minute."

Soon, we find ourselves sitting in a booth, giving the waitress our orders. After the waitress walks away, we sit eerily quiet while I desperately try to think of something to say.

"How are your parents doing?" I ask.

"Good. Both are retired and doing a lot of traveling. How about yours?"

"They're retired, too, and living down at the bay."

"It was nice meeting Keegan the other night. Boy, she sure isn't the type of girl I thought you would end up marrying."

"Why do you say that?" I ask curiously.

"I don't know. I mean, the whole bit at the bar and then that guy making a scene. It just shocks me a little to see you've ended up with someone like that."

I chuckle a little, shaking my head. "Once you get to know her better, you'll see that she's pretty amazing. She's been through a lot."

"Yeah? Like what?"

"She was in a car accident. While she was in the hospital, the doctors found a brain tumor. Her first husband, who was a state cop, died while she was recovering from the accident and surgery."

"A tumor? Wow. Is she okay?"

"Keegan's fine. The tumor was benign. There was no need for any further treatment."

"Thank God. And you were together when all of this happened?"

"Yeah, my station responded to the car accident."

"That must have been tough for you."

"Worst day of my life. So, tell me, why did you decide to come back?"

"I got divorced and needed a new beginning somewhere else. I wanted to be closer to my parents, so when the administrative chief position came open, I put in for it."

I'm not paying attention to the comings and goings of the diner's customers, so I'm surprised when Keegan unexpectedly shows up to our booth.

"Hey, guys," she says.

I stand and greet her with a hug. "Hey, babe. Here, have a seat, and join us." I step aside, so she can slide into the booth.

"Sorry. I need to get back to the studio. Marcy is leaving early today, and I'm covering for her. I just left a consignment shop a few doors down and stopped in to get something to drink."

"You have a studio?" Chelsey asks.

"Yeah, a pottery studio and store. You should stop in sometime and check them out. Hey, I need to get out of here. I'll let the two of you get back to your lunch."

"Chelsey, I'll be right back." I leave her sitting as I walk Keegan out.

Once outside on the sidewalk, I take her in my arms. "I didn't want to miss out on an opportunity to kiss you."

She smiles after I give her a kiss, and tells me, "I love you beyond the stars and back."

"I love you, too. Thanks for stopping by and making my day better."

"Any special requests for dinner?"

"You?"

Keegan giggles as she walks away backward and says, "Kyle might have a little bit of a problem with that one. Maybe I could be dessert later tonight."

"With some cherry cheesecake?" I shout back.

She laughs and waves as she turns to go to her car.

When I return to the booth, Chelsey asks, "Everything okay?"

"Yeah, everything is great." I grin back at her as I think back to Keegan's comments about dessert later this evening.

"Jack, I still can't believe you got married. You really seem happy."

"You have no idea."

Kirby greets me as I come in through the back door to the kitchen. There, waiting for me on the counter, is a cherry cheesecake with a note scribbled beside it.

Kyle decided to spend the night with Joyce. Thought we could skip dinner and go straight to dessert. If you're game, meet me upstairs. Don't forget to bring the cheesecake and a couple of forks!

K

"Hell yeah!"

After grabbing the cheesecake in one hand and a couple of forks in the other, I almost trip over Kirby while taking the stairs two steps at a time.

II

Keegan

Stretching the next morning, I discover a note on Jack's pillow.

> *To my Sleeping Beauty,*
>
> *I didn't have the heart to wake you this morning.*
>
> *Thank you for the amazing dessert last night. It's the best I've ever tasted.*
>
> *Love you beyond the stars and back.*
>
> *Your loving Prince Charming*

I lie there, smiling like a silly schoolgirl. I pick up my phone from the nightstand next to me and text Jack.

Me: To my Prince Charming, I love you. Have a wonderful day at work.

> *Jack: In a boring staff meeting. Wish I were back in bed with you. Talk to you later.*

I wonder if Chelsey is in the meeting with him. There is something about her that strikes me as odd. It might be the whole old-girlfriend-meeting-the-new-wife thing, but I sense there's more to it than that.

Jack's love note will join other special keepsakes from him that are safely tucked away in a lidded porcelain box creation of mine that sits on my dresser.

I get ready for the day and then head to the basement to a room that was originally Jack's study but is now our shared office. I pull out all my notes that I've taken to date for the book and spread them across the desk, contemplating the best way to start organizing my thoughts.

I read over them and sit for a couple of moments, thinking about the book. *Should it begin at Will's birth or later as a teenager during his drug arrest?*

I didn't enter his life until his senior year in college. I only have his mother's version of his earlier years, except for the firsthand account that Will wrote in the letter he left me.

Suddenly, it all clicks in place. I change my original concept of the book from one focused on Will's undercover work to a story about us, starting with the first day we met in the college library. I start jotting down a rough outline to use as a road map, purposely keeping it brief.

Once satisfied with it, I open my laptop and type.

ULTIMATE COST BY KEEGAN GRADY

Chapter 1

I was standing at the counter of the college library, getting ready to check out a book when…

It feels like a dam has burst wide open, and the words come flowing out faster than I can type them.

Before I know it, Kyle is walking through the front door, announcing he's home from school. He is now officially a senior in high school. Being so immersed in my writing, it slipped my mind that today was the last day of school and the start of summer break. Six hours passed in a blink, and I've already written four chapters of the book. It is killing me to stop, but I have dinner to fix and things to tend to before Jack gets home from work.

I shut down my laptop, filled with a sense of accomplishment, and I'm anxious to get back to it. Deciding to keep quiet about my writing today, I tuck my notes and computer away. For the moment, I'm not ready for anyone to know that I've started to write it.

It's Jack's evening with Sean, and they enter our home, laughing about something they saw while driving home.

We decide to celebrate the end of school by going out to play some miniature golf. Afterward, we stop for some ice cream on the way home.

As we sit at our table, waiting for our orders, Chelsey walks in with a couple of friends. As her group passes us on the way to their table, she acts as if it is a chore to acknowledge us with her brief hello. She is gone so fast that Jack didn't have a chance to introduce the boys to her.

"Who was that?" Kyle asks.

"It's someone Jack knows from work. I guess she's in a hurry to catch up with her friends," I reply in an attempt to make an excuse for her rude behavior, looking over to Jack.

He only shrugs his shoulders in response and picks up the conversation where we left off.

Once home and settled in bed, I ask Jack, "Back when you and Chelsey were together, was she always so uptight? Is it me, or is she like that all the time?"

"No, *uptight* is the last word I would use to describe Chelsey when we were together. In fact, she could be pretty wild at times. A woman working in a firehouse needs to have a good sense of humor and not take herself too seriously to survive."

"So, wild, huh? Would you like to elaborate?"

"Um, no, I wouldn't. Let's just say, when it comes to being wild, you've got Chelsey beat by a mile."

"Good save." I snicker.

"Mama didn't raise any dummies," Jack mutters under his breath.

A few weeks later, I stop by the coffee shop with my laptop in hand to write a little while enjoying an early morning chai latte. The book is coming together much faster than expected, and I find myself writing whenever I have a few free moments. I glance up while typing mid sentence to see Seth plop down in front of me on the other side of the booth.

"May I help you?" I ask while saving my work.

"Are you avoiding me?"

"No. So, what's new?" I ask, trying hard to change the topic of our conversation.

"Come on, let's just put it all out here on the table and deal with it," Seth persists.

"Can we please not do this now? I love you and don't want to upset you," I appeal to him.

"Keegan, I know your history with Annie. Her head was in a different place back then. She's not that person. She is a good—"

Frowning at him, I interrupt, "She's a *bitch*! Annie did her best to destroy what Jack and I had. For God's sake, Seth, who in the hell would make someone think the person they loved had died? Only deranged sickos do that kind of crap! You saw what it did to me, and now, you're sleeping with the enemy. Thanks a lot, *friend*!"

"Jesus! Now, why don't you tell me how you really feel?"

Throwing a piercing look in his direction, I snap back at him, "You asked for it."

"Okay, now, let me have my say. Think back to when Cassidy dumped me. How did I act? Did my actions back then remind you of anyone we know? People act out when someone has hurt you like that."

"I didn't," I gloat.

"Oh no, you just had a nervous breakdown and dumped Jack when Will died; that's all."

"Go to hell, Seth. You know there was more to it than that." I start to pack up my things to get as far away from him as possible.

"Keegan, wait," he responds, grabbing my arm. "Just hear me out, please?"

I stop packing and turn my attention back to him.

He continues, "I'm sorry. That was a rotten thing to say to you. It's just...the person you met four years ago is not who Annie is. She was trying to save the family that she had with Jack and Sean."

"Bullshit! Jack had already left her."

"No, they weren't together as a couple, but they were still a happy family. You don't get it, do you? It was never about her being in love with Jack. She wanted to keep her family intact. After they broke up, Jack kept going over to her house every night he was off to have dinner with them and help out with Sean. The only thing that changed was him sleeping with her. It was never about the love or sex but the bond they shared as Sean's parents. She was being a mama bear and saw you as a threat to her family."

During the weekend up at the lake when we got back together, I remember Jack telling me how easy it was to fall back into the old routine of going over to her house every night. Jack and Annie ended up in bed only once during the three years we were apart, and both of them were drunk when that happened.

"If what you're saying is true, maybe you're just a filler to complete the family she needs."

"I've gone to counseling with her. I know what's in her heart," Seth defensively says to me.

"I hope so because I would hate to see you go through what you did with Cassidy."

"Keegan, I'm going to ask Annie to marry me one day," he announces.

"*What?* Just promise me, you'll give it some serious thought before doing that."

"I will." He smiles at me.

I've lost all desire to write after Seth leaves the coffee shop. I decide to walk down to the studio, only to find Annie there, glazing some pieces during open studio time. I politely acknowledge her and go back to the office to see Marcy.

"Hey, how are things going?" I ask her.

"Great! No problems with the kilns. The clay order came in, and it was perfect. Open studio is running smoothly. As I said, everything is great. Must be the excellent management running this joint," she says jokingly. "Why are you here? You got all the receipts yesterday, and it's not payday."

"I was down at the coffee shop. Seth crashed my happy place by pleading Annie's case to me. God, Marcy, it's Cassidy all over again."

"What do you mean, it's Cassidy all over again?"

"I mean, that bitch out there in the studio is going to do a number on him, and we'll be the ones left to pick up the pieces."

"Have you seen those two together? I thought you and Jack were sickening. They have you guys beat by a mile. I hate to tell you, Keegan, but they're the real thing. She's not using him."

"Yeah, and there's a Santa Claus and an Easter Bunny, too! You saw how she played Jack every chance she could. Do you think that, all of a sudden, she's miraculously changed?"

"Sorry, but from what I see, it's real," Marcy says, walking back to the stockroom.

I stand there, astonished that Annie has not only fooled Seth, but now also Marcy.

As I am getting ready to leave, Annie enters, walking over to the inventory of clay for a package of Red Rock.

"Hi, Annie. Marcy will be right with you." I sling the strap of my laptop carrier over my shoulder to make a quick exit.

"Do you have a minute to talk?" she asks.

"I'm kind of in a hurry. Is it something you can discuss with Jack when he picks up Sean this week?" I ask, praying to God she says yes.

"No, this involves you. I promise, it will take only a sec."

"Okay, shoot," I say, crossing my arms.

"I just want you to know that I am in love with Seth. I'm sorry for my past behavior. I hope, one day, we can put it behind us and move on from it. I know we will never be best friends, but I'd like to at least be able to tolerate each other enough to be civil for Seth's and Sean's sake. That's all I wanted to say."

"You can understand me being a little skeptical of this whole thing you have with Seth. I hope what you're saying is true. Guess we'll just have to wait and see."

"All I'm asking for is a chance to prove myself. Thanks for hearing me out." Annie turns and heads back to the glazing room without her clay.

I leave the studio to go home to salvage what is left of the day to write. Usually, once I get in my groove, away from interruptions, the words flow smoothly. Sadly, I'm unable to switch my focus from Seth and Annie to writing. Instead, I decide to read the chapters I've written to check the flow of the story. With any luck, it might get me inspired to write some more before everyone comes home for the evening.

After I've finished reading the last sentence, I find myself irritable and restless. I blame it on all the day's drama and decide an evening to chill up at the lake is what's needed.

I text Jack.

> *Me: Think I'll check on things up at the lake tonight. I'm taking Kirby with me. You and Kyle are on your own for dinner.*

> *Jack: What's going on?*

> *Me: Nothing. Just taking a break and going up to check on the house. Will see you tomorrow morning before Kyle leaves for the beach.*

> *Jack: Bullshit! Talk to me.*

> *Me: Really, I'm good.*

Then, there is nothing more from Jack.

The moment I drive through the gates and pass the guardhouse at the lake's entrance, I feel the tension disappear from my shoulders. I pull into the garage and unpack the car of all the goodies I picked up at a local farmers market.

Kirby is anxious to run down to visit the lake, so I take him down to the dock. I get comfy on the lounger as he sniffs around the dock, making sure everything is in order.

Just as I doze off, the sound of Jack's voice wakes me up.

"What the hell do you mean by taking a break? What's going on that you felt the need to run away up here tonight? This is bullshit!" Jack bellows out, towering over me with his hands on his hips.

I stand up, wrapping my arms around him. "Shh…calm down. I just needed some quiet; that's all."

"Talk to me," Jack tells me as he sits on the end of the lounger.

Taking a seat next to him, I try to explain, "Things have been crazy since we've gotten back from our honeymoon. I've been interviewing people for the book. Then, there was Chelsey's happy-hour fiasco. And, today, to top it off, Seth wanted to talk to me about Annie. I needed some peace and quiet. So, I came up here to check on things."

Jack stares at me, saying nothing.

"No comment?" I ask him.

"What do you want me to say? Poor baby?"

"Excuse me? What's crawled up your butt?" I ask, now becoming annoyed with his lack of sympathy for me.

"I'm sorry, Keegan, but what you just described to me is life. Shit happens to all of us, and we learn to deal with it. So, I'll tell you what. Take your break, and come home when you're ready. I'm out of here," Jack says in a huff. He gets up and walks toward the house.

Stunned by his response, I watch him walk away as painful regret comes over me.

Jumping up, I run to him, yelling, "Jack, wait a minute!"

He stops and turns to face me with a type of anger in his eyes that I don't ever remember seeing before. It is then I know how badly my actions and words have hurt him. Since buying the lake house, it's become my habit to use it as a retreat to recharge when the crazy of everyday life starts to take over. It occurs to me, by coming here today, I shut him out, exactly like I had on the day of my breakdown.

"Baby, I'm sorry. It's become a habit of mine to come up here when things get a little nutty at home. I didn't mean to exclude you or shut you out. I'm sorry."

He responds by taking me in his arms. "We're a team, goddamn it! When are you going to get that through your head? We're here for each other when things get to be too much to handle. There's no taking a break or running away. We're in this together."

As calmly as possible, I attempt to explain, "For years, I've used this place as my escape from the outside world. When I came here today by myself, I never gave it a thought as to how it would make you feel. Again, I'm sorry."

"Keegan, you've got to stop running away. That's all you've been doing since the day we met."

"No, I haven't."

"What do you call your cigarette breaks down at the dock? It was one thing when you lived with your parents, but you left me at the bar the other night to run over there."

"Your little announcement to the bar about Cameron fucking your wife was humiliating. There was no way I was going to go back in that bar, especially with Chelsey being there. She had already told me how inappropriate our joke was earlier that night. I can only imagine what she thought about the whole thing with Cameron!"

"If anyone was humiliated, it should have been me since I was the one who was making an ass out of myself. I went back in and manned up for my actions while you went running off, feeling sorry for yourself."

"Well, whoop-de-do for you! How dare you even think that about me! If that's the person you see standing here in front of you, then you have no idea who I am! At this rate, our marriage might have a shorter life span than either of my ones with Will. I guess the good news is, since Annie's with Seth, at least you'll have Chelsey close by to run back to!" I turn and call out to Kirby, "Come on, Kirby. Time to go inside."

Kirby scampers up the hill behind me as I run up to the house because I have lost all desire to continue this asinine conversation with Jack.

A few minutes later, Jack enters our bedroom where I have ended up lying on the bed with Kirby in my arms.

"I'm not sure how we got from you taking a break to our marriage ending and me going back to Chelsey."

I lie curled up in a ball with my back to him, so he can't see the tears streaming down my face.

"Keegan, I need to understand what just happened between us."

I continue to remain quiet.

"Talk to me, Keegan. I'm getting tired of always asking what you're thinking. Just tell me, so we can deal with this shit."

"All I wanted was to come up here and turn off the noise for five fucking minutes. Instead, it's followed me up here."

Jack leaves without saying another word to me.

12

Jack

After hearing Keegan's last comment, I knew it was time for me to go back home. I heard nothing from her for the remainder of the night.

The next morning, after little sleep, I get ready for work and head downstairs for my morning cup of coffee. Kyle is downstairs, all set to leave for his weeklong stay with his uncle's family at their beach house. I've just finished telling him good morning and to have a safe trip when Keegan walks in through the back door.

"Ready for the beach?" she asks Kyle, acting as if nothing happened between us.

"Yeah, I'm getting ready to head out now."

"Are you following Uncle Ryan down in your car?" Since Keegan purchased a new Jeep that matches mine, she gave Kyle her Mustang convertible to drive.

"Yeah, all of us guys are riding together," he says, referring to his two cousins.

"Well, be careful. You're carrying precious cargo in your car," she warns him.

"I will," he promises. "How are things up at the lake?"

"Great! The boat is all ready for when you get back home. Here's some money. Remember, you don't have to spend it all, but have fun," she says, smiling at him. She gives him a hug, "Bye, sweetie. I'll miss you. Be sure to call me when you get down there."

"Will do. Bye, Jack. See you guys next Friday," Kyle says as he walks out the door to his car.

I say my final good-bye to Kyle as Keegan walks past me and goes upstairs without saying another word.

Standing in the kitchen, torn over what to do next, I decide to go about my business and leave for work.

The day drags on at work, and still, there's no word from Keegan all day. I'm not sure what to do at this point. I decide, when I get home from work, a run might help me put things in perspective.

As I pack up for the day, my office phone rings. Immediately, I grab the receiver in hopes that it's Keegan, only to find out it's Chelsey calling.

"Good, I caught you. I was afraid you had left for the day," she says.

"I was just getting ready to leave for home and go for a run," I tell her.

"That's what I was going to do after work, too. You want some company?"

"Sure. A park close to where I live has a great trail. You might know it. It's the park off of Emerson."

"I know it well. I love running there."

"See you there in about an hour?" I suggest.

"Great. That gives me plenty of time to go home and change."

"Hey, why did you call?" I ask.

"We can talk at the park," she says before we hang up.

When I arrive home from work, Kirby is the only one there, anxiously waiting to be let out.

Keegan still isn't here when I am ready to go meet up with Chelsey at the park for our run. By now, I'm getting worried. No matter how upset Keegan is with me, she always lets me know when she's running late. I shoot her a quick text before leaving.

> Me: *Is everything okay other than you being pissed off at me? Can we talk when you get home? I'm going for a run.*

There's no reply back from her.

As I jog into the park, I see Chelsey off in the distance, doing her stretches beside a bench.

Once I reach her, I ask, "Ready?"

"Don't you want to stretch?"

"Nah, I jogged here. I'm ready to go," I reply while patiently waiting as she finishes up. I ask her, "Why did you call me?"

Chelsey stands up straight. "To tell you that I've reviewed firefighter Rogers's grievance against his captain. I don't see anything that substantiates his claims. You should be getting a copy of my decision in writing this week. Rogers can appeal my decision further up the chain of command."

"If I know Rogers, he'll probably do that. Thanks for the heads-up."

"Not a problem."

We start out on the trail, not saying much, setting our pace.

I can't resist teasing Chelsey, "It's good to see that you can still keep up with me after all these years."

"Same ego problem as always. I think we've proven too many times who has more stamina between the two of us."

"Is that so?"

"I believe it was me who always beat you in the marathons we ran. You still run them?"

"Nah. How about you?"

"Yeah. In fact, I have one coming up next month. Are you interested in joining me?"

"Too out of shape."

"Married life made you soft?"

"No, fatherhood."

Chelsey becomes quiet as we continue with our run.

The trail twists and turns for several miles until we are heading back to the bench where we started, slowing our pace to cool down. A few yards away from where we began, I pull my left calf muscle, causing me to stumble down onto the path.

Standing over me with her hands on her hips, Chelsey asks in her all-familiar I-told-you-so voice, "Okay, Mr. I Don't Need to Stretch, how bad is it?"

"It's not bad. Just help me up," I answer while holding my arm up for her to grab. Once back on my feet, I try to work out the cramp in my leg but with no success. It's then I start to consider how painful the short walk home is going to be and how to manage it.

"Come on. My car is over there. I'll give you a ride home. You know the drill. RICE—rest, ice, compression, and elevation."

Chelsey helps me hobble over to her car, and she drives me home. I find Keegan still isn't here.

Chelsey helps me over to the couch, so I can elevate my leg. Then, she gets a bag of frozen peas from the freezer.

After my leg is resting on a bag of peas wrapped in a tea towel and I've taken some pain relievers, Chelsey asks, "Are you expecting Keegan home soon? I'm not sure if it's a good idea to leave you here alone."

Not wanting to confess that I have no idea as to where my wife is or even if she's coming home, I lie to her, "She should be here any minute. You can take off."

"Nah, I'll stick around for a few more minutes. It's okay. Can I get you anything else?"

"Yeah, my phone is lying over there on the kitchen island."

The second Chelsey hands it to me, I check my phone for texts. Still nothing from Keegan, but there is a message from Marcy.

> *Marcy: Keegan wanted me to let you know she's running late tonight. She'll explain when she gets home.*

"Everything okay?" Chelsey asks.

Feeling a small bit of relief from Marcy's message, I answer, "Yeah, Keegan is running a little late. Listen, there's no reason for you to hang around here and ruin your evening. Seriously, I'm all right."

Before Chelsey can answer, Keegan comes in through the back door. She looks at Chelsey and then over to me. Without even saying hello, she sets the bag she's carrying on the kitchen counter.

Keegan walks over to the two of us. "Hi, Chelsey. What happened here?"

"We went running together"—Chelsey giggles—"and someone didn't do any stretches before we started, and he ended up straining a calf muscle. I've given him a couple of pain relievers and applied a bag of peas to the strain. Just do the RICE protocol, and he should be fine."

"Rice?" Keegan questions.

"Yeah. Rest, ice, compression, and elevation—RICE."

"Oh, and here I thought, we were going to have to order out for Chinese tonight," Keegan says sarcastically while looking at me.

From Chelsey's expression, I can tell she senses something is off between Keegan and me. "Well, time for me to get out of here. Take care of the strain. Talk to you soon, Jack. Nice seeing you, Keegan."

As Keegan follows Chelsey to the front door, I hear her say, "Thanks for taking care of Jack."

"No problem. Once a paramedic, always a paramedic. Night," Chelsey tells Keegan as she leaves.

Keegan walks back in the room and looks at me for a moment, as if she's sizing up the situation. "You need anything else, or has Chelsey taken care of everything?"

"Nope, I'm good."

Without another word, Keegan goes out to the kitchen and feeds Kirby. It takes him two minutes to inhale his food. She then lets him out to do his business. Once back in the house, without saying anything to me, Keegan picks up the bag off the kitchen island and goes upstairs, like she did this morning.

What the hell is going on? I'm sitting here, injured, and my wife leaves, not giving a damn about me. Even though we're not talking to each other, you'd think she could muster up a little sympathy.

I hear water running upstairs, and by the sound of it, I determine she's taking a shower. I'll give her time to get out of the shower before hobbling up the stairs to find out what's going on. A few minutes later, after hearing the blow-dryer being shut off, I hear footsteps coming down the stairs. Keegan walks in, wrapped in a towel that's showing off an abundant amount of cleavage and barely covering her ass. She might as well not bother to wear anything.

Ah, now, I know the game we're playing. It's called punishment. Keegan knows how it affects me, watching her walking around, knowing she's naked under that towel. She also knows, there's not a whole lot I can do about it.

Now, the question is, exactly why am I being punished?

Keegan walks up to the couch while biting into an apple, much like Eve did to Adam. "You want anything?"

"You?" I ask with a smirk.

She responds without a hint of a smile, "Not in your wildest dreams, bud!"

"Okay, what game are you playing? Just spit it out. My leg hurts, you haven't said one damn word to me all day, and now, you're parading around here like that." I nod my head in her direction.

"*Me? Playing games!* I apologized to you last night and tried to explain how going up to the lake was nothing but a habit of mine. You started accusing me of all sorts of stuff and then left. No, wait, *you ran away* to feel sorry for yourself. After giving us both time to calm down, I came home this morning, thinking we could talk and clear things up between us. I went upstairs after Kyle left for the beach, thinking you would follow. Instead, you left again! Excuse me. *You ran away again.* To top it all off, I come home this evening, only to be greeted by your new little jogging buddy, Chelsey, playing doctor with you. So, exactly who's the one playing games around here, Jack?"

She stops long enough to catch a breath and then continues, "Let me know if and when you get the urge to talk because, by the looks of things, you're in no shape to run away anymore. Until then, if you don't need anything else, I'm going to bed. Good night. Come on, Kirby."

I sit for a moment, considering her comments. Although a little overly stated, she was right about the sequence of things. My bruised ego couldn't handle her going up to the lake instead of coming to me. She did apologize and try to explain her actions.

After removing the bag now filled with thawed peas, I limp over and pitch it in the kitchen sink. Then, I slowly make my way upstairs to our bedroom. I find Keegan curled up in bed with Kirby snuggled up against her chest.

Damn lucky dog!

Using furniture in our bedroom for support, I make my way to the bathroom to shower. The hot water helps loosen up my sore muscle and makes it feel better.

After my shower, I find some pain-reliever ointment in the medicine cabinet and apply it to my calf. I would kill for one of Keegan's deep-muscle massages right about now.

I climb into bed to find Keegan's back to me. I don't ever remember falling asleep like this with her, and I don't like it.

Lying on my back, not being able to handle the silence any longer, I ask, "Can we talk?"

"I'm listening."

"I'm sorry for accusing you of running away from things. I was hurt you left for the lake, never thinking to ask me to come with you."

"During the years we were apart, it was second nature for me to go to the lake whenever the mood struck. I meant nothing by it, and I'm sorry you took it personally. I guess it's kind of like how I was sensitive to the stuff you did with Annie when we first started dating. I'll try to be more considerate of your feelings in the future. If I screw it up again, please just tell me."

"Okay, but the killer was when you threw ending our marriage and Chelsey in my face. There was no call for it. You need to stop doing that to me. I'm not Will or any of those other guys in your past."

I hear the rustling of the sheets as Keegan rolls over to face me.

"I'm sorry, but there was something else going on that day."

I look over at her. "What?"

"I started writing the book."

"Yeah, I know."

"How did you know?" she asks.

"You're never without your laptop. I also hear when you get up in the middle of the night to work on it."

"Why haven't you asked me about it?"

"Because I knew you'd eventually tell me. My guess, it's been pretty hard to write and kind of personal. How's it going?"

"The writing isn't the problem. Yesterday, I read what I had written up to now."

"And?"

"And, even though it was me, I didn't recognize myself. Reading it all back…" Keegan pauses.

"Tell me."

"It made me realize how much I've gone through to get to where I am today."

"How does that make you feel?"

A slow smile spreads across Keegan's face. "It feels good. The problem was having this great revelation up at the lake last night, and I couldn't tell you. When you didn't come upstairs to talk this morning, I thought I had really screwed things up between us. Then, tonight, walking in on Chelsey taking care of you pissed me off. It's my job to take care of you, not hers."

"Why didn't you call me? Marcy sent a text about you explaining something to me."

"I had to get a new phone today because I found out that recycling clay and cell phones don't mix. I'm still not sure how it happened, but my phone ended up in the hopper of the pug mill. It wasn't pretty."

"What's a pug mill?"

"You know that thing in the glazing room that looks like a huge meat grinder on steroids?"

"Yeah."

"It's called a pug mill, and it's used to recycle clay."

Jack starts laughing. "Sounds like your day was just about as bad as mine."

"By the looks of things, yours was going pretty good when I walked in."

I look up at the ceiling and run my hands through my hair in frustration. "God, she wouldn't go home. Chelsey insisted on staying until you got home."

"So, is running a thing with the two of you?"

"Yeah, we used to do marathons together. Chelsey invited me to go with her to one next month."

"Are you going?"

"Nah, I never enjoyed them. I only did it because she liked doing them. Not really my thing."

"Why do we do that? Do things or change who we are to please other people? Why can't we be ourselves, flaws and all?"

I look back over at her. "Are you saying you aren't yourself around me?"

"No, the exact opposite. What I'm trying to say is, the person in this bed with you, right this very minute, is the real Keegan Grady. I lost her years ago, and it feels good to have her back. I hope you never feel the need to be anyone other than yourself around me."

It then occurs to me why my relationship with Chelsey or Annie never worked out. I was always trying to please them. The guilt consumed me when I couldn't live up to their expectations. I have never felt that way with Keegan.

Snapping me out of my thoughts, she asks, "How's the leg?"

"Hurts like a son of a bitch. Will you massage it for me?"

Keegan laughs out loud. "How many times have I heard that line before?"

13

Keegan

Today, Kyle and I are making our annual pilgrimage to Will's grave on the anniversary of his death. When we come here, memories of that brutally hot August day flood my thoughts. I remember the honor guard, who represents police departments from all around the state, leading the funeral possession to the gravesite. I can still see the state troopers along with other law enforcement officers saluting Will one last time as his Maryland flag-draped casket passed by them.

I hold my breath when Kyle sets the vase upright for the flowers we brought from Mom's garden. Seeing that it's empty, I'm able to breathe normally again.

After tending to the flowers, Kyle stands and stares at the gravestone in silence.

I glance over to him and ask, "You okay?"

With his head hanging down, he nods. "Yeah. I was thinking how it would be if Dad were still here. I miss him."

"I do, too." I put my arm around him for support and comfort.

It might be a dreary September afternoon outside, but it couldn't be more beautiful inside my home as I sit in front of my laptop, looking at the last sentence of my book *Ultimate Cost*. The feeling of accomplishment is indescribable as I stare at the final period of the manuscript. Gone is the unrest I felt before my wedding, replaced with resolve and peace. What started as a quest to fill in gaps of missing information has turned into an understanding that there are times we have no control over where our lives take us.

It will be a year next Friday when I unexpectedly ran into Jack at Donnelly's for the first time in three years. Little did I know during our brief encounter that night at the bar, I would not only marry Jack, but he'd also encourage me to write a book about Will.

With a smile, I save my work, close my laptop, and run down to the studio to pick up some invoices and fired pottery that I made to sell at the store.

I find Marcy sitting at the desk in the back office when I arrive.

I mention to her, "You know, it will be a year next Friday when Jack and I got back together."

"Really? My God, a hell of a lot has happened. Girlfriend, no one could ever accuse you of allowing grass to grow under your feet," Marcy says with a laugh.

Seth and Annie walk in—the very two people I do not want to involve in this conversation.

"Hey, did you know, it has been a year since Jack and Keegan got back together?" Marcy shouts out to them.

Just kill me now.

"Really? A year? Any special plans?" Seth asks.

Standing there, I nervously look over at Annie as memories of her watching my meltdown on Jack's front steps that night flash through my mind.

Marcy answers Seth, paying no attention to the death stares I'm giving her to shut up, "No, we're trying to come up with some ideas. Any thoughts?"

Seth continues this inane conversation while Annie and I grow more uncomfortable with each passing minute, "You could have dinner somewhere that has sentimental meaning to you guys."

Again, Marcy spouts off, "Yeah, maybe Jack's tenants would let you use his front step?"

The words no sooner leave Marcy's mouth than it occurs to both her and Seth the discomfort their whole exchange is causing Annie and me.

Marcy comes up with an excuse to leave before I can do bodily harm to her by saying, "Think I'll go check on the kilns."

"Good idea." I glare back at her.

Seth turns his attention to Annie and me. "I'm sorry. I wasn't thinking."

I try to reassure Seth, "Don't worry about it."

Annie is a little more forgiving than me by saying, "It's okay, hon. Things like that are bound to happen when we're all together."

I try to change the subject by asking, "Was there something you needed, Annie?"

Annie tries to act as if nothing has happened. "Um, yeah. I wanted to sign up for the wood firing class."

I quickly take care of her registration and payment. Seth and Annie waste no time in leaving once I complete the transaction.

As I sit alone in the now-empty office, it starts clicking into place as to what I want to do next Friday. Now, all I have to do is figure out a way to get Jack up to the lake that night and surprise him.

By the time we sit down to dinner, I'm convinced I've thought of everything, and I am ready to put my plan into action.

I ask Jack, "Hey, babe, do you have anything going on next weekend?"

"I don't think so. Why?"

"I thought we could go up to the lake next Friday night and spend the weekend there. The boat needs cleaning before we take it down to the marina for winter storage. If the weather is nice, we might even be able to go out for one last cruise around the lake."

"What about Kyle?"

"He said something about going over to Joyce's to help with some things around the house. I don't know what she's going to do when Kyle goes to college. One of these days, she's going to have to think about selling her place and moving into a condo."

Jack shrugs. "Maybe. She'll figure it out."

"So, this weekend? Can we go up to the lake on Friday night?"

"Sure. It works for me."

Everything is going according to plan until Jack comes home Wednesday night and announces as he walks in the back door, "Hey, babe. I've got some bad news. There's a mock emergency drill planned for Saturday, and I'm required to be there. Sorry, but it doesn't look like the boat is going to get done this weekend."

"What? You've got to be kidding!" I cry out at him in disappointment.

"Can't it wait until next weekend?" Jack asks, confused by my reaction.

I decide to take advantage of my time alone by going ahead with my plans of going up to the lake. "It's okay. I'll still go up on Friday to take care of things."

"Maybe I can come up on Sunday and help."

Knowing Jack will be tired after being at the drill all day, I let him off the hook by saying. "Nah, don't bother. I'll get it done and come back home Saturday evening."

Friday morning, I lie in bed, watching Jack through the master bath door. He's shaving in front of the mirror, wearing only a towel around his waist. I get out of bed, walk up behind him, and wrap my arms around his waist.

"It's going to be hard, leaving this tonight," I tell him as I gently kiss his back.

He turns to face me. "You're making it awfully difficult to go to work this morning." He gives me the sweetest kiss back.

I try to take things to the next level when Jack says, "As much as I want to stay and finish this, I've got to get out of here. I have an early meeting at headquarters this morning."

"Will Chelsey be there?"

"I don't think so. It's a meeting with all the county's battalion chiefs about tomorrow's drill."

"I guess I'll have to take a rain check until tomorrow night, huh?" I ask, resting my head against his rock-hard chest.

"I guess so." He breaks off from our hold and turns to finish at the bathroom sink.

Although I'm disappointed that Jack has forgotten the significance of today's date, I decide not to mention anything to him.

Jack leaves for his meeting, and before I can get out the door, my cell phone rings with a call from Marcy.

"What's up, Marcy?"

"Have you left for the lake yet?"

"No. I was getting ready to walk out the door now. Why?"

"The kilns aren't working."

"What do you mean, the kilns aren't working?"

"They're not working. I've flipped the switch on each of them and nothing. They're plugged in, but neither is coming on. What do you want me to do?"

"Shit! I'm on my way."

When I walk in the studio's office, I find Marcy on the phone.

"I've got to go. Keegan is here." After Marcy disconnects from her call, she says to me, "I called Roger to see if he had any idea what could be the problem."

"And what did your sweet hubby say?"

"He thinks it's a bad outlet, and we should call an electrician."

"Let me take a look before we do that."

I walk in the kiln room and flip the switches on each of the two kilns, hoping they will magically start working again.

Maybe Roger is right, and it's a bad outlet.

I turn to leave to go back to the office, and the electrical panel box catches my eye. I say a silent prayer as I open it to see if there are any tripped breakers.

Bingo!

The two breakers for the kilns were both tripped.

After flipping the breakers back on, I go back to the office.

As I enter, Marcy says, "You know, Roger's brother is an electrician. I could call him."

"Don't bother. Two of the breakers were tripped. The kilns are up and running. I'm out of here."

I no sooner get in my Jeep than Carly is calling out to me from the back door of the shop.

She runs up to my open window. "Boy, I'm glad I caught you. I can't find the paperwork on the shipment that came in. Did you take it when you were in yesterday?"

"No."

"Damn. I wonder what happened to it."

"I'll come in and help you look for it."

A few minutes later, I find the missing paperwork was misfiled.

As I walk to the car, my cell phone rings, and I see Mom is calling.

"Hi, Mom."

"Hi, sweetie. Are you busy?"

"I was just leaving to go up to the lake."

"So, you're still in town?"

"Yes. Why?"

"Your dad is getting the boat ready to pull it out of the water for the season. I pulled a muscle in my back and can't help him. Ryan is busy with work. I was wondering if you could stop by and give your dad a hand with the boat."

"I want to get up to the lake to take care of our boat. Can it wait until Sunday?"

"You know your father. Once he gets something in his head, there's no stopping him. It's such a big job for him to do without any help, especially with his bad knee."

Now feeling guilty, especially after all the help Dad's given me at the lake house, I finally give in. "Okay, I'll be over in a few minutes."

"Thanks, sweetie! I'll even have some lunch ready for you. Bye."

"Bye."

I finally get on the road a little after four o'clock, frustrated that this weekend is turning out to be a total bust.

For a couple of minutes, I reconsider my plans of going up to the lake. After further thought, I decide that chilling out with a nice glass of wine down at the dock is exactly what I need right now.

I arrive at the lake a little after five o'clock, feeling tired and irritated that nothing has gone according to plan. Once in the house, I begin to unpack the groceries that I brought when there is a knock at the front door.

When I open it, I find Jack standing there, holding a pizza box in one hand and Kirby on a leash in the other. I'm speechless.

"Just going to stand there with your mouth gaping open, or are you going to invite us in?"

I'm overwhelmed that Jack remembered the date we got back together and chose to reenact him delivering pizza to me.

As he walks past me, Jack hands me the leash. "Do me a favor, and take care of the hairball."

I take the leash off of Kirby and then join Jack in the kitchen.

He opens the pizza box with a wink. "Would you like some pizza?"

I grab a couple of beers and paper towels, and I set us up on the floor in front of the kitchen's fireplace, just like we did that day.

Taking a slice, I ask, "You had this planned all along, didn't you?"

"Yeah, don't get mad, but I wanted to surprise you."

I start to laugh. "This was the menu I planned, except it was going to be served on fine bone china with beautiful crystal with candlelight down at the dock."

"Guess it's true what they say about great minds thinking alike." Jack chuckles.

"And the drill tomorrow?" I ask, hoping that it was also a part of his con.

"Sorry, but I have to leave early in the morning and then come back afterward. I figured we could stay until late Sunday afternoon."

"What if I had chosen to stay home?"

"I had a plan all figured out to get you up here for the weekend."

"What was it?"

"Think I'll keep it to myself in case I ever need to fall back on it in the future." Jack laughs.

"So, what else is happening tonight other than this gourmet dinner of pizza and beer?"

"I thought you would never ask." Jack stands, holding his hand out to me to help me up from the floor.

We go downstairs in the direction of the hot tub on the patio. When we enter the study to go out the sliding glass door, I see the drapes drawn across them.

Jack stops and says to me as he sits down in the study's oversize leather chair. "Strip for me, baby."

As I take off each piece of clothing for Jack, a grin spreads across his face.

After I shimmy out of my panties and stand, unashamedly exposed to him, he takes a moment before speaking, "If someone asked me at the bar last year what I would be doing tonight, this would never have made the list. God, I'm a lucky man!" Slowly rising from the chair, Jack takes me in his arms and begins passionately kissing me.

I break away to pull his T-shirt over his head. "Now, it's my turn to get you out of your clothes."

In short order, I strip Jack's clothes off of him. He pulls the drapes back and leads me out to a candlelit patio with the hot tub bubbling, ready for us to climb in. I notice towels laying on the patio loungers, and there's more beer in a cooler only a short reach away.

Looking around in amazement, I ask, "Have you been up here all day, setting this up?"

"Yep. I was scared you would catch me. That's why I had Marcy and your parents find things to keep you busy all day to delay you from coming up here."

Once in the hot tub, I straddle Jack and begin to make sweet love to him. Neither of us takes our eyes off of each other or says a word. My intense orgasm causes me to fall limp against Jack, and he kisses the nape of my neck as we recover.

"I love you to the stars and back," I softly whisper in his ear.

Jack answers back, "*Gra Go Deo*," which is the Celtic inscription inside my engagement ring that means *love forever*.

14

Jack

It's mid-December with Christmas fast approaching. It's been a year since I moved in with Keegan a couple of months after we got back together. Last Christmas, we weren't married, and we were living among some of my unpacked boxes with only a minimum amount of decorating done.

This year, Keegan has outdone herself by decking out our home with beautiful decorations along with establishing holiday traditions for our newly blended family.

This morning, she gets us all up bright and early for a hearty breakfast. We then go hiking through the fields at a local tree farm in search of the perfect tree. Once we find it, Keegan memorializes the moment with a picture. She ambushes an unsuspecting family, minding their own business, to take the photo of us standing in front of our first tree before chopping it down. It took only minutes for the photograph to be proudly posted on her social media pages for all to see.

As soon as we get home, she insists that we bring the tree inside, set it up, and string the lights on it. I watch as she and the boys decorate it with both ornaments from our pasts and the ones we purchased together last weekend.

I catch a private moment between Keegan and Kyle, looking at an ornament with a picture of him and his dad. It's then I gain a better understanding of Keegan's actions today. I silently promise myself to do everything in my power to make sure our first Christmas together as a married couple is one we will never forget.

I become exhausted as Keegan shares with me everything she plans to jam into the week of Christmas and the few days that follow. Beginning with Christmas Eve, we will be attending church with her family along with Marcy, Roger, and Keegan's godchild, Aaron. Everyone will come back to our townhouse after church for a buffet and more holiday cheer. We decide to include Seth and Annie since it's my year to have Sean on Christmas Eve and morning. Then, on Christmas Day, the plan is to drop Sean off at Annie's on our way over to my in-laws' for dinner. The day after Christmas, we'll pick up Sean and drive down to my parents' to spend the day.

What Keegan doesn't know is one of my gifts to her is a weekend stay at the National Harbor where we spent our first night as man and wife. I've already arranged for the boys to stay with my parents' while I whisk Keegan off to enjoy a quiet weekend alone.

At work the following Monday, I'm sitting at my desk, finishing a report before breaking for lunch, when Chelsey walks in, unannounced.

"Hey, this is a surprise. Do we have a meeting today?" I ask while checking my calendar on the computer.

"No, I was in the area. I was wondering if you would like to attend the fire chiefs conference in San Diego in April?" Chelsey continues, "The chief usually goes, but he has a schedule conflict this year. There is enough money in the budget to send two people. The chief wants to send his new highest-ranking officers, which are you and me."

"Are you okay with that?" I ask.

"Yeah, sure. The question is, will Keegan be all right with us going together?" Chelsey asks.

"She'll be okay with it. I'll probably ask her to come with me if that works with you and the finances."

"Sure, as long as she pays for her expenses. You'll just have to separate them from yours on the reimbursement paperwork."

"Then, go ahead and register me. I'll talk it over with Keegan tonight, and I'll let you know if she decides to come with me."

As Keegan and I eat dinner with Kyle at the dining room table that evening, I share the details about the conference with her.

"Sure I won't be a third wheel?" she asks.

"Never, especially at night." I give her a wink.

Kyle wastes no time in protesting, "Ew, please, not at the dinner table. That's all I've ever asked you guys; don't say that kind of stuff while I'm trying to eat."

We both laugh and purposely carry on.

"Well, if you're a good boy, one night, I might wear that little number made of nothing but black lace for you," Keegan teases.

"That's it. I'm out of here. I don't need to hear anything else. I'm going over to Jerry's. See you guys later," Kyle says as he pushes his chair back and quickly exits the room.

Once we stop laughing, Keegan says, "Yeah, I would love to tag along with you to San Diego. First, let me double-check the dates to make sure it doesn't conflict with any of Kyle's year-end senior activities."

With Kyle gone for the evening, it is a good time for us to review our shopping lists and map out a strategy for getting everything done in the next two weeks before Christmas.

Then, Keegan says, "Not to change the subject, but I contacted Aiden today to set up another meeting with Brittany."

"Why? I thought you were done writing the book."

"It's not because of the book but to discuss her feelings concerning Kyle and Jace knowing about each other."

It never occurred to me—the need to inform Kyle about Jace or vice versa. So far, it has been a relatively smooth transition of our two families melding together. Both of our sons have adjusted with no major issues. I'm skeptical of doing something that could upset the delicate balance of our family, especially during the holidays.

"I don't know, Keegan. Do you think it's a good idea to tell Kyle about Jace? Kyle has had to deal with so much these past few years. Finding out his dad had a son with another woman might be the last straw for him."

She becomes defensive. "Jack, how can I not tell him? Isn't it better for him to hear it from me than finding out about it on his own?"

"If things are okay with Brittany, when are you planning to tell Kyle?" I ask.

"First, I've already decided to tell Kyle. This meeting is not about getting permission but finding out her intentions on ever telling Jace. If she doesn't want Jace to know about Kyle, that's her business. Bottom line, I feel Kyle has every right to know he has a brother, no matter how Brittany feels about it."

"Promise me one thing. Wait until after the New Year to tell him. It's our first Christmas together as a family, and I want it to be as drama-free as possible."

Keegan laughs out loud. "Well, if you wanted a drama-free holiday, then why in the hell did we invite your baby's mama over on Christmas Eve? Do I have to remind you what happened the last time we had the brilliant idea to do that? The only thing missing is asking Chelsey to join us, and don't you even dare think about doing that! One ex in the house during the holidays is one too many as it is."

"You're the one who invited her!"

"Oh, come on, Jack. What was I supposed to do? I couldn't very well invite Marcy's family without asking Seth, and there was no way for Seth and Sean to come without including Annie. The truth is, if I had it my way, that bitch wouldn't be here."

"Well, it's one hell of a time to find out all of this. By the way, do me a favor, and stop referring to Annie as a bitch. She's the mother of my son, and I would like you to remember that. I've never once disrespected Will the way you do Annie."

"Will never pulled the kind of crap that she has."

"Do I have to remind you of his letters that broke us up for three years? Oh, and let's not forget that kiss on the dock. I admit Annie did some inexcusable shit to us, but Will has her beat by a mile!"

Keegan just gives me a cold death stare and quietly asks, "So, is there anything else you would like to get off your chest about my dead ex-husband who is the father of my child?"

"No, that's it," I answer, knowing all hell is about to break loose.

Keegan continues in that eerily calm tone of hers when she's beyond pissed off, "Let me refresh your memory of all of the little goodies that Annie has pulled—"

135

I interrupt by holding my hand up to her, "You don't have to bother. Remember, I was there. All I'm saying is, she's Sean's mother, and she deserves a little respect. You can think it all you want, but please stop calling her a bitch. It might accidentally slip out in front of Sean; that's all."

"And here we are again with you coming to Annie's defense. Fine, I will no longer call the bitch a bitch because everyone knows she's a bitch, so there's no need to reiterate the bitch is a bitch since it would be redundant to keep calling her a bitch. Sorry, I have to get out as many bitches out as possible since I've been forbidden to ever use the word *bitch* in the same sentence as that bitch's name."

"Do you feel better now?" I ask angrily.

"A little. Now, what would you like me to call the bitch? Her Royal Highness? Queen Annie? Mother Superior?"

"By her name would be fine. Think I'll go downstairs if your little temper tantrum is over. You got anything else for me?" I ask.

"Nope," she says.

I push back from the table to leave as she sits, fuming over our conversation. I think she muttered the word *asshole* under her breath as I left the room, but I chose to ignore it.

Later that evening, Kyle comes downstairs to my man cave in the basement to let me know he's home before heading off to bed. I let Kirby out for the last time before going to bed myself. Once he comes back in, I turn off all the lights and lock up for the evening. I take a deep breath before going upstairs to face the music with Keegan. I find she's already in bed, and she appears to be asleep.

I shower and then crawl into bed. As I settle in to get comfortable, I might have *unintentionally*—meaning, on purpose—jostled the bed a little more than usual.

"You can stop. I'm still awake," she says in the darkness with her back to me.

"Sorry," I respond.

"For what? Being a jerk or for trying to wake me up?"

"Not doing this with you again, Keegan. If there was a problem with Annie being here on Christmas Eve, then you should have told me, and we could have avoided all of this bullshit tonight."

She rolls over to her side, facing me, and says, "Jack, everyone else in the world might have accepted Seth and Annie, but I haven't. I wish everybody would be a little more sensitive to my feelings."

"I understand that you and Annie will never be great friends. But, eventually, you need to move on from the past, babe."

"In my head, I know everything you're saying is true, but it's my heart that can't get on board with things. It still hurts when I think back to what she did to us. All the times she manipulated the truth to cause problems between us keeps me from trusting her."

"You've got to find a way to let go of it, babe. If you don't, you'll only end up with a bunch of regret to deal with down the road."

"Sounds like you're speaking from experience."

"My anger toward Chelsey kept me from trusting anyone enough to fall in love again. You want to know how I got past it?"

"How?"

"You."

Keegan's eyes grow wide with surprise.

"Yep, it was all you, babe."

"You need to stop giving me so much credit. It was only a couple of hours ago that I was going for the world's record of saying *bitch* as many times as possible in one sentence."

"So, do I need to find a nice way to uninvite Annie to Christmas Eve?"

"No. If I start to say something bitchy, just stick a cheese puff in my mouth, okay?"

"Okay. It's getting late. Scoot over here, and let me hold you while we fall asleep."

I kiss Keegan good night, and we find comfort in each other's arms as the rise and fall of our breathing gently rocks us to sleep.

15

Keegan

As Jack and I sit in Aiden's conference room a few days before Christmas, it feels like déjà vu of our last meeting with Brittany and him sitting across the table from us. The only difference is, this time, we're here to talk about Will's sons instead of my book.

I had no idea how upset Brittany would be over this meeting until I say to her, "Thank you for agreeing to meet with me to discuss Kyle and Jace."

"No need to thank me. I'm only here because of Aiden. As far as I'm concerned, there is no reason for us to have this conversation. You had no right to remove the letter. I want it back! It was for Will, not you," she snaps back at me.

Now becoming annoyed with her, I say, "Brittany, we both know that's a bunch of bull. Maybe it was your intent for Joyce, not me, to find it, but you wanted someone in the family to know about Jace. Please understand, I'm not asking for your permission to tell my son about his brother. My plan is to tell Kyle after the holidays before the release of my book. All I want to know is, what would you like me to say if he asks to meet Jace?"

Aiden interjects, "What happened to our agreement of you letting us read the book before you publish it? I can get an injunction from the court to stop you from moving forward with it without us seeing it first."

Jack then comes to my defense, "Calm down. No one has read the book."

I add, "I'm not going back on my word of letting you two read it. Your copies are being delivered here within the week. I decided to change the approach to the book after our last meeting. The few times you're mentioned, it's only by your roles, like the Feds or informer, not by name."

"Thank you for that," Brittany says. "Back to your question, it has never been my intention to tell Jace about Kyle."

"Then, why the letter, Brittany?" I ask. "Help me understand why you left it."

"You want to know the truth? I'm tired of being a dirty little secret. Will and I had plans for the future until his mother and father turned their noses up at me. I wanted Joyce to find out that all their manipulating little head games with Will didn't work. His marriages to you were feeble attempts to make it up to that son of a bitch he called a father. Will's last words that he loved me are proof of it." By now, Brittany is choking on her tears as she spits out her venom at me.

I feel no anger toward Brittany, nor do I harbor any responsibility for any of the unhappiness that my relationship with Will might have caused her. I have only a deep sadness for Brittany's incapability of not being able to find a way to move on with her life for Jace's benefit.

Instead of lashing back at her, I quietly try to share what I've learned from my writing. "Brittany, at some point in time, he was in love with both of us for different reasons. It took me a long time to understand that, and eventually, you will, too. Out of his love, we each have a part of him in our sons. I will respect your wishes by telling Kyle you don't want Jace to know about him."

Brittany wipes a lone tear from her eye. "Thank you."

"One last thing, Brittany, you're right. The letter is Will's. In the spring, I plan to plant a flower at the foot of his headstone with your note buried underneath it. Does that work for you?" I ask her.

Brittany nods in agreement. "Yeah, that works."

"Is there a particular type of flower you would like me to plant?"

"A white daisy."

"A white daisy, it is. Do you want to be there when I do it?"

"Yes, please. Thank you."

"Please know, it was never my intent to ruin the holidays for you. It's just that Kyle will want to read my book. Knowing my son, he'll have questions. I wanted to hear your plans on how you were going to handle things with Jace, nothing more. Thank you for seeing me today."

As Jack and I walk toward the door, Brittany says, "Tell Kyle whatever you think is best, but I'm not ready for the boys to meet."

"I understand. Take care, Brittany," are my final words before I walk out of the conference room with Jack.

After the beautiful Christmas Eve service, we walk out into the cold winter night, full of Christmas spirit, as a few snowflakes drift down around us.

I hold on to Jack as we carefully navigate the steps of the church.

I ask, "Do you think we might have a white Christmas?"

"No. It isn't supposed to amount to anything," he answers back, looking up at the dark sky.

Family and friends gather at the bottom of the steps as I tell them before walking away, "So, I guess we'll see all of you at the house. Be careful driving. It could be a little slippery."

Once reaching home, Jack turns on both the outside and tree lights to welcome our guests as I pop goodies into the oven to warm them up.

Soon, all arrive safely and start to enjoy the food I've prepared as Christmas music fills the air. I look over at Marcy and her four year-old son, Aaron, lying on their bellies, watching the train go around the bottom of the tree. Roger is at the controls, making the engine occasionally blow its whistle, each time making his son laugh as it passes him. Mom and Dad are over in the corner, talking to Kyle about college, with Seth and Annie laughing about something with Sean.

Familiar arms reach around me, taking me into a warm embrace. "Everything okay?"

"Everything is awesome, even with Annie here," I tell Jack as I rest my head back on his shoulder.

He continues, "You seem different. I don't believe I've ever seen you so…"

"At peace?"

"Yeah. At peace." He nods.

"It feels good," I tell him while turning in his arms. "Merry Christmas, baby."

"Merry Christmas," Jack answers back with a kiss.

"Ew, get a room," Kyle says in disgust as he walks past us.

All who are within hearing range crack up laughing, including Annie.

After everyone has gone home, the boys are in bed, and the presents are placed under the tree. Jack is waiting for me in bed when I enter the bedroom from the bath, wearing red lingerie, a Santa hat, and furry, spiked white heels, with a Christmas stocking dangling from my fingertip.

"What the hell?" Jack says while choking on his laughter.

Although not the reaction I was looking for, I walk over to his side of the bed, bend over for him to get the full view, and ask, "Have you been a good boy?"

"You do remember that both boys are across the hall?" His response isn't quite what I expected.

"The door's locked. You want to see what goodies are in your stocking?" I pull out some sex toys, a red scarf, and some oils and lotions.

"Sorry, babe. It's not happening tonight."

"Why?" I whine like a disappointed, spoiled child.

"Because you would never be quiet enough to do any of this. Hell, I'm not even sure what you do with some of this stuff. Do I have to worry about losing my job because of the porn sites you had to go on to get some of this?"

We hear the doorknob jiggle with Sean saying on the other side, "Can I come in?"

Jack starts laughing as I scurry around, gathering everything off the bed, and I nearly break my neck when running back in the bathroom in my spiked heels.

Patiently, I wait as Jack opens the door and does his best to convince Sean to go back to his bed.

"Hey, buddy, what's up?"

Sean answers, "I don't know. I just can't fall asleep."

I then hear some movement, as if Sean has come into our room and climbed up onto our bed.

"Are you excited about Christmas tomorrow?" Jack asks.

Sean answers so softly that I can barely hear him, "I miss Mom."

"You miss Mom? Why?" Jack asks.

"This is the first time I've been away from her on Christmas Eve," Sean answers.

My heart is now breaking. *Poor Sean.* I never once thought about how he always spends Christmas with his mom and Jack, opening gifts at her house.

"I wonder what Mom is doing," Sean ponders out loud to Jack.

"I bet you she's fast asleep, so Santa can come."

"Dad, there's no Santa Claus."

I can just imagine the eye roll Sean is giving his father right now.

"Sure there is."

"Prove it."

"I've never told anyone this. Last year, I wished for something so big that I was sure I would never get it."

"You did? What was it?"

"To be with Keegan and to spend Christmas with her."

I quietly giggle as Jack draws me into his story.

"Next to you, it was the best gift I have ever gotten," he says.

My hand flies to my mouth, so neither of them can hear my audible gasp.

"Can I stay here and sleep with you, Dad?"

"What about Keegan?"

"She can sleep in my bed."

"No, I think you need to sleep in your bed tonight."

"Can I stay here until Keegan comes to bed?"

"Sure, buddy, but you have to go back to yours when she finishes up in the bathroom."

"Okay."

I desperately look around the bathroom for something to wear because there is no way I can go out there, looking like this. I spot one of Jack's tees and his sweats hanging on a hook on the back of the door. I wash off my makeup and brush out my hair before changing out of my lingerie.

The T-shirt comes mid thigh, and Jack's sweatpants start to fall off my hips. I pull the drawstring tight along with rolling the waistband down and the legs up so as not to trip when walking. I check myself to see if I'm presentable enough to leave the bathroom, and I pray to God that Sean won't ask why I'm wearing his dad's clothes. I jam my lingerie into one of the vanity drawers before turning off the light.

What I see when I reach the bed is too adorable for words. Both Jack and Sean are sound asleep, lying smack dab in the middle of the bed, leaving no room for me. Jack is on his back, snoring, with one arm across his eyes and the other around Sean, who is snuggled up close.

Kirby is at the foot of the bed, looking at me, as if asking me, *Where am I going to sleep?*

Quietly, I get a pair of pajamas that fit me out of my dresser and pick up my phone. Then, I quietly tiptoe out of the bedroom so as not to disturb either Jack or Sean.

Once downstairs and changed, I make myself comfy on the couch beside our Christmas tree and the gifts placed around its base.

I lie there in the dark with my phone in hand, knowing all too well what I need to do.

I find myself hesitating until I hear Sean's voice in my head saying, *"I miss Mom."*

Even though it's past midnight, I pull Annie's number up and press the icon on the screen to dial it.

She answers on the first ring in a panic, "Is Sean all right?"

"Yeah, he's fine. I'm calling to see if you would like to come over in the morning to open presents with us."

"You're okay with that?" she asks in astonishment.

"This evening, I overheard Sean telling Jack he misses you. I thought it would be a fun surprise for him if you were here."

I hear Annie sniffle. "You have no idea how much I've missed not having that little guy home tonight."

"I can imagine. By the way, you can tell Seth he can come, too."

Annie giggles a little. "I have no idea what you're talking about."

"See you around eight?"

"Eight would be good."

"Merry Christmas, Annie."

"Merry Christmas. And, Keegan, thank you."

After settling under the quilt that was folded neatly at the end of the couch, I doze off to sleep, thinking how happy Sean will be to have his mom here tomorrow morning.

Sound asleep, facing the back of the sofa, I'm startled awake in the dark by someone lifting the quilt and lying close behind me. Instantly, I know it is Jack by the feel of his all-too-familiar body up next to me.

"Hey, why are you down here?" he asks.

"You and Sean were hogging the bed, so this is where I ended up."

"I missed you," he whispers in my ear as he nuzzles his nose in my hair.

"I heard Sean and you talking last night. I never once gave it a thought about this being his first Christmas away from home. I called Annie and invited her and Seth over to open presents with us."

Jack becomes very still, saying nothing at first. "Are you sure?" he asks.

"Yeah, I'm sure. Sean needs her here."

"Thank you."

"For what?"

"For loving my son, me. For everything."

"What time is it?"

"Around six. Why?"

"I need to get up and figure out what I'm going to feed everyone since Annie and Seth are coming over. I don't think the pastries I have will be enough."

"We still have time."

Jack gets up as I roll to my other side, and I watch him turn on the tree lights and some holiday music to play softly in the background.

He crawls back under the cover and kisses me. "Merry Christmas, Mrs. Grady."

"Merry Christmas, Mr. Grady."

The boys come downstairs around a quarter till eight, ready to dig into the piles of gifts waiting for them under the tree. They can't understand why they aren't allowed to go at it yet.

Our stalling is thankfully interrupted by the doorbell.

Kyle asks, "Who's that?"

I wink at Jack and answer, "Maybe it's Santa, and he forgot to leave something."

Kyle looks over at me. "Ho, ho, ho, Mom."

Jack then tells Sean, "Hey, buddy. Go answer the door."

There are no words to describe my joy while watching Sean open the door to see Annie standing there, on the other side. He looks back to Jack and me, as if silently asking if it is okay for her to be here.

Our beaming smiles must be all the answer he needs because he jumps into her arms as she tells him, "Merry Christmas, sweetie."

I look over to Kyle when it becomes apparent he's oblivious to everything that's happening as he asks, "Now, can we open our gifts?"

Jack and I promised each other we'd keep our gift-giving to two presents each. I've given him a new laptop and a digital frame full of photos of us for his desk at work. He's given me a beautiful necklace with two entwined hearts with our family's four birthstones. The other box has a sexy black dress with a note informing me to wear it during our weekend getaway at National Harbor.

After Annie and Seth leave with Sean, we go over to my parents' for an early dinner with my brother's family and Joyce Henderson.

Since my first marriage to Will, it has become a tradition for Joyce to join my family for Christmas dinner, and it's continued after his death. I feared it would be awkward this year with me being married to Jack, but Joyce greets all of us with warm hugs.

The first order of business is opening gifts while enjoying drinks and appetizers. Dad gives his annual Christmas toast before anyone is allowed to open any presents.

After the exchange of gifts, as everyone sits around, talking, I retrieve a large box out of Dad's office that I secretly placed in there when we arrived. Anxiously, everyone looks at me as I distribute the six wrapped boxes inside it to my parents, Jack, Kyle, Ryan, and Joyce.

I explain, "Before opening these, please know how special you are to me and that I couldn't have done this without your love and support."

They rip off the paper, each finding a personal hardback copy of my book, *Ultimate Cost*.

All are speechless.

Dad comes up and pulls me into a hug, saying, "I'm so proud of you, princess."

"Thanks, Daddy."

After helping Mom clean up from dinner, there's talk of packing up and leaving for home.

Joyce takes me aside and asks, "Can you drive me to the cemetery?"

"Now?" I ask, surprised by Joyce's question because she hasn't been there since Will's funeral.

"Yes, if you don't mind. Just for a few minutes. I just need to go there now. Holding your book in my hand made me see, if you could do that, then I can visit Will's grave. I just can't go by myself. Can you take me?"

"It's getting awfully late. You won't have much time to spend there before the cemetery closes. Wouldn't you rather go when you'd have more time, so you wouldn't feel rushed?"

"I know. It's just…if I don't go now, I'm not sure I'll have the courage to go again."

"Okay. Give me a minute to tell Jack and Kyle."

As I park the Jeep at the cemetery, my entire focus is on Joyce, preparing myself for the grief that I expect will overcome her at any moment.

I see a look come over her face as I hear her shriek out Will's nickname as a child, "Oh my God, it's Willy!"

As Joyce unbuckles her seat belt and bolts out of the vehicle, I look to see what caused her to react like this. It's then I see a child playing and Annie at Will's grave with her back to us.

Immediately, I realize the boy is Jace. Dumbfounded, I try to get to Joyce as fast as possible to stop her.

She reaches Jace, takes him in her arms, and says, "Willy, it's Mommy."

Once reaching them, I try to reason with her, "Let go of him. That's not Will."

She either doesn't hear me or chooses to ignore me as she tries to comfort the little boy who is now terrified, crying out for his mother. "Shh, there's no need to cry, sweetheart. Mommy is here to take care of you."

Brittany is now tearing over to us, shouting, "Let go of my son!"

Joyce, now embarrassed, sees her mistake and takes a step back from the child. "I'm so sorry. I don't know what came over me. He looks so much like my son at that age. My son is dead and—" She stops mid sentence as she stares at Brittany and then down at the Jace. Joyce starts to connect the dots when she recognizes her. "Brittany? Is this your son?"

Knowing that we're just moments away before Joyce realizes that Jace is her grandson, I stand frozen, unsure of what to do next.

Brittany nervously looks to me and then back at Joyce as she puts a protective arm around Jace. "Yes, it is."

"I didn't mean to scare him. I'm sorry. I guess, when I saw him…well, he looks so much like Will, and it was…" And then it happens. "Oh my God, he's Will's son," she whispers her discovery out loud.

As though things could not get any worse, Jace tearfully asks, "Mommy, are we done visiting Daddy? I want to go home."

16

Brittany

A woman's screeching turns my attention in the direction where Jace is playing.

Oh my God! It's Joyce!

Without wasting a single second, I rush over to my son to rescue him from Joyce's clutches. Fearing my moment of reckoning has arrived, I brace myself for it.

After Joyce realizes who Jace is, she asks, "How old is he?"

"He turned three a few months ago."

I can see her doing the math in her head.

"Will never knew you were pregnant, did he?"

I just shake my head.

"What's his name?"

"Jace William Peters."

"Why didn't you tell me about my grandson?"

"I didn't tell anyone. It's nobody's business but mine," I defiantly respond back.

Then, Joyce turns to Keegan. "Did you know about this?"

"Yes. I found out after my honeymoon when I read a note that Brittany had left in the headstone's vase."

"A note? And you didn't show it to me?" Joyce says to Keegan, as though she has been betrayed in some manner.

"I'm sorry, but it wasn't my place to tell you. Kyle doesn't even know yet. I'm planning on telling him after he finishes reading the book."

"And if Kyle wants to meet Jace?" Joyce asks Keegan.

"Brittany's not interested in the boys meeting at this time, and I'm respecting her wishes."

Joyce then focuses her attention back on me. "But he has family—a brother and me. We have a right to know him."

My fear turns to anger, as this woman has the nerve to lecture me about her rights. Nobody has given a damn about me and my rights.

I can't take her holier-than-thou bullshit a minute longer. "You gave up all rights to know anything about my life the day your husband said I wasn't good enough for your son."

"That was my husband, not me. I've done nothing to deserve this."

"Except for not stopping that son of a bitch from humiliating me."

"And what did you expect me to do? My husband was a womanizing bastard that I had to tolerate for the sake of our son."

I didn't notice until now that Keegan had left, taking Jace back toward Will's headstone, out of hearing range. It looks as if she is entertaining him with her cell phone. I have to stop this with Joyce and get as far away as possible from her.

"My only concern right now is to get my little boy home and try to salvage what little bit of Christmas that is left."

"Are you going to allow me to see him? Spend time with him?"

I try to dismiss her questions by saying, "Joyce, this isn't the place or the time to discuss this. I need to get Jace out of the cold."

"You either promise me now that I get to see my grandson or we can see what my attorney has to say about my rights as a grandmother. It's your choice, Brittany."

Out of the corner of my eye, I see a truck and car pull up. Aiden jumps out of the car and runs over to me as Jack and an older gentleman get out of the truck. The older man walks toward Joyce and me while Jack quickly walks over to Keegan and Jace. I notice Jack hugs Keegan. Then, he stoops down to Jace's level, holding out his hand, as if he's introducing himself.

Bewildered, Joyce asks, "Aiden Collins. What in the world are you doing here?"

Ignoring her question, Aiden asks me, "Britt, are you okay?"

"Yeah. How did you even know what was going on here?"

"Keegan called."

Joyce jerks her head in Keegan's direction and glares at her.

The older man offers his hand as he introduces himself to me, "Hi. I'm Mitch Fitzgerald, Keegan's dad."

I shake his hand. "Brittany Peters, and this is Aiden Collins."

He then looks over to Joyce. "Are you okay?"

"No, I'm not okay. I have a grandson, whom she's keeping from me."

It's apparent that Mitch knows how to handle Joyce as he suggests to her, "Why don't you tell me about everything while I take you home? You and Brittany can work this all out at a more appropriate time." He then asks me, "Brittany, is there a way to contact you?"

Aiden speaks up, "Yeah, through me. Keegan has my number."

"Good. Keegan can contact Aiden when everyone has had time to calm down."

Before leaving with Mitch, Joyce threatens me one more time, "You haven't heard the last of this, Brittany. Either we come up with a plan for me to spend time with my grandson or I'll take legal action."

As Mitch assists Joyce in his truck before driving off, I walk over to Keegan and say, "Thanks for calling in the cavalry."

Keegan apologetically looks at me and says, "You're welcome. I'm sorry. Joyce hasn't been to Will's grave since his funeral, and out of the blue, she asked me to bring her today at the same time you happened to be here. What are the odds of that happening? Brittany, you know Joyce is not going to stop until she's allowed to see Jace. It might be in your best interest to talk to her."

"Yeah, I know."

Keegan sees Jace yawning. "Hey, it looks like your little guy is ready to go home. You can deal with all of this later."

I agree and call over to Jace, who's being entertained by Aiden and Jack, "Come on, Jace. Time to go home." Turning back to Keegan, I tell her, "Merry Christmas, Keegan, and thanks."

"Merry Christmas, Brittany," she answers back with a small smile.

After saying good night to the Gradys and securing Jace in his car seat, I tell Aiden as we stand outside of my car, "It seems as if you're always coming to my rescue. Thank you. I'm sorry for ruining your Christmas."

"Brittany, you know I'm here whenever you need me." He takes me in his arms for one of his special hugs. "I'll follow you home."

"Thanks, but I'm okay. There's no need to do that. Go back to your parents' and enjoy what's left of Christmas with them."

"No, I'm following you home. No arguments."

17

Keegan

Jack slides behind the wheel of his Jeep as I get in the front passenger seat. Driving in silence as we leave the cemetery, I stare aimlessly out of my window, exhausted by the scene that played out between Joyce and Brittany.

Jack asks, "Are you all right?"

"Yeah. How did Daddy end up coming with you?"

"The only way I could get out of the house was to say you were having car trouble. I asked Mitch if I could borrow his truck. Of course, Mitch, Ryan, and Kyle all wanted to come along to help. Liz stopped Ryan by telling him it was time to go home. I asked Kyle to stay behind and give your mom a hand with cleaning up, but there was no stopping Mitch, especially with his little princess in distress," he says, chuckling under his breath. "Your dad knew something was up. As soon as we got in his truck, he demanded to know what was going on. Since he was going to find out when we got here, I told him everything about finding the letter and that Will had a son with Brittany."

Heaving out a sigh, I say, "I hope Kyle bought the whole car-trouble story."

"What are you going to do if he starts to ask questions?"

"I guess play it by ear."

We pull into my parents' driveway, and I see Kyle outside with Kirby, waiting for us.

"Everything okay?" asks Kyle, suspiciously eyeing both the Jeep and me.

"Yeah, everything is fine."

Kyle looks down the drive. "Where's Granddad?"

"Taking your grandmother home."

"Is she okay?"

"Yeah, she's fine."

"I should have gone along with you guys."

I take Kyle in a hug. "Oh, sweetie. You can't always be there to make things better for your grandmother."

Jack calls over from the front steps of the house, "Hey, Kyle. Why don't you and I start loading up our gifts, so we can head home?"

As the guys enter the house, the garage door starts to rise, and Dad pulls inside.

I walk into the garage to meet him. "How's Joyce doing?" I ask.

Dad first checks to see if anyone is around, and in a low voice, he tells me, "She's calmed down. Keegan, you need to make Brittany understand that Joyce will do whatever it takes to see Jace. I know you don't want to be in the middle of all of this, but someone needs to talk a little sense into both of them. You do understand that I need to tell your mom about what happened tonight."

"Yeah, I know. It's turned out to be one hell of a Christmas! We're getting ready to go home. Thanks for helping out with Joyce. I don't know what I would do without you guys. I love you." I give my dad a hug.

"I love you, too, princess."

I hear the interior door to the garage open and see Kyle carrying out a bag of trash.

Thankful that he didn't come out a few minutes earlier, I joke with him, "So, Grandma has you on trash duty, huh?"

Kyle nods and jokes back, "Yeah, it's a dirty job, but somebody has to do it."

Back at our townhouse, we quickly unpack the Jeep, not caring where we drop our gifts from the family once inside. While I'm hanging up my coat in the hall closet, Kyle comes up to give me a long hug.

As he breaks away, he says, "Mom, I know."

With Jack standing only a few steps away, we give each other a guarded look.

"You know what?" I ask, not daring to make any assumptions.

"I know about Brittany and her son," he answers back.

"What? But how?"

"A few weeks before Dad died, I overheard him on the phone with Brittany. He didn't know I was in the hallway, outside of his bedroom door. He called her Britt, and by the things he was saying, I could tell they were more than just friends," Kyle says, his face reddening.

He continues, "At the viewing, I saw a woman who was really upset. I knew it had to be her by the way she was acting. I went up to offer her a tissue and introduced myself, hoping she would tell me her name. When she did, I figured Britt was short for Brittany. A few months after Dad's funeral, I saw her at the mall one day, and she was pregnant."

"Oh my God," I cry out while taking him into my arms for a hug. "Why didn't you tell me?"

"Mom, you were in no shape to hear any of this back then. When you got better, I didn't want to do anything to upset you."

Jack takes a step closer to the two of us. "Let's all go into the TV room and talk."

Once settled, I turn to Kyle and say, "Sweetheart, I don't know what to say. I'm so sorry you didn't feel as if you could talk to me about this. It must have been awful for you. Why did you decide to tell me tonight?"

"I heard you and Granddad talking about it in the garage. You guys didn't hear the first time I opened the door to come out. I waited until you were finished talking before bringing the trash out."

"Kyle, you need to stop eavesdropping on private conversations," I scold him.

"I didn't mean to, Mom," he tries to defend himself.

"How are you doing?" Jack asks Kyle.

"I'm okay," Kyle answers, "but I think it was a crappy thing that Dad did this."

"Kyle, please don't say that about your dad. He never knew Brittany was pregnant. She found out after he died."

"So, what happened at the cemetery tonight with Grandma?" Kyle asks.

After I finish sharing the details with him, he says nothing.

"You okay?" I ask.

"Yeah, I was thinking about how sad Grandma must be feeling right now. Jack, would you be mad if I didn't go to see your parents tomorrow? I'd rather go over to Grandma's tonight and stay with her. I know she's probably upset over everything that's happened today."

"It's fine with me if it's okay with your mom."

"Sounds perfect to me." I smile back at the both of them.

Kyle leaves to run upstairs to call Joyce and pack some clothes.

When he returns downstairs, he says, "Grandma sounded happy that I was coming over. I'm staying with her until you guys get back."

I answer back, "Thank you, Kyle."

"For what?" he asks with a puzzled look.

I take him in for a hug. "For just being you. I love you."

"I love you, too, Mom."

Kyle slings his bag over his shoulder and says to me before walking out the door, "Merry Christmas, Mom."

I wave to him. "Merry Christmas."

The first thing the next morning, I call Kyle to check in with him before leaving to pick up Sean to head down to Jack's parents' home.

Kyle answers his phone, "Hi, Mom."

"Hi. How is everything?"

"Grandma is better. We talked a little bit about Jace. I'm not sure how I feel about it all."

"Kyle, no one expects you to feel one way or the other. The important thing is that everything is out in the open, and there are no more secrets."

"I guess. Tell Grandma Pat and Grandma John merry Christmas for me."

I smile, hearing Kyle's names for Pat and John Grady that he came up with by himself. "I'll be sure to tell them. See you when we get back. Bye."

Jack and I leave to pick up Sean and head down to the Gradys' to celebrate Christmas with them.

Although the Gradys are disappointed that Kyle isn't with us, they understand once the situation has been explained to them. It is fun, watching Sean open his presents from them. As always, the day flies by way too quickly, and it's time for Jack and me to leave for our weekend getaway at National Harbor.

Pulling up to the entrance of the hotel, Jack turns to me and says, "Are you ready to have a little fun?"

I laugh at him and say, "I'm always ready for a little fun with you."

Once settled in our room, Jack reaches into his duffel bag and pulls out the stocking I tried to give him on Christmas Eve. "Look what I found in our bedroom closet."

"I was looking for that! Well, I'm glad you found it because look what I packed." Reaching into my overnight bag, I hold up my red lingerie in one hand and the furry, spiked heels in the other.

Although our weekend getaway was perfect in every way and exactly what I needed, it is nice to get back home before New Year's Eve.

I wake up on the morning of New Year's Eve with Kirby giving me the I-need-to-do-my-business stare. I look over to Jack, hoping to persuade him to take Kirby out, only to see he's still asleep. Carefully, I climb out of bed so as not to disturb Jack, and I go to the bathroom before tending to Kirby. While finishing up in the bathroom, through the crack of the door, I see Jack scratching Kirby's belly. I walk back out to our room to find Jack pretending to be asleep, throwing in a little snoring for good measure.

I quietly walk over to the bed, grabbing one of the pillows from my side, and hit Jack as hard as I can with it. Kirby starts to bark as I let out a small scream when Jack grabs me by the waist and playfully throws me down on the bed. He rolls on top of me, pinning my arms down above my head. I'm trapped and at his mercy, lying on my back, unable to move.

"So, you want to play rough this morning, huh?" he asks.

Laughing so hard that I can barely speak, I squeak out, "You weren't asleep! I saw you scratching Kirby's belly."

Jack then gives me a slow, enticing kiss, making me want this moment to turn into so much more than this lighthearted exchange between us.

I remind him, "You know, it's five years today when we met for the first time for coffee. I was going to ask if you wanted to go for coffee this morning, but I kind of like it here in bed with you."

A sexy grin spreads across his face. "Did you forget that we have to take Sean to basketball practice this morning?"

"Damn! These rec leagues need to stop interfering in my sex life!"

Jack laughs. "I'll be sure to tell Sean's coach that. We can go for coffee during practice."

Regretting that this moment with Jack has to come to an end because Kirby is now begging to be taken out, I tell him, "Okay. I need to take Kirby out before I have a mess to clean up."

He gives me one last kiss before getting up. I watch him from the bed as he walks into the bathroom, wearing only his boxer briefs. As Jack reaches the door, he pauses just long enough to give me a wink and one of his damn wicked smiles that makes me melt.

God, I love this man!

An hour later, Jack and I are sitting in the same booth we did five years ago, reminiscing about the first time we met, when my phone pings, signaling an incoming text.

> *Brittany: Can we meet for lunch sometime this week to talk about what happened at the cemetery?*

"Shit!" I let slip from under my breath after reading it.

"What?" Jack asks.

"Brittany wants to meet for lunch this week to talk about Joyce."

"Keegan, do you really want to get involved in that?"

"Not really, but Dad thinks I might be able to convince Brittany to at least talk to Joyce."

"This isn't your problem. With you in the middle of it, I see it turning into a bigger shitstorm than it already is."

I consider what Jack said for a moment while sipping my chai latte. "You might be right, but I think I should meet her for lunch. I feel a little sorry for Jace and Joyce."

"Why?"

I shrug. "Even though I might not be very close to Joyce, she's been a wonderful grandmother to Kyle. I would hate to see Jace miss out on knowing her. Plus, I can't help to have a little empathy for her in this situation. I'm not sure how I would respond if I were ever kept from seeing a grandchild of mine."

I text Brittany back.

> *Me: I'm pretty much open for lunch all week. You pick the place and the time.*

> *Brittany: How about Wednesday at noon at The Sandwich Shop?*

> *Me: Works for me. See you then.*

A few days later, I walk into the restaurant and find Brittany is there, waiting for me.

Once I take my seat at the table, I ask, "Hi. How are you holding up?"

"I've been better. Thank you for coming today. You're the last person I want to drag into this mess, but Aiden suggested that I talk to you."

The waitress comes to take our drink order. To limit any further interruptions, we stop to take a look at the menu and place our lunch orders.

Once the waitress leaves us, I pick up the conversation again. "I'm confused. You left the letter for Joyce to find out about Jace. Now that Joyce knows, you want to keep Jace away from her. I don't understand."

Brittany confesses, "I needed to show Joyce that I was good enough for her son. I never thought she would accept Jace as her grandson since I was his mother."

Thinking to myself that Brittany was unbelievably naive to think Joyce wouldn't care, I point out, "It's obvious that you don't know her very well. You need to find a way to come to terms with her."

Brittany then asks the question I've feared the most, "Would you be willing to go with me to talk to her?"

Shaking my head, I answer, "I'd rather not, Brittany. What happens between the two of you isn't any of my business. Can't Aiden go with you?"

"I saw how your dad was able to handle her. I thought maybe…"

"So, it's not me that you want there but my dad."

"I want both of you."

"Why?"

"So, Joyce will at least hear me out."

After further persuading, I eventually give in to Brittany. We come up with a plan to meet at my parents' house on Saturday, and then I call Dad to make the necessary arrangements.

I leave the restaurant, silently cursing Will for still causing chaos in my life after all these years.

As I sit on the bed and slip on my shoes on Saturday, I mumble out loud to myself, "I can't believe I got sucked into this mess."

Jack walks out of the bathroom and into the bedroom. "Did you say something?"

"Not of any importance. I'm just annoyed that I got pulled into this thing between Joyce and Brittany."

"Hey, I hate to say it, but I told you not to get involved."

"Yeah, I know."

"Just promise me today is it for you. Please, don't get any deeper into this mess between the two of them."

"That's the plan." I give Jack a kiss. "Well, I'm out of here. Wish me luck."

Jack chuckles. "Good luck, and try to come back home in one piece."

I know Jack is joking, but I can't help but worry about the outcome of this afternoon's little meeting.

I see that Joyce is already here as I pull in beside her parked car in my parents' drive. When I go inside, I find her standing in the study off the entrance of the foyer.

"Hi, Joyce. Where's Daddy?" I ask.

164

Before she has a chance to answer, Dad enters with Joyce's favorite drink, bourbon on ice, in hand.

"Thanks, Mitch, but I'm driving today," Joyce says to Dad.

"Come on, Joyce, you know I won't let you get drunk. One drink won't hurt." He winks at her.

My thoughts go back to the evening Dad got Jack drunk on purpose to keep him from apologizing to Annie for not telling her about our engagement.

"Well, I certainly could use a nice stiff drink about now," Joyce says as she takes the drink from Dad before she begins to sip on it.

A few minutes later, the doorbell rings. When I open the door, I find Brittany standing with Aiden at her side as she fidgets with the bracelets on her arm, looking scared to death and ready to bolt.

"Hi, Brittany and Aiden. I didn't realize you were coming, Aiden. It's good to see you again."

"It was the only way to get Brittany here. She's terrified. Is it okay for me to be here?" he asks.

"This is Brittany's show, not mine. If she's good with it, I am, too. Come on in. Joyce is waiting in the study with my dad."

As we enter the room, Joyce says snippily, "Aiden, first, you show up at the cemetery, and now, today. Maybe Keegan would like to explain why since she didn't even know who you were a few months ago when we had lunch together."

I don't give Aiden a chance to respond. "Joyce, I met Aiden briefly after Will died. I'm sorry I lied to you."

Joyce ignores my feeble attempt to apologize as she continues to question Aiden, "What does this have to do with you?"

This time, Brittany answers, "I asked him to come with me, and that's all you need to know."

Dad then takes charge by saying, "This isn't getting us anywhere. Let's all sit down and see if we can come to some common ground. Aiden, can I get you a beer?"

"Yeah, a beer would be good. Thanks."

"Brittany and Keegan, can I get anything for you?" Dad asks.

"A bottled water for me," I answer.

Brittany then says, "I'll take one, too."

Awkwardly, everyone finds a seat while Dad gets Aiden his beer along with bottled waters for Brittany and me. Once everyone has their drinks, we look at each other, not knowing where to begin.

God bless my father, as he decides to speak first, "Well, nothing is going to get settled without some good, honest conversation. Okay, you first, Brittany. What are your concerns?"

Brittany glances over to Aiden for moral support, and he nods for her to proceed.

She says in a meek voice, "I know Joyce has never thought very highly of me. Jace is all I have. I don't want him to hear any of her lies about me."

Indignantly, Joyce says, "I beg your pardon! I don't appreciate your attitude, young lady! Where do you get—"

Dad interrupts her, "Settle down, Joyce, and let's hear Brittany out. Go ahead and tell us why you think Joyce would tell Jace lies about you."

"Because I know what she and her husband thought of me back when Will and I were dating in college. They told me once that I was nothing but white trash." Brittany turns to Joyce. "Well, let me tell you something. I busted my ass getting my master's in social work to help others have a better life than I did. Yes, after college, I did some things I'm not very proud of, and it brought Troy Martin into my life, but I kept Will safe from Troy. I was the one there with him until he took his last breath! I loved Will!" By now, the tears are flowing down Brittany's face as she chokes on her words while crying.

As Aiden sits next to Brittany on the couch, he takes her hand into his, trying his best to comfort her. I see the pained look on his face and the love he has for her.

Joyce's mouth is hanging open.

After a few moments of silence, Joyce gets up and sits on the other side of Brittany, pulling her into a hug. "You listen to me very carefully, young lady. Those were my husband's words that day, not mine. Yes, I should have stopped him from saying all those ugly things to you. Please forgive me. I will never say or do anything to my grandson that would ever degrade you or put you in a bad light. I promise."

"But how can I believe you?"

Joyce looks around, desperate to find the right words to convince Brittany.

I speak up, "Brittany, I can vouch for Joyce. With everything that has happened, Joyce has never said anything inappropriate about me to Kyle. She might not always like me, but she respects me as Kyle's mother. She's a good grandmother, and Jace would be missing out on something pretty special if he never had the chance to know her."

My words bring tears to Joyce's eyes as we exchange a look of unspoken thanks to each other.

Joyce looks back to Brittany. "Please, Brittany? I'm begging you. Please let me see Jace."

Overcome with emotion, Brittany is incapable of speaking, and she only nods.

Dad breaks the silence by suddenly clapping his hands together once, causing us all to jump in our seats. He announces, "Good! Since we have that cleared up, let's get down to details."

Within the hour, a plan is in place for Joyce to be reintroduced to Jace. First, Brittany will be in attendance, and then they'll slowly work up to overnight visits. We all agree that Jace will set the pace as to how fast things happen with Joyce.

At one point during the conversation, Joyce turns to me and says, "I think Kyle should be a part of all of this. After all, he'll want to meet his brother, too."

"That's Kyle's decision, not mine. We'll cross that bridge if and when he ever shows any interest in meeting Jace."

After everything is mapped out, I sense Brittany can use a break. "It seems as if everything is all set. I'm going to take Brittany down to the dock and show her the lake."

Dad agrees, "That sounds like a good idea."

Aiden then stands. "Brittany, do you want me to go along with you?"

She shakes her head. "No, it's okay."

We no sooner get outside than I anxiously ask Brittany, "So, are you okay with everything?"

"I still don't trust Joyce, but it's only fair to give her a chance to prove me wrong. And I do mean, a chance, as in one. If she tries to undermine me, I'll shut it all down."

We find our way down to the dock. The sun is shining brightly over the gray tone of the beautiful winter landscape, void of all color that other seasons bring to it.

We stand, taking in the scenery, when Brittany says, "The first time we ran into each other at the cemetery, you mentioned something about letters from Will. What did he say in them?"

"There were two of them. The first was written right after our second divorce and read more like a confessional, telling me all about his undercover work and his investigation into Troy. He also wrote about the two of you getting back together."

"And the second one?"

Not wanting to hurt Brittany any further but knowing she won't be happy until she's heard what it said, I quote it to her word for word, "All it said was, '*My dearest Keegan, I'm sorry. I love you with all my heart. Be happy. Will.*'"

Brittany jerks her head in my direction and asks, "When did he write the second letter?"

I know it is going to break her heart, but for her to move on from Will's death, she needs to know the truth about everything.

The pain becomes evident on Brittany's face as I tell her, "I had been home from the hospital for about a week after my surgery. I was still in a lot of pain and was having problems with focusing on things. Dad had set up a place for me here, at the dock. Will came over one afternoon when I was down here. We spent a good part of the afternoon laughing and talking about anything and everything. Before he left that day, Will apologized and then kissed me. It was the last time I saw him, and it was also the day he wrote the second letter." I brush away a lone tear from my cheek.

Brittany turns back to the lake and asks, "Will kissed you?"

"Yes." In an attempt to make Brittany feel better, I add, "Will was in love with you."

"He kept us a secret from the world. At first, I thought it was because he was ashamed of me. It wasn't until later that I understood he was doing it to protect me from Troy and the cartel, much like he was protecting you by getting divorced. After your second divorce, things were different between Will and me. For a short time, we were like any other normal couple. God, we were happy during those last few weeks together. You know that envelope you gave Aiden?"

"Yes."

"The key in it was to a safe deposit box. It had a deed to a house and a letter to Aiden in it. Will never liked the neighborhood where I lived. He was always telling me to find someplace safer to live. In the letter, Will told Aiden that his plan was to surprise me with the house on my birthday. He wanted to make sure I got it in case something went wrong with his undercover assignment. Will always said he would make it up to me for helping him out. I think he knew all along how it was going to end.

"I don't know why he planted that stupid bug in Troy's office. If only I had been able to convince Troy that we weren't trying to take over his business, Will would still be alive today," Brittany says, sobbing to me. "I'm sorry."

I pull her into a hug. "Brittany, it's not your fault. Will's choices ended his life too soon. You need to understand that to be able to move on."

Brittany says nothing as she takes in my words.

I then tell her, "Come on. We'd better get back up to the house."

Standing on the front porch with my dad, we say our good-byes to Brittany and Aiden as they walk out to their car to leave.

When I go back inside, Joyce grabs my arm and pulls me into Dad's empty study, asking, "What do you mean by, if Kyle ever shows any interest in meeting Jace? Of course Kyle will want to know his brother."

"I'm not forcing the issue with Kyle. He knows about Jace. If and when Kyle expresses any interest in meeting Jace, then I'll make arrangements with Brittany for it to happen."

In her typical overbearing manner, Joyce tells me, "I'll talk to him."

"I'm warning you, Joyce. You'll never see Kyle again if I get any hint of you pressuring him about this," I threaten her.

"You wouldn't dare!" Joyce exclaims.

"Try me. No one screws around with the well-being of my son! Not even you!" I then exit the room, leaving her speechless.

18

Jack

It's the beginning of April, and my trip with Chelsey to the conference in San Diego is in a couple of weeks. Since Keegan is also going, there will be an equal amount of fun to balance out the sometimes boring sessions. I think Keegan is more excited over our reservation at a highly acclaimed restaurant of a celebrity chef she loves watching on TV than anything else.

I'm anxious to get home tonight because Keegan and I have the whole weekend to ourselves. It's Sean's weekend with Annie, and Kyle is away, working out with his future college soccer team.

Walking in the front door, I get my usual greeting from Kirby, but I see no sign of my wife. I immediately go upstairs, and when I reach our bedroom, I hear the blow-dryer from the bathroom. I stand in the open doorway and lean against it with my arms crossed, watching the show that Keegan is unaware she's putting on for me. Naked, bending over slightly at the waist, with her beautiful, long auburn hair covering her face as it blows freely in the air, she runs her fingers through it as it dries. Keegan then stands, throwing her hair back so that it gently cascades down her back.

She then sees me in the mirror and screams, "Sweet Jesus! Why don't you just scare me half to death?"

"Now, that's not a very nice way to greet your husband after a hard day at work. Speaking of hard, your little show caused a problem here that needs some attention," I remark, looking down to my pants.

Keegan glances down to the area I'm referring to and then back up. "Seriously? Why don't you just demand me to drop to my knees and service you?"

I immediately straighten up from my stance, acting as if I'm about to unbuckle my belt. "Well, if you insist."

"Not so fast, buddy. I think we need to do a little role reversal," Keegan comments as she pulls on her robe that was hanging on a hook by the door.

She casually saunters by me to the bedroom and takes a seat at the end of the bed, crossing her legs. I follow her as I start to unbutton my shirt.

Keegan shouts, "Stop!"

A mischievous smile spreads across her face as I freeze in place.

"You have to wait for my command."

A second or two passes before she throws back the words I've said to her more than once, "Strip for me, baby."

I fully embrace the moment and decide to accept her challenge by putting on a show she'll never forget.

I walk over to the dresser where a docking station sits, charging several of our devices, and select the perfect music for the occasion. As the music fills the air, I begin to make a few dance moves with my hips gyrating to the beat. It isn't long before Keegan is hooting and hollering for more. I start to pull my shirt out from the waistband of my pants and soon have it off, swinging it in the air and then dropping it to the floor. My T-shirt follows as I reach over my shoulder, grabbing it from the back. I teasingly pull it over my head, revealing my abs, inch by inch. I continue with a few more hip thrusts in male stripper–style, causing Keegan to scramble for her purse to pull bills from her wallet. She holds the money like a fan and waves them in front of her face, as if cooling herself off. I unbutton and gradually unzip my pants. Keegan motions me over to stick some bills in my open fly.

It isn't long until I'm totally naked with Keegan reclining on the bed, undoing the belt of her robe, letting it fall off her shoulders.

As I cover her body with mine, I ask, "What's your next command?"

"Make love to me, baby," she answers.

As we lie in bed, recovering from our fun, Keegan's cell phone starts to ring. Once she begins to talk, I soon realize it's her literary agent, Jerry. A short time after Keegan's book, *Ultimate Cost*, went live online, a publisher contacted her to find out who her agent was to discuss a book deal. When the publisher found out she didn't have one, Keegan was given a list of reputable agents to consider if she was interested in pursuing their offer.

I get up to take a shower, and when I'm done, I find Keegan waiting outside the shower's glass door with a towel in her hand.

I suspiciously eye her. "What's going on?"

"You will never believe what that phone call was about."

"What?"

"It was my agent. He said that Alison Kennedy and Keith Steele want to buy the options to my book!" Keegan is now bouncing on her tippy-toes, excited over Hollywood's hottest couple wanting to adapt her book into a movie.

"Okay, let me grab my sweats. You need to get dressed, too, or I'll never be able to concentrate on what you're telling me."

After we're both dressed, we take a seat on the bed, facing each other, with Kirby stretched out between us. As Keegan pets hairball, she shares the details of her phone call. It seems Keith Steele and his actress wife, Alison Kennedy, are looking for a project for him to break out from the chick flicks that he's famous for making. They think *Ultimate Cost* would make the perfect movie to feature Keith's more dramatic talents.

Keegan asks, "So, what do you think?"

"Isn't it a little soon for this to be happening? Don't get me wrong. It's a great book, but it's only been out since the first of the year." She looks as though I just killed her puppy, so I try to recover. "Hey, it's great news, sweetheart. It's just…the moment your book went live online, some publisher contacted you, and now, this."

"Now, the bad news," she says, ignoring my comment.

"What?"

"They want to meet with me the week I'm supposed to go to San Diego with you."

"Who?"

"Alison Kennedy and Keith Steele."

"Really? After one phone call, you're dumping our plans to meet with them?"

"They want to talk to me about being a consultant on the script. They're only available that week because of their work schedules and some film festival."

"So, you've already decided to sell the options to your book to them?"

"Well, I guess so. Jerry said it's a really good offer. We're supposed to do some kind of web conference with Jerry while I'm out there. I guess I'll decide after that."

"And you have to go out there to do this? You can't web conference with them in San Diego?"

"Jack, this is the way they want to handle it. I'm not in a position to make demands on Alison Kennedy and Keith Steele."

"Sure you are. You have something they want."

"And so do a million other authors."

"Will you need to be in LA during filming? What kind of time commitment are we talking about?"

"According to Jerry, they want to fast-track the project—whatever the hell that means. They already have the screenwriter lined up. It's my understanding that, when someone buys the options to a book, they have a set amount of time to move forward with the movie. It's a unique opportunity for me because authors usually don't have a whole lot to do with their book's movie."

"I don't know, Keegan. It's all happening so fast, and it could have a significant impact on our lives. I'm not sure if I can go along with you doing something that could put you on the West Coast for months at a time."

"Wait a second. Are you telling me I need your permission to do this?"

"No, but I do think we need to discuss how it could affect our lives before you go traipsing off to Hollywood," I say defensively.

"Why can't you just be happy for me?" Keegan asks.

"What happens if you get out to LA and a few days turn into a month? A month turns into six? I don't want our marriage to be one where we only see each other when we can fit it into our schedules," I counter.

She stares at me, shakes her head, and walks out of the bedroom. I see her grab her keys as I catch up with her downstairs.

"Don't leave while we're talking about this, Keegan. Going to your parents' dock isn't going to give you any damn magical answers."

"For your information, I'm going to the studio to throw some clay on the wheel. I'll be back later," she says, walking out the door.

In the morning, I wake up on the couch where I fell asleep, waiting for Keegan to come home last night. Kirby is staring at me to be let outside. I notice a quilt is spread over me. Keegan must have covered me when she came home last night.

After letting Kirby out and then back in, I put on a fresh pot of coffee. Then, I go upstairs to get ready for my morning run. I find Keegan asleep in bed. My first inclination is to crawl under the covers with her but not this time. I'm still upset she left during our argument instead of staying to sort things out between us.

Quietly going about my business, I hear Keegan ask, "Can we talk?"

I sit on the edge of the bed to put my running shoes on. "Yeah. What's up?"

She sits up in bed. "Please try to understand that, when I heard someone wanted to make a movie out of my book—*my book*—my first thought was to share this news with you. Then, you ruined it all with some off-the-wall bullshit about never seeing me because, somehow, I was going to end up living on the West Coast for months. I went to the studio to throw some clay and to clear my head."

Turning to her, I ask, "And?"

"And, while I was there, it occurred to me that, after all we've been through, you don't believe in us. Why?"

I frown at her. "What do you mean? Of course I believe in us."

"Are you sure about that? When you proposed to me, you said that the tattoos we got that day symbolized our never-ending love for each other. If you truly believed that and in us, why couldn't you simply be happy for me instead of seeing how it could destroy us? I see our marriage as an adventure of endless possibilities. If we allow our fears to get in the way of considering all life has to offer, then a part of us will die."

Touching the tattoo on my wrist before looking back up at Keegan, I say, "You left for three years, and it just about killed me. I don't want to find out what would happen if you left me again."

"So, that call yesterday made you jump to the conclusion that I might leave you?"

I shrug. "It's just that I'm getting a bad feeling about all of this California stuff. Maybe I'm afraid the creative side of you might want to stay in Hollywood and make movies."

"It's more than that. I can't think of anything—wait a minute. Does this have anything to do with Chelsey?"

I say nothing.

"Jack, please answer me."

I hang my head. "The night of her happy hour, Chelsey said our relationship had turned into us being roomies because we never saw each other." I sheepishly glance up at Keegan. "I just don't want that to happen to us."

On her hands and knees, Keegan crawls closer to me at the end of the bed, wrapping her arms around me. "Oh, baby, is that what's behind all of this? I'm not Chelsey. What we have is so much more. Remember, I'm your paradigm shift."

I confess my insecurities out loud, "There's no way I can compete with Hollywood if they end up making your book into a movie."

"Are you kidding me? After that striptease last night? Babe, you've got nothing to worry about." She giggles.

19

Keegan

Booked on the same airline, Jack and I patiently stand in line with Chelsey, waiting to check in for our flights. Although my flight departs an hour after Jack's, we will be able to stay together since our gates are on the same concourse.

At the security checkpoint, none of us sets off any alarms as we each step through the scanner. After gathering up our carry-ons from the conveyer, we slip our shoes back on and head in the direction of Chelsey and Jack's gate. I stop at a coffee kiosk on the way to grab a chai latte.

As we sit, anticipating the boarding announcement at any moment, butterflies begin to take flight in my stomach, and I start nervously bouncing my knee up and down. Jack firmly places his large hand on my upper thigh to stop it.

He tries to calm me. "You can do this. It's going to be all right. They're just people, like you and me."

"I wish you were going with me."

"Sorry, babe."

The gate agent speaks into a handheld microphone, "Good morning, passengers. This is the preboarding announcement for flight three twenty-two to San Diego, California. We are now inviting business-class passengers along with those passengers with small children and anyone requiring special assistance to begin boarding at this time. Please have your boarding pass ready. Thank you."

"That's us, Chelsey," Jack says as he stands. He pulls his boarding pass from the side pocket of his carry-on before slinging its strap over his shoulder.

Chelsey stands and fumbles with her laptop as she puts it in a leather case.

"Can I help with anything?" Jack asks.

"No, I got it. Thanks," Chelsey answers, double-checking that she has everything.

Jack then turns his attention back to me, taking me into his arms. "Let me know when you land, okay?"

"Okay." I nod.

"See you in a few days. I love you." Jack gives me a quick good-bye kiss.

"Love you to the stars and back." I smile back.

I watch Chelsey and Jack walk together toward the gate, and then each one hands their pass to the agent. Jack pauses for a moment to turn back toward me for one last look before disappearing down the jet bridge to board the aircraft.

Quickly grabbing my bag, I make my way over to the huge window to watch their plane depart. A slight ping of jealousy hits as I picture Chelsey taking her seat next to Jack.

Not even knowing if he can see me, I wave as the plane pulls out and slowly taxies away to the runway for takeoff. It isn't long before I see it off in the distance, speeding down the runway until it is airborne.

Walking a few gates down the concourse where my flight will depart in another hour, I check the posted flight information to make sure it will be leaving on time. Then, I make myself comfortable in one of the many rows of seats.

I pull out my laptop from my carry-on and try to entertain myself as time slowly passes. I double-check the schedule of the train that I plan on taking from LA to San Diego. I thought the ride would be a great way to see the scenic Pacific Coastline.

The gate agent finally announces, "Ladies and gentlemen, at this time I would like to begin boarding for flight four thirty-two to Los Angeles, California."

After landing in sunny California, I walk through LAX and find a gentleman in a dark suit holding a sign with my name. Soon, I'm being chauffeured to Malibu in a luxurious black limo with a stocked bar. Pulling out my phone, I take a picture to send to Jack with a text.

> *Me: Check out my ride.*

>> *Jack: Sweet! I just got to my room. Kind of boring compared to your ride.*

> *Me: How was your flight?*

>> *Jack: Okay. I slept a good part of the way.*

> *Me: What about Chelsey?*

>> *Jack: Our seats weren't together. I sat beside some old guy who kept waking me up with his snoring.*

> *Me: ☺ Sounds exciting.*

Jack: That's me. Mr. Excitement.

Me: Wait until I get there. I'll spice things up for you.

Jack: That's what I'm counting on.

Me: I miss you.

Jack: I miss you, too. Good luck with your meeting. I love you.

Me: I love you, too.

The drive from the airport takes me up the Pacific Coast Highway, eventually ending at an impressive beach house. My anxiety heightens as I look at the place, knowing who is waiting inside for me.

A woman greets me at the door. "Hi, I'm Charlotte, Alison's assistant. You must be exhausted from your flight and the drive. I'll show you to your room. Here, let me help you with your bag," she offers.

"Thanks, but I've got it," I tell Charlotte as I hold the handle of my suitcase even tighter, much like a child would with a security blanket.

She continues as I follow her down a hallway, "Alison and Keith wanted me to extend their apologies for not being here to greet you personally. Their shooting schedule is causing them to run late this afternoon. You can get unpacked and settled in until they arrive."

I think to myself as I take in my surroundings with fascination, *They're ordinary people, like me. They put on their pants one leg at a time, just like me. Pants? Bikinis are probably more like it. Oh my God! I've seen Alison in a bikini. Did I pack my cover-up? Stop it! They're just like me. Yeah, right. Keep telling yourself that, Keegan.*

Charlotte opens the door to the room I'll be staying in for the next few days. Stepping inside, I find it spacious and beautifully appointed with a large deck overlooking a breathtaking view of the Pacific Ocean. The color palette is a variation of soft, soothing gray tones with white accents. Looking at the king-size bed overflowing with layers of pillows stacked up against the headboard, I can't help but think about who else has slept here.

If only these walls could talk.

"Make yourself comfortable. I'll be back for you as soon as Alison and Keith arrive," Charlotte says before pulling the door shut as she leaves my room.

I take a moment to step out onto the deck to drink in the view. As over the top as all of this is, my awe and excitement start to fade as I wish Jack were here with me to see it, too.

I come back in and unpack my toiletries and makeup to freshen up a bit before my big meeting. As I enter the en suite bathroom, I'm taken aback by its understated elegance. There is marble everywhere, and French doors lead outside to the bedroom's adjoining balcony. An antique upholstered chaise lounge with a luxurious white robe draped over it sits in the corner of the room.

Jack and I could have a ton of fun in here!

As I close up my suitcase after changing my clothes, I hear a soft tapping on the door, followed by Charlotte asking from the other side, "May I come in?"

Walking to the door, I open it, motioning for her to come in. "Come on in."

"Alison and Keith are waiting for you downstairs. If you're ready, I'll take you to them."

Within minutes, I'm being led to a great room with a fireplace with what I believe is an original canvas from one of my favorite artists hanging from the stonework. Across from it is an enormous wall of windows looking out onto another incredible view of the ocean. Alison and Keith are there, waiting for me, dressed in casual clothes, looking unassuming. This puts me a little more at ease.

After introductions, I'm invited to have a seat on a comfy curved sofa that takes up the center portion of the spacious room in front of the hearth. We quickly address all the niceties about my flight and the guest room meeting my needs. It's then the conversation turns to the reason I'm here.

Alison starts by saying, "I've been wanting to get into directing, and Keith has been looking for a more challenging dramatic role. After reading *Ultimate Cost*, we thought it was the perfect vehicle for our needs. Our friend who brought your book to our attention is also the screenwriter for the project. We were hoping he would be here by now. Traffic must be delaying him."

"Um, can I ask, who is the writer?" The words are no sooner out of my mouth than a man I know all too well steps into the room.

"Alex!" Alison exclaims.

I stand up, shocked to see my ex Alex Parker strolling across the room, straight toward me, as if we were a couple of long-lost old friends.

He pulls me into a hug and says, "Keegan, it's so good to see you after all these years."

Feeling as though this is a setup of some kind, I snap back, "I wish the feeling were mutual. Don't tell me, you're the screenwriter."

"Well, yes, I am." He smiles brightly at me, clueless as to how upset I am with the whole situation.

Now turning my attention to my host and hostess, I say, "I'm sorry. Um, here's the deal. There's some history between Alex and me. I'd rather not work with him. My husband is waiting for me in San Diego. If you'll excuse me, I need to make arrangements to get to the train station."

I quickly exit the room, leaving everyone flabbergasted by my words.

Once back in my bedroom, I start gathering the few items I unpacked.

I hear a light knock at my door.

Assuming it's Charlotte checking to see if I need any assistance, I yell, "Come on in, Charlotte."

Alex enters my room and asks, "Can we talk about this like two reasonable adults?"

"For the life of me, I can't think of anything we have to say to each other. I've been able to live without you in my life for, what? About ten years? Guess what? I've been doing just fine without you."

"Are you finished, Ginger?"

"You don't get to call me that anymore."

"Please give me a few minutes to explain. I'll leave if you still don't want anything to do with me."

"Hurry up. I have a train to catch."

"I'm sorry about how things ended with us. I got scared. When Ashley reached out to me, it was an easy out. I heard about your book and read it. I thought it would be perfect for Alison and Keith's project, so I told them about it. Please don't walk out on this opportunity because of me. Just hear them out. I'll make sure you get to wherever you want after you listen to their pitch."

It is rude to leave without even hearing what Alison and Keith have to say. "Okay, I'll go back down but only under one condition."

"What's that?" Alex asks.

"I have no further contact with you after today."

"What are you so afraid of, Ginger? Are you worried that, deep down, you might still have some feelings for me?"

"Go to hell, Alex. I got you out of my system a long time ago."

"Yeah, I know. Remember, I read your book. You went back to Will, and that certainly turned out well for you."

"As a matter of fact, it did. Through all the heartache, I found Jack and discovered what real love was all about."

"Well, so did I," he says, lifting his finger to show me his wedding band.

"Congratulations. I hope you don't get scared again and screw it up."

By Alex's expression, I've hit a nerve.

He curtly responds back, "Alison and Keith are waiting for us. Are you going back down with me or not?"

"Didn't I say I would?" I snap back.

I close up my suitcase and then follow Alex out of my room.

I hear voices off in the distance as we get closer to where Alison and Keith are waiting for us. I see they have gone ahead with the planned web conference with Jerry, my agent, even though I walked out on them.

Quietly taking a seat on the couch, I hear terms like *options payments*, *extension periods*, *rights granted*, and I know I'm way out of my element. I will have to trust Jerry and hope that he's representing my best interests. The web conference ends with an agreement that their people will get paperwork to my people to review and sign.

I never even knew I had people.

As the director, Alison starts to share her vision of the movie with me. "Keegan, it's important to me that you're a part of the development process of the script to make sure the soul of the book doesn't get lost in the dialogue."

Looking at Alex and then back to Alison, I shake my head. "I'm sorry. I'm flattered, but I know nothing about writing a movie script, and I refuse to work with Alex."

I can tell by Alison's expression that she is slowly losing her patience with me.

Keith steps in and offers, "We don't want you to do any of the writing. That's Alex's job. We need you to help with editing the screenplay to make sure it stays true to the characters and the story. You wouldn't have to have any contact with Alex. We could do it all electronically."

"How much of a time commitment are we talking about?" I ask.

Alex then interjects, "My wife, Madeline, and I split our time between here and my mother's place back in Maryland that I inherited when she died last year. We'll be staying there while I write the screenplay. Other than the time it'd take for you to read what I wrote, there would be a minimum time commitment."

"Alex, I'm sorry to hear about your mother," I tell him, remembering the dear woman I grew to care about so long ago.

Our discussion is interrupted by the news that dinner is ready for us outside on the main deck of the house. As we sit down to the table, a woman serves plates of fresh fruits, salad, and grilled salmon with glasses of white wine to each of us.

Dinner conversation centers on the movie and an estimated production timeline. By now, my head is spinning with the ideas being thrown out for consideration. During dessert, personal calendars are being pulled up on phones with talks of deadlines, and thoughts on casting fill the ocean breeze.

Jack was right about my rush to commit to the project and getting in too deep without giving it serious thought.

When I interrupt their discussion, it occurs to me that they have forgotten I'm even here, "Um, excuse me. I'm new to all of this. You might as well be speaking a foreign language right now. I need to discuss all of this with my husband before agreeing to anything."

Keith speaks up, "I know you want to get to San Diego to meet…"

"Jack. His name is Jack."

"Jack. We were wondering if you could stay at least until tomorrow. I want to take you to the set where Alison is currently filming. It would give you a chance to see firsthand how everything works."

"Okay, that would be great. By the way, why do you want me working on this project? I didn't think authors usually got involved at this level of a movie."

Alison answers, "First impressions are the ones that last in the film industry. I want this script to be perfect to make sure Keith has the best opportunity to show people his range of talent. You'll find that I'm a controlling bitch who can be quite demanding. Do I care? No. Not if it gives me the final product that I want. It's my understanding that Alex knows the asshole side of your ex-husband. You, however, know the caring side of him. I don't want Alex's biases to show in the script. I need you to be a part of this movie to make sure we don't take too much literary license with it. Bottom line, I want a flawless adaptation of the book. The best way to achieve that is to have both of you working on the project. If you two disagree on something, I'm a telephone call away. Understand?"

I nod. "Yeah, totally. Well, if you'll excuse me, I'm exhausted, and I need to turn in. What time should I be up and ready to go tomorrow morning?"

Keith tells me, "Five."

As I lie in bed, missing Jack, I call him, but there's no answer, so I text instead.

> *Me: Hey, baby, I'm missing you right now. Where are you?*

>> *Jack: In an evening session that's about to end. How are things going?*

> *Me: I have a lot to tell you.*

>> *Jack: When will you be here?*

> *Me: Looks like the day after tomorrow.*

>*Jack: Damn it! Looks like Chelsey &
I will be using the dinner reservation for
tomorrow night.*

Me: What?

>*Jack: Sorry. I never canceled it. I was
hoping you would make it down in time
for us to go. Without thinking, I said
something to Chelsey about it. Come to
find out, she likes this chef as much as
you. She offered to go in your place. I
couldn't find a nice way out of it.*

Me: Well, that sucks big time!

>*Jack: We're going dutch. Does that
make you feel any better?*

Me: Nope.

>*Jack: I have a key card waiting for you
at the front desk in case you get in
while I'm at the conference.*

*Me: Busy day tomorrow. Not sure if I'll get time
to text you.*

>*Jack: Okay. I've got to go. Love you.*

Me: Love you, too.

Instead of the texts making me feel better, it only causes me to miss Jack more, and I'm beginning to regret ever coming here. They can do the movie with or without me, but I can't be without Jack. I fire up my laptop and book the five forty-five train to San Diego tomorrow evening. Although I won't be able to make it in time for our dinner reservation, I'll still be able to tour the studio, and then I'll be waiting for Jack when he gets back to the hotel.

The next morning on the way to the studio, I share my plans with Alison and Keith. They generously make arrangements for a car to take me from the movie set to the station and another one to meet me in San Diego.

My day is hectic with visiting the set and then rushing to meet the train. I don't have any time to check my phone for messages until I'm in my seat on the train. I smile as I read Jack's text from this morning.

> *Jack: Hi, baby. God, I missed you last night. Can't wait until tomorrow. Don't plan on leaving the room when you get here. Making sweet love to my girl is the first thing on my agenda.*

I decide to surprise Jack and not text him about my change of plans.

20

Jack

When we arrive at the restaurant, the hostess escorts Chelsey and me to a table overlooking the marina that turns out to be the perfect spot to take in this evening's sunset. I don't think it's possible to miss Keegan any more than I do right now.

"Wow! This place is even more over the top than what I imagined," Chelsey says, distracting me from my thoughts.

I nod in agreement, trying my best to appear that I'm enjoying myself but failing miserably. "Yeah, it is."

"Maybe this isn't such a good idea after all. It's okay if you want to leave and go back to the hotel."

"Nah, I'm good. Let's get a bottle of wine and enjoy some good food."

Surprisingly, the evening with Chelsey turns out to be a lot of fun. I'm not sure if it's the drinks, the food, the setting, or the combination of all three, but our conversation is easy and lighthearted.

It could be the wine served during dinner that is the cause of our laughter during the walk back to the hotel as the conversation slowly turns into one about our past.

"Remember the first time we met?" Chelsey asks, giggling.

"God, you were such a bitch to me." I laugh as I recall sitting next to Chelsey in class, trying to hit on her.

"You had it coming."

"Excuse me?"

"I was the only woman in a lot of the classes. Do you have any idea how many times I heard those sorry-ass lines?"

"But not as good or as smooth as my delivery," I answer back with a wink and smile.

She laughs. "Yeah, I guess that's why I ended up going for coffee with you after class that day."

We both turn quiet as we near the hotel.

Then Chelsey says, "I never thought we would be able to enjoy an evening out like this again. It feels good. Thank you."

"You know, Chelsey, to this day, I still don't know what the hell happened."

"I know. After all these years, I don't even know where to start. I had to sort some things out. It wasn't anything that you did wrong. It was all me. I do have a question for you."

"Shoot."

"Why Keegan?"

"She-she—hell, it's hard to put into words. From the moment we met, I knew there was something different about her. I just wanted—no, I needed to be with her."

Chelsey doesn't say anything else as we join other guests in the hotel elevator.

The elevator stops at our floor, and as we exit, I say, "Night, Chelsey. I had a good time tonight."

"Me, too. Night, Jack."

We turn away from each other to walk in different directions to our rooms.

After entering my room, I empty my pockets and get ready to take a long, hot shower. Afterward, I pull on only my cutoff sweats and crawl into bed, glad that today is over, as I look forward to seeing Keegan tomorrow. I check my phone one last time to see if there are any texts or missed calls from her before turning off the light to go to sleep.

Nothing.

I no sooner start dozing off than there is a knock at the door. Turning on the light on the nightstand, I get up and go over to the door to look through the peephole. I see Chelsey in her robe, standing out in the hallway.

Opening the door, I ask, "Something wrong?"

"We need to talk."

"Now? I just went to bed. Can't it wait until tomorrow?"

"No, it has to be now before I lose my nerve. I have just enough buzz left from the wine to tell you the truth." She pushes past me before I can say anything else. Once inside my room, Chelsey turns toward me and shocks me with her next words. "I screwed up by not telling you I was pregnant."

"What?"

Chelsey takes a deep breath and continues, "I was pregnant, Jack. I never told you because I was scared. I wasn't ready to be a mother. I'd worked so hard to become a paramedic. A baby was the last thing either of us needed. But the joke was on me. I had a miscarriage before I could figure out a way to explain my feelings to you about having a baby."

I drop down onto the edge of the bed in disbelief.

Chelsey kneels in front of me and starts crying. "It was as if God was punishing me for not being happy about my pregnancy. I was so messed up. I had to leave."

"What the hell? We were living together! I would have known if you had a miscarriage."

"Our work schedules had us hardly ever seeing each other. Hiding it from you was easy. I was afraid to tell you."

"Afraid of what?"

"That you would propose to me for all the wrong reasons. I wasn't ready to get married or have a child. Other than our work schedules, my life with you was perfect. I didn't want to ruin what we had with a baby or marriage."

I stand up and start pacing around the room, not knowing what to do or how to respond to everything Chelsey just said to me. She remains kneeling on the floor, sitting back on her heels, watching me.

I stop my pacing and return to where I was sitting on the bed in front of Chelsey. I notice the tears streaming down her face.

The emotions of losing our child that I had no knowledge of until a few minutes ago overcome me. "We lost our baby?"

Chelsey brings herself up onto her knees, nodding, as she gently wipes my tears away. "I'm so sorry for losing our baby. Please forgive me. I'm so—" She stops mid sentence, looking over my shoulder.

I follow her gaze and see Keegan standing just inside the room with a horrified look on her face.

21

Keegan

After inserting my key card in the door, the red light flashes, seemingly mocking me and denying me access.

Damn it! I never seem to slide these things in right the first time.

I look at the card and find I had it upside down. I flip it around to try again.

The door opens up to a scene that there are no words to describe. Devastation consumes me as I see Jack sitting on the edge of the bed, bare-chested with only his sweat shorts on, and Chelsey is kneeling in front of him at his feet, wearing a robe.

"I'm so sorry for losing our baby. Please forgive me. I'm so—"

I physically force down the bile that burns my throat as Chelsey's words register.

Chelsey then sees me.

Jack looks over his shoulder at me with tears streaming down his face. *"Keegan!"*

Chelsey stands up and says, "I'm so sorry, Keegan." She goes tearing past me and out of the room.

I stand frozen, taking in Jack's state of undress and the rumpled bed. I don't dare speak, for fear of getting physically ill.

Jack stands, and in a panic, he says, "It's not what it looks like. You've got to believe me."

I find my voice. "What does Chelsey mean by *our* baby? *What baby, Jack?*" I shout.

Jack cries out, "My baby! Chelsey was pregnant with my baby and lost it! *Please, just give me a goddamn minute to explain!*"

I'm now visibly shaking, not believing what I heard. In a cold, deadly calm voice, I respond back, "Take all the fucking time you need."

I hear Jack calling out to me as I run out of the room with only my purse over my shoulder, leaving my suitcase behind. I reach the elevator and push the button, hoping it comes before Jack catches up to me. The doors open, and I board the empty elevator. I press the button with the icon to shut the doors, forcing them to close before Jack appears. Through the crack of the shutting doors, I see Jack now wearing a T-shirt. Knowing he will take the stairs, I get off two floors down and wait in the snack machine area until I think there's no chance of running into him downstairs.

I decide to take the stairs, and I pause to listen at each level to hear if anyone is coming before proceeding. Once reaching the main floor of the hotel, I stop at the front desk to see if there are any other rooms available. The hotel is full due to the conference. Not sure what to do next, I walk over to the hotel's coffee shop for a chai latte and somewhere to sit to rest my drained, achy body.

My phone is blowing up with texts and phone calls from Jack.

Screw him.

There is no way I can talk to him right now.

I stare at the cup, turning it in my hands, as the scene keeps playing in my head—Chelsey on her knees, touching

Jack's face, as he sat on the edge of the bed in front of her. It was all so intimate between them that it made me feel like an interloper in my own room. The latte does nothing to calm me or to take away the feeling of being sick.

I begin to feel all my insecurities about the men in my past and their need to leave me for others come creeping back in, one by one. I look down at the Celtic love knot tattoo that matches the one Jack has on his inner left wrist. He promised that our love would be endless because of the honesty and trust that we shared. Discovering his words were meaningless cuts me to the core. The hurt is unbearable as the tears run down my face, and anger surges through me.

I continue to ignore Jack's attempts to contact me while I pull up the schedule of flights back to Maryland. I find nothing is departing from San Diego until early tomorrow morning. It then occurs to me that I left my suitcase behind when fleeing the room. I take a deep breath as it sinks in that I need to go back upstairs to retrieve my luggage and confront Jack.

As I stand at our room's door, afraid of the heartache waiting for me on the other side, I power through my emotions and open the door.

I no sooner enter the room than I'm slammed up against the wall by Jack. As he cages me in with his body, he starts to forcibly kiss me while ripping my blouse open at the same time, causing buttons to fly across the rug. My hurt and anger are now replaced with fear as it starts to feel as if my husband might rape me.

Trying to jerk my head away while pushing him off of me, I scream out, "Stop! You're hurting me. Get off!"

The second Jack hears me, he stops, pushes himself off the wall, and drops down, defeated, on the bed. Sitting hunched over with his elbows on his knees and his head hanging down, he sobs, "I thought you left me. I'm sorry. Please, forgive me."

Trembling, I yank my blouse closed with one hand and hold it in place as I escape into the bathroom to pull myself together. I look at my reflection in the mirror and see the redness caused by the scruff of Jack's beard. I gently run my shaking hands over it, still not quite believing what just occurred between us. After throwing some cold water on my face, I see my blouse is ruined. The thought of going back out to the room for my suitcase is terrifying, and it takes me a few minutes to find the courage to do it.

As I walk out to retrieve my bag, Jack watches my every move. I feel as though I'm an animal being stalked by a predator.

Once back in the bathroom, I pull out an oversize tee and a pair of yoga pants along with some flats to put on. Knowing I can't stay in the bathroom forever, I take a few deep breaths to try to calm myself before opening the door to confront Jack.

When I reenter the room, I see Jack standing, staring out the window into the darkness of the night.

Feeling safe with the distance between us, I ask, "When did you and Chelsey hook up again?"

Jack continues to stare out the window as he speaks, "What you heard tonight was Chelsey explaining why she left me. She had a miscarriage."

"*What?*" I ask, stunned.

"She was pregnant and had a miscarriage. I didn't find out about it until tonight."

"But you said—after I pushed you off, you-you were apologizing to me for doing it," I stammer back in tears.

With his hands on his hips, Jack drops his head. "Chelsey had just told me everything when you walked in. I was messed up. I thought I had lost you forever. I was apologizing for the way I attacked you a few minutes ago."

I know in my heart that Jack is telling the truth.

I walk up to him and take his hand in mine. "Come sit down. Tell me everything from the beginning." I lead him over to the bed.

First, we sit on the edge. Eventually, I lie on my back with my head propped up by pillows against the headboard. Jack is beside me with his head resting on my stomach and his right arm holding me tight, making it impossible for me to run off again.

As I listen, I hear the raw pain in his voice. My man is broken, and I'm not sure how to fix him. I try to soothe him by running my fingers through his hair as he talks. It isn't long until he falls asleep.

Remembering my wedding vows, I whisper to him, "I will share in the joy of our good times together and be your beacon of light when you are struggling to find your way out of the fog."

The next morning, I wake up as I feel someone gently shifting my body in bed. I open my eyes to see Jack standing over me.

Sleepily, I ask, "Hey, how are you doing this morning?"

Jack squats down beside the bed to my level. He tenderly brushes a few strands of hair off my face. "Shh, go back to sleep. When I woke up, we were in the same position as last night. You looked uncomfortable, so I tried to reposition you. Sorry I woke you up."

"Talk to me, Jack."

He sighs. "I'm feeling pretty shitty right now. I thought a run might clear my head."

"So, who's running away now?"

"What do you mean by that?"

"Well, that's what you always accuse me of doing."

"Yeah, I guess you're right. What do you suggest?"

"I don't know. Do you think finishing your talk with Chelsey might help?"

"What else is there left to say? Over eighteen years ago, Chelsey had a miscarriage, and she didn't bother to tell me. Anyhow, it doesn't matter now. I'm more upset over what I did to you. I can only imagine how much I scared you. Are we okay?"

I nod. "Yeah, we're good."

"Thank God. I think I'm still going to go for a run and let you get some more sleep."

Now fully awake, I sit up in bed. "Jack, wait a minute. Can you answer a question for me?"

"Sure."

"What would have happened if Chelsey had told you about her pregnancy instead of leaving you?"

"I would have been shocked, happy, and probably asked her to marry me."

"Okay, what if you two got married after she lost the baby, and she got pregnant again? What would have happened?"

Jack shrugs. "I guess we would have had a baby." His irritation over my questions is beginning to show in his tone.

"What about the firehouse? What would you have done when both of you were scheduled to work on the same day? I don't know too many twenty-four-hour daycare centers."

"I don't know. Women in the department have babies all the time. We would have figured it out. Chelsey might have needed to find another job with regular hours or be a stay-at-home mom."

Jack's chauvinistic viewpoint surprises me.

"Why Chelsey and not you? I mean, what if Chelsey had said she wasn't going to give up her career? That you'd need to be the one to get a job with regular hours or be a stay-at-home-dad? Would you have done it?"

"That wouldn't have been an option. I'd worked too hard to earn my fire science degree. It's the only thing I've ever wanted to do."

"What if Chelsey felt the same way?"

"What's your point, Keegan?"

"When I was pregnant, at the top of my list of worries was how to juggle a career while being a good mom. I can only imagine what was going through Chelsey's head when she discovered she was having a baby. And then to lose the baby? Her emotions must have been off the charts."

Jack sits down, facing me on the bed. "Maybe, if she had told me, the miscarriage wouldn't have happened."

"There was nothing you could have done to prevent it. They happen because there's something wrong with the pregnancy."

"What about you?"

"What about me?"

"What if you got pregnant? You weren't sure how you felt about it when we talked after your car accident. With Kyle going to college and Sean in middle school, would you want to have a baby?"

I sit there for a minute before answering, "I would be scared but also excited to be having our child."

"I love you." Jack takes me in his arms to kiss me.

As we break from the kiss, I tell him, "I love you, too. I hate to ruin the moment, but you need to get out of here if you're going to go for a run before the conference starts today."

"I was thinking about playing hooky."

"Why don't you go to the sessions while I get some sleep?"

As Jack puts on his running shoes, he asks, "So, how was Hollywood? From your texts, it sounds as if you have a lot to tell me."

"You have no idea. We'll talk later."

With all the drama with Chelsey, I think it's best to delay telling Jack the news about working with Alex. I yawn, feigning sleep, and I snuggle deep under the covers to put off that conversation for a little while longer.

22

Jack

When I walk out of the hotel, Chelsey is across the street, doing stretches before her run. She doesn't see me at first, and I consider slipping back inside until she jogs off. My luck runs out as Chelsey spots me, and she walks over.

"Morning. Do you have time to talk?" she asks.

I nod. "Yeah, sure."

"How are things with Keegan?"

"Everything is fine."

"Ah, come on, Jack. Unless she's a saint, no woman is going to be okay with finding her husband half-dressed with another woman kneeling in a robe in front of him. How bad is it? Do you need me to talk to her?"

Chelsey is starting to piss me off.

"No, you don't need to talk to Keegan. I explained everything to her."

Suddenly, Chelsey becomes defensive, raising her voice a little too loud for my liking. "What? That I'm a bitch for never telling you that I was pregnant and that I lost the baby?"

Through a clenched jaw, I tell her, "Will you lower your damn voice? I'm not getting into all of this with you out here on the street."

Chelsey looks around to see if anyone notices us and then continues, "It wasn't your damn career in jeopardy. Being a woman, I had to work twice as hard as you to land a job in the fire department. You had a cakewalk compared to me."

I can't take any more, and I let it rip. "What a load of crap! Women in the fire service have babies all the time, and you know it. Losing the baby gave you an out for not telling me about the pregnancy, and hell, maybe it was even an excuse to leave me." Chelsey stands with tears welling up in her eyes as I continue, "My only regret is that you went through all of that by yourself. It didn't have to be that way."

"Yes, it did because you would have been the good guy by asking me to marry you, and I would have said yes. We would never have made it. I think, deep down, that's why I never told you."

"You know what? You're probably right about that. Strange how things have a way of working out for the best. I'll see you later," are my final words before I jog off along the waterfront, feeling free from the baggage that I was lugging around for all those years.

Returning to the hotel room, I see Keegan is asleep in bed. I hop in the shower, deciding to blow off the conference today and join her.

I hear the bathroom door open and watch Keegan step in the shower, asking, "Mind if I join you?"

"I was hoping you would."

I notice a small mark on her neck from last night. Touching it, I apologize, "I'm sorry."

She places the tip of her index finger to my lips. "Shh, everything is okay," she reassures me.

Tenderly, I take her into my arms as the water pelts against our skin. It's almost as if we meld into one. The intensity of the moment is almost too much for me to handle.

Keegan looks into my eyes and says, "I need you."

I gently push her back up against the tiled wall of the shower. I lift her legs, so they wrap around me. I softly start to kiss Keegan as I enter her. Her back arches off the wall as the movement between us quickens, taking us both to ecstasy in a matter of minutes.

It's late morning, and Keegan and I haven't left the protective cocoon we've created in bed, blocking out the rest of the world.

"So, tell me about Hollywood."

"Before I do that, did you get a chance to speak to Chelsey?"

"Yeah. I'm still pissed off at her for not telling me. How could I not have seen she was capable of doing something like that?"

"You're asking me that question? Remember, I'm the one who married a man not once but twice, and he still ended up shocking the hell out of me. I think, sometimes, we're so focused on the dream that it prevents us from seeing reality."

"I don't know. Maybe. Now, tell me what happened in Hollywood. I know when you're stalling."

Keegan breaks from our embrace to sit up in bed. "Promise me you won't lose it."

"No promises. Start talking. Now!"

"No, not if you're going to have that kind of attitude before I get a single word out."

"I'm getting an attitude because you're not telling me what happened. It's starting to piss me off."

She starts talking with her hands flying about in the air, "Okay, first, the house was amazeballs! I mean, it had all these levels that opened out to decks facing the ocean. Charlotte, Alison's assistant, took me to the great room that was the size of the whole downstairs of our townhouse. It had these enormous windows—"

I interrupt, "Keegan, the meeting. I don't give three shits about the house."

She pauses long enough to roll her eyes at me and heaves out a sigh. "The meeting started off with just Alison and Keith. When I asked who the writer was, it was as if on cue, Alex Parker came waltzing in the room."

With raised eyebrows, Jack asks, "Alex Parker? As in your former boyfriend Alex Parker?"

"The one and only. What are the chances of that happening?"

Jack mutters under his breath, "Yeah, what are the chances?"

"You know, he had the nerve to walk up and hug me like we were old buds. Anyhow, I set everyone straight, telling them that there was no way I would work with him. He convinced me to listen to Alison and Keith's pitch. They want me to consult on the script, so the—how did they put it? So the soul of the book isn't lost. I can do it all from home. Alex and his wife—did I tell you he was married?"

"No, you didn't."

"Well, he's married now. He inherited his parents' place in Maryland and splits his time between there and LA. Alex and his wife, Madeline, will be staying in Maryland while he writes the script."

"Where's his house in Maryland?"

"Not far from where we live."

"So, what are you going to do?"

"I don't know. Writing the book was hard enough. Seeing it in print is one thing, but up on the big screen is a whole different ballgame. During our meeting yesterday, there was a web conference with Jerry. They lost me with all their legal jargon. Alison and Keith are going to submit their offer to Jerry for review and my signature. If I sign off on it, they'll move forward with the movie."

"It sounds like you're having doubts about selling the options to the book."

"It's a catch-twenty-two. The reason for writing the book was to tell Will's story. What better way to get it out there than in a movie? If I sell the rights to Alison and Keith, I have the opportunity to have a say in the screenplay. To do that, I have to work with Alex, whom I don't trust."

"Can you ask them to get another writer?"

"I could, but I'm not sure if I have that kind of clout. I get the feeling that Alison is the one running the show. If I start making demands like that, she might think it's more hassle than what it's worth. Plus, Alex is a phenomenal writer, and I know he would do a fantastic job. What do you think?"

"You told me not too long ago that a part of us could die if we didn't consider the possibilities out there, waiting for us. I think, if you give Alex the power to keep you from doing this, you'll regret it for the rest of your life."

"I haven't thought about it that way. I'm not deciding anything until I see how Kyle feels about all of this." Keegan snuggles back into my arms under the covers.

We're lying in the quiet when I ask, "Do you think Alex is doing this to try to make up for what he did to you?"

The words are no sooner out of my mouth than I regret saying them. I feel Keegan's body go tense before she throws back the covers to get up and stomp over to her suitcase.

She rummages through it, pulling out clothes to get dressed, as she sarcastically replies over her shoulder, "Yeah, it couldn't possibly be that my book would make a good movie. Alex must have asked Alison and Keith to waste a few million to set things straight with a girl he screwed over years ago."

Keegan is now dressed, standing at the end of the bed, with her hands on her hips and the dirtiest go-to-hell look on her face.

Saying nothing, I get out of bed to put on my T-shirt and sweats. Walking over to Keegan, I put my arms around her. "Hey, calm down. That's not what I meant, and you know it."

Keegan takes a moment before answering, "When I saw Alex, I figured it was a setup, and that's why I walked out of the meeting. I was packing up to leave when he came up to my room to explain how it all happened."

"To your room? As in your bedroom?" I inquire.

"Yeah, Mr. You Were Half-Naked with Your Ex in Only a Robe on Her Knees at Your Feet. Any other questions?"

"God, sometimes, you're such a damn smart-ass!"

"According to Alex, he heard that I had written a book. He read it and told Alison and Keith about it. They thought it was a perfect fit for their needs, and the rest is history."

I give Keegan a soft kiss. "Tell you what. Why don't we forget all this bullshit and enjoy what's left of our trip?"

"Sounds perfect," Keegan answers back.

But I know it will remain in the back of her mind until she makes a final decision.

Returning to work is always an adjustment after being away for a week. While I sit at my desk at work on the first day back, catching up on the backlog of paperwork, an email pops up on the computer screen, announcing that Chelsey has accepted a position in another county.

Immediately, I pick up the phone to call her.

"I was wondering how long it would take for you to call. Wow, it was a whole five minutes," Chelsey says after answering the phone.

"What's going on?"

"A few months ago, I applied for the head of an emergency management division closer to Mom and Dad. They offered me the position while I was at the conference. I couldn't say anything until I spoke to the chief."

"When are you leaving?"

"I'm sticking around until the first of July."

"You've only been here for a year. Why are you leaving?"

"Jack, you know I can't stay. It was wrong for me to ever come back."

We say our good-byes, both knowing this is probably the last time we ever speak to each other.

Walking in the townhouse's back door after work this evening, I find only Kirby and some envelopes scattered all over the top of the counter. There is a note in Keegan's handwriting lying beside them, instructing me to select three and then come upstairs to our bedroom.

Reaching down to scratch Kirby behind his ears, I ask him, "Hey, buddy, do you know what this is all about?"

I swear, the dog just shrugged back at me.

After picking out three, the hairball and I head to the bedroom. There stands Keegan in the lingerie she wore on Christmas Eve, sans the Santa hat, next to a huge box sitting on the bed, wrapped up with a big bow on top.

Keegan shouts, "Happy anniversary!"

"Thanks, but our anniversary isn't for a couple of more weeks. Remember, we're heading to the beach for the weekend to celebrate? Shouldn't you be giving me this down there?"

She giggles. "Oh, don't worry; there will be more gifts down there. In each envelope is an activity for us to do at the beach that requires a reservation."

"Are you going to tell me what's in the envelopes that I left downstairs?"

"Nope. They'll all be tucked away for safekeeping for the next time we play this game." She smiles back at me.

"But what if there's something in one of those I'd rather do than what's in these?" I try to negotiate.

"Um, hello? Wife is standing in front of you with hardly anything on, except some flimsy lace! Do you want to waste time on debating this?" Keegan asks in exasperation.

"Okay, continue," I tell her.

"In this box are numbered items with clues attached to them. Now, if you haven't noticed, you have three envelopes, and I happen to be wearing three items of clothing. Any thought as to where this is going?"

"Your version of strip poker?"

"My version of strip gift-giving! If you get the clue right, I lose a piece of clothing. If you get it wrong, you lose a piece of clothing."

I start ripping off my clothes.

She yells at me, "Hold on! What do you think you're doing?"

"Leveling the playing field, baby," I tell her as I stand in only my T-shirt, boxers, and socks.

Keegan laughs and then holds out her hand to me. "Give me your envelopes."

She looks at the number on the outside of the first one and then reaches into the box. She pulls out what looks like one of Sean's superhero figurines dangling from a scarf by some string along with a piece of paper.

Keegan reads the clue attached to it out loud, "*This gift is my way of showing you my love is to the stars and back. Be sure to wear your swim trunks because we could get wet by taking a little dip along the way.*"

I mutter the clue over and over under my breath, but I have no idea what it means. "I give up. What is it?"

She rips open the envelope and pulls out an ad for a parasailing company.

"We're going parasailing! Take the shirt off, baby. Let me see that hot, sexy six-pack of yours!" Keegan is now doing her little happy dance that I love to watch.

Laughing, I oblige. I begin to worry that Keegan won't be losing any parts of her skimpy outfit that leaves little to the imagination.

The next envelope has the number six on it.

Keegan pulls a string of glittering stars and reads the paper on the end, "*Don't be blue when I tell you the stars will light the way as we enjoy the bounties of the sea beneath them.*"

"I know this one!" I jump up and down, pointing at her. "We're having dinner at that place you love called Blue something up on the roof deck. Right? I know I'm right. Just take your top off now!"

By now, Keegan is laughing so hard, she can barely breathe, much less show the answer and take off her top in a seductive way.

The last envelope has the number ten on it. She pulls out a bottle of suntan lotion and reads the clue taped on it, "*Come float with me for the day.*"

My thoughts go back to the weekend when we got back together and floated all afternoon on the lake. It then comes to me, and I ask, "We're renting a pontoon boat to take out on the bay, aren't we?"

Keegan nods as she shimmies out of her thong. She wraps her arms around me, wearing only the fur heels, kissing my neck, "Did you have fun playing?"

"Baby, we've only started playing," I tell her as I lay her down on the bed.

23

Keegan

Jack knows how I love to spend time at the beach that is approximately a three-and-a-half-hour drive away from where we live. The Delmarva Peninsula runs along the coastline of Delaware, through Maryland, down to Virginia with the Atlantic Ocean on one side and an assortment of inlet waterways on the other. It houses numerous beach communities that dot the coastline through the three states. For our first wedding anniversary, Jack has rented a place that someone in the department owns, and we will be staying there for a long weekend.

I'm surprised when Jack turns down a street of a house located in an inlet neighborhood that borders one of the local bays. Jack pulls into the driveway of a beach bungalow that sits on top of tall, massive wooden stilts, creating a large carport to park vehicles underneath.

After unpacking the car, I take a moment to explore the house's bedrooms, loft, tastefully decorated living area, and cute retro kitchen with all its modern amenities.

"Well, what do you think?" Jack asks anxiously.

"It's gorgeous! I've always dreamed of owning a place like this," I answer, still looking around in amazement.

"Great! By the way, happy anniversary," he says, extending a set of keys to me on a beautiful engraved key chain. "It's yours—well, I mean, ours, but it's my anniversary gift to you."

"Holy shit! No, you didn't!" I shout as I playfully smack his shoulder. Then, I take the keys from him, and I read the engraving that says *Beach Shack* on the key chain.

"Are you kidding me? How did you do this without me knowing about it?" I ask him as I look around the great room in shock, trying to take in that it belongs to us.

"Well, it's time for me to fess up to a few things. I tucked away the rent money from my townhouse, and eventually, I sold it to my tenant. I know this was all done behind your back, but there's a good reason for it. Since Ryan and Liz have a place down here, I've been having them keep an eye out for a good deal on some bayside waterfront property. A local realtor, who is a friend of Ryan's, has been working with me on it. I didn't think he would ever find anything in my price range.

"A little while ago, he called me about this property. I got it for a song because of its condition. You know all of those trips your parents have been taking to the beach? Mitch and Ryan have been getting this place ready to surprise you this weekend. The kitchen and bathrooms still need some work. Your parents along with Ryan and Liz cleaned up the place and got most of the painting done. Last weekend, they came down with the furniture. If you look under those slipcovers, you'll find my old furniture from the townhouse. Also, my tables and dressers were given fresh coats of paint to fit in better with the beach theme."

"So, you made up that whole story about someone in the department owning this place?"

"No. Someone in the department does own it. Me."

"I'm totally blown away," I say, giving him a kiss that doesn't begin to show my appreciation. "I think this is the perfect time for me to give my gift to you."

"You did the other week. Remember, strip gift-giving?"

"How could I ever forget that?" I ask, laughing at him. "I told you I had other gifts for you."

"I just thought you meant great sex," Jack says, raising his eyebrows up and down.

While scanning the room, I say, "Well, that goes without saying, but I do have one more to give you. Now, give me a second to find the perfect spot for it."

Taking Jack's hand, I lead him over to the couch facing the fireplace in the living area with its high-vaulted ceilings and exposed beams. I look for something to use as a blindfold but see nothing other than the T-shirt he's wearing.

"Take your T-shirt off, and have a seat," I tell Jack.

He eagerly obliges, thinking this is going in an entirely different direction. I'm sure my blindfolding him only heightens the fantasy he's conjuring up in his head. I instruct him not to move or peek as I run to the bedroom to open one of my suitcases that contains a large, flat package in brown paper. Once the paper is off, I carry it back out to the living room where Jack is patiently waiting. I remove the items off the mantel to make room for the gift.

Striking a pose in front of the fireplace, facing Jack, I tell him, "You can take off your blindfold."

He wastes no time in pulling the shirt off his head. "What the hell? You still have your clothes on. You're not even wearing any sexy lingerie," Jack whines like a baby.

Rolling my eyes at him, I point to the mantel. He takes in the poster-size framed black-and-white photo of a magnificent lighthouse, taken at dusk with its light brightly shining. It looks perfect in its new home. An envelope is taped to the glass.

Jack stands to walk over to it for a closer look. "Wow, that is an incredible photograph," he says while carefully removing the envelope with his name. He slowly drops down onto a nearby chair and starts to read the enclosed notecard.

> *My dearest husband,*
>
> *Your light appearing out of the fog changed my life as it led me through troubled waters to you. Yes, you were my lighthouse then, and you continue to be today as my husband.*
>
> *I cherish your love and feel blessed to have found you.*
>
> *Happy first anniversary!*
>
> *Your devoted wife*

Jack slowly shakes his head, looking up at me with glassy eyes. "You've got this all wrong. It's you who is my light."

I go to him, falling to my knees. "Isn't that the way it's supposed to be? Us being each other's light to help get through bad times?"

Jack nods. He lifts me onto his lap, and we begin to show our love for each other with passionate, deep kisses.

He pulls back. "I think it's time we christen our bedroom."

The deck outside spans across the back of the house with half of it enclosed in a screened-in porch, giving us privacy from the neighbors on each side of us. Within the screened section is a comfy bed swing. Jack must have remembered that I showed him a similar swing in a magazine, and he ordered one for here. It is hanging from the porch rafters in a strategic position for the sole purpose of watching the sunsets out over the bay.

On our last night at the beach, Jack and I are stretched out on the bed swing, lazily watching the show of colors from the sunset. Jack looks over at me and starts to repeat his wedding vows, and I respond in kind. The love that fills my heart is indescribable.

I straddle him, taking off my top, exposing my breasts, as he intently watches. It doesn't take long for Jack to roll me over onto my back. He removes the rest of my clothes, and then he strips out of his. As we make love, I have never felt more as one with this man, who is my lover, friend, and soul mate.

We fall asleep under a cozy quilt on the swing and wake up to the sounds of seagulls searching for their breakfast along the beach in the morning. It's the perfect ending to a perfect night of a perfect first anniversary.

Our long weekend ends too soon for my liking. My only comfort in leaving today is knowing we can come back to this magical place whenever the mood strikes us because it's ours.

On the drive home, my decision to sell the options to my book and work on the film is the topic of our conversation.

"So, how is this supposed to work? Will you and Alex hammer out the script together?" Jack asks me.

"My understanding is, after Alex completes a scene, he'll send it to me electronically for me to review. I'm to note any inconsistencies with the book."

Jack then asks, "You remember when you told Kyle about Alex and the movie?"

"Yeah. What about it?"

"Didn't you think his reaction was strange when he heard about it all?"

"In what way?"

"I don't know. Kyle didn't seem overly surprised about it. I mean, this is a guy he hasn't seen in years. I'd thought he'd act differently."

"I don't know. It's been a long time since we lived with Alex."

"Hmm, maybe."

"He's graduating from high school next month. I'm sure he has college and other things on his mind."

Once home, I check my emails and find one from Alex with an attached file. Assuming it's the first scenes of the movie for me to review, I decide to wait until after Jack goes to work tomorrow to open and read it. I will have the whole house to myself and be able to focus on it without interruption.

After saying good-bye to Jack the next morning, I fill my coffee mug, get comfy on the couch with my laptop, and open Alex's email. I read his instructions on how to make notations on the attached script and then begin reading it. The randomness of the scenes is unexpected. I assumed Alex would start to write the script in chronological order, starting at page one. I'm taken aback by the insightfulness of Alex's writing, and I'm shaken by his ability to capture the book's essence.

An hour later, after typing several notations, I begin to read the last scene in the file. It's about Kyle having a run-in at school with a teammate on the soccer team, culminating in a locker-room fight. It ends with him having an emotional heart-to-heart talk with his coach in private about all the heartache in his life.

Not recognizing anything that is transpiring in this part of the script, I'm confused as to where it came from or how it fits into the movie.

I'm stunned that Alex took such liberties with the story, creating a fabrication like this at Kyle's expense. It goes way beyond taking literary license with the story for the sake of the movie. Out of anger, I hit the Delete key, making the words disappear on the screen. This action does nothing to calm me.

Since Alex is staying only a few miles away, I waste no time in jumping into my car to confront him face-to-face about the scene.

Alex's parents' former estate is just as beautiful as I remember. I drive up the sweeping driveway to the massive home, and after parking my car, I quickly make my way to the front door and ring the doorbell.

An attractive woman answers.

I introduce myself, "Hi, I'm Keegan Grady. I was wondering if Alex was home."

"Keegan! It's so nice to meet you. I'm Madeline, Alex's wife. Please come in. Alex ran to the store for me, and he should be back any minute."

I follow her to the living room of the house.

"Can I get you something to drink while you wait?" Madeline offers.

"No, I'm fine. Alex wasn't expecting me. I'm sorry. I can come—"

Alex walks in, surprised to see me waiting for him. "Hi, Keegan."

"We need to talk."

He looks at me and then over to Madeline, as if to get a clue as to what's going on, but she only gives her head a slight shake in response.

He then says, "Yeah, sure. Let's go to my study."

Once in his office, closing the door behind us, Alex takes a seat at his desk. "Please have a seat."

"That's okay. I won't be staying that long."

He looks at me with furrowed brows as he asks, "So, what's on your mind?"

"I read what you sent me. Where do you get off, making up shit at Kyle's expense?"

"What are you talking about?" Alex asks.

"The locker-room scene where Kyle gets in a fight. That never happened, and it wasn't in the book. I know adaptations of books aren't exact, but that scene is way off the mark."

At first, Alex says nothing as he stares at me. He then carefully chooses his words as he begins to speak, "Someone I know mentioned something about Kyle having an issue at school. I might have taken a few liberties here, but it's not as far off the mark as you might think. It's important to the story for the audience to see how Kyle was affected by everything."

"Who?"

"What?"

"You said *someone* mentioned Kyle having issues in school. I want to know who was spreading lies about stuff they knew nothing about!"

"Calm down, Keegan. It's not that big of a deal."

"The hell it isn't! If someone is talking shit about my child, I want to know who it is, so I can set them straight. Now, whom did you talk to?"

Alex drops his head in resolve. "It was Kyle."

"What? When did you speak to him? He hasn't mentioned anything about talking to or seeing you."

"Christ! I told him to tell you."

"Tell me what, Alex?" I demand.

"Kyle and I have been in touch with each other for years. It all started back when you were in your car accident and had surgery. He contacted me online. We've been talking to each other ever since. He even knew about the screenplay before you did because I wasn't going to pursue it unless he was okay with it. It'd killed me when we broke up because Kyle was like a son to me. My stupid choices not only made me lose you, but Kyle, too."

My anger turns to shock as I wonder why Kyle kept something this important from me. Here I thought, my relationship with my son was an open and honest one. In reality, I'm finding it's much like the one I had with his father—full of secrets.

All the emotions I felt while reading Will's letters are resurfacing, especially the paranoia. I can't help but wonder if Jack is in on this conspiracy, too.

Can I not trust anyone in my life?

"I've got to get out of here," are the only words that come out of my mouth.

"Wait, Keegan. Please, let me explain."

I don't bother to listen to any more and hastily leave Alex's house to get back to mine before Kyle gets home from school.

Once back home, waiting for Kyle, I try to talk myself down so as not to pounce the second he walks in from school.

Sitting at the kitchen island, I hear him enter through the front door, and I call out to him, "Kyle, could you please come to the kitchen for a moment?"

At first, there's no response.

Then, I hear, "Mom, can we do this later?"

I get up from the barstool and go to the hallway stairs where he is standing with one foot resting on the first step, ready to make a hasty getaway.

"No, I don't believe we can. Alex told me today that you two have been in contact with each other since my car accident."

"Yeah, I know. He sent me a text before I left school."

"So, what do you have to say about it?"

He guiltily looks up at me. "What's there to say? My fucking world was falling apart. I missed Alex. I found him online. End of story."

Stunned by Kyle's language and tone, I try to remain calm and say, "Excuse me? Would you like to try that again, young man?"

"I'm sorry, Mom, but what's the problem? I saw Alex's name in some movie credits right before your car accident. I did some research and came across his email address. I sent a message to him, and we've been in contact ever since."

"Why didn't you tell me?"

"Like I told Jack, I was waiting for the right time."

"Jack knows about this?"

I didn't hear Jack come home, but he walks up from behind and asks, "Knows what?"

I spin on my heels, glaring at him. "That Alex and Kyle have been in touch with each other?"

Jack mutters under his breath, "Ah, shit!"

Kyle stammers, "I-I—man, I'm sorry, Jack. I didn't mean to throw you under the bus."

I take a deep breath and demand, "Everyone, stop! Both of you, in the TV room. Now!"

Jack tries to intervene once we're all seated. "Keegan, please listen. I—"

Looking at Kyle, I hold my hand up in Jack's direction, signaling him to stop. "Kyle, I want to hear everything. Start talking."

He looks up at me with tears in his eyes. "Mom, I missed Alex ever since we moved out of his house. Dad hadn't been around much, and I had connected with Alex. You never took into account how leaving both Dad and Alex affected me. You just made all of these decisions for the both of us. I wanted to stay in touch with him, but you were so angry and hurt, I knew you wouldn't allow it. I contacted him through his website."

"How did I not know all of this?" I wonder out loud.

"I don't know, Mom, because Alex was at both the viewing and Dad's funeral for me!"

"*What?*"

"Yeah, Mom. Alex was there for me! You looked right at him, but it never even registered with you that it was Alex. That's how much you had checked out on me!" Kyle defiantly stands up, ready to make his escape. "Can I go to my room?"

"Yeah, go ahead," I respond. I watch my son leave the room, angry and hurt.

My tears start to flow. "Oh my God, I suck as a mother!"

Jack comes and sits down on the couch beside me. With my back turned to him, he tries to put his arm around me to comfort me, but I pull away from him.

"Don't. You knew and never said a word. What about all of your talk about how there's no room for secrets in a marriage? It was nothing but a bunch of bullshit."

"Don't do this, Keegan. You let Kyle explain. Now, let me."

I face him. "Go ahead. Just try to talk your way out of this one."

"Remember when we got back from San Diego, and you told Kyle about the movie? I thought he was a little too laid-back about the whole thing. It didn't make sense until yesterday when I was walking past his bedroom and found him FaceTiming with someone. As soon as Kyle heard me, he slammed his computer shut to end the conversation. I asked whom he was talking to, and he fessed up and said that it was Alex. When I found out you didn't know about it, I told him he had until the weekend to tell you, or I would. Maybe I handled it wrong, but I'm on shaky ground here, being the new stepdad. I thought I needed to give Kyle a chance to tell you instead of me ratting him out. I'm sorry if I screwed this one up, but it was never my intention to keep a secret or be dishonest with you."

Saying nothing in response, I leave Jack alone in the TV room, and I go upstairs to Kyle.

I tap on his closed bedroom door. "May I come in?"

At first, there's silence on the other side, and then he answers, "Yeah, come on in, Mom."

Once inside, I find Kyle lying on his bed with tears streaming down his face. I crawl up behind him, wrap my arms around him, and hold him tight. He starts sobbing hard.

I try to soothe him. "Shh, it's okay."

"Mom, I didn't mean to hurt you. I just wanted all the crap in my life to stop."

Through my own tears, I hold Kyle tighter. "I know, I know. I'm sorry I wasn't there for you. You're right. I did check out on you. I'm sorry. Please forgive me, baby."

"Mom, that was a shitty thing for me to say to you. You didn't check out. You were still recovering from your accident and surgery when Dad died. I'm sorry. I love you, Mom."

"I love you, too, sweetie. Kyle, promise me one thing."

"What?"

"Don't ever be afraid to tell me things. Yeah, it took time for me to get better, but you have been talking to Alex for years. You've had a lot of opportunities to tell me. I don't like secrets. Even though the truth can be the harder road to take, it's always the best way to go. Okay?"

"Okay."

"Always remember, I will love you, no matter what happens. So, tell me all about you and Alex."

For the next hour, I find out that it was Alex's plan to write a book, and he even started the research for it. Listening to Kyle, I start questioning Alex's motives for rekindling their connection. I can't help but wonder how many other little scenes Alex has squirreled away for the movie that came from Kyle and not the book. I also learn it was Alex who reached out to his publisher friend about my book, and he was responsible for me getting signed on.

How foolish was it of me to think my book had stood on its own merits?

Jack's suspicions were right, and I was too stupid to see it.

I leave Kyle's bedroom to find Jack sitting on the floor in the hallway with his legs stretched out with Kirby nestled in his lap.

"So, how's he doing?" he asks.

Sitting down next to Jack, taking Kirby into my arms to snuggle up to, I answer, "He's good. But I found out a lot of stuff. I owe you an apology."

"For what?"

"Can we go somewhere else to talk? I've got a lot to tell you."

Jack nods and helps me up, and we go downstairs to his man cave in the basement. There, I share what happened today between Alex and me along with what Kyle told me.

"So, what do you think I should do? Cut my ties to the movie?" I ask Jack.

"I don't know. It's a tough call. If you quit, God only knows what kind of stuff Alex will put in the movie that's not in the book."

"Yeah, but with his close ties to Alison, nothing says she'll listen to me. Her only focus is making the best movie to showcase her husband. If it's a juicy scene, I'm not sure if she'll care if it's from the book or not."

"If she doesn't listen to you, is there any legal action you can take?"

"Probably not."

"Then, the only option I see is you trying to appeal to Alison's good judgment and hope she listens. Are you going to talk to Alex about this?"

"No. I don't trust him. If I confront him, he could influence Alison's opinion before I even get a chance to talk to her. I'll deal with all of this tomorrow. Right now, I just need you to hold me."

"Yes, ma'am!"

24

Alex

"**A**lex, what the hell is going on between you and Keegan?" Alison shouts over the phone. "You told me all your bullshit with her was in the past. That you would be able to deliver the kind of screenplay I needed to get backing for this movie. I swear, if you fuck things up for Keith, you will never write another fucking word in this town!"

"What the hell are you talking about, Alison? Calm the hell down, and tell me what happened."

"I've been on the phone with Keegan all morning, listening to some boohoo story about how you wrote a scene that wasn't in her book, and supposedly, it exploits her son. Something about how she found out you've been talking to her son for years, and she's quitting if you don't stick to the book. I told her I knew nothing about the scene and promised her we would stick to the book. Alex, I don't know what you've done, but just fix it. Do you hear me? If you do anything to screw this up for Keith, I swear, I'll make your life a living hell!"

"Jesus! All I did was write a scene about a fight Kyle had at school over his dad's death. It adds some depth to the story. Keegan had a fit when she read it, and then she found out that I'd been talking to Kyle for the past few years. She stormed out of here yesterday before I could explain things to her."

"Well, it seems that Keegan has some trust issues with you because she told me that you were repeating the same kind of behavior from back when you two were together. Something about how you were now talking to her son behind her back instead of some bimbo. Whatever you're doing, cut it out! If it doesn't meet with her approval, then it doesn't go into the movie. I know the movie will be picked up by a studio because it's my and Keith's project. Studios love this kind of shit. I want everyone happy and on board when we market the film. Got it? If not, I'll find someone who does understand!" Alison threatens.

"Yeah, I got it. I'll go make nice with Keegan."

"Call me once you two talk." Alison hangs up.

God, how does Keith put up with her?

I immediately text Keegan.

> *Me: Hey, can we talk?*

> *Keegan: Sure. I'm home. Come on over.*

> *Me: Your house? I was thinking more neutral ground, like a coffee shop or something.*

> *Keegan: Here. Time?*

> *Me: In an hour?*

> *Keegan: Okay.*

An hour later, I'm sitting at Keegan's dining room table with a cup of coffee in hand.

"So, talk," she says with her arms crossed, sitting back in her chair.

I begin by saying, "Hey, I think there's been a huge misunderstanding, and—"

"Misunderstanding? Is that what you're calling your deceitfulness these days?"

"Excuse me? Where in the hell did that come from?" I ask.

"Um, where do I start? Reconnecting with Kyle behind my back. Deciding to write a book while conveniently being Internet buds with him. Then, when you found out I had already written a book, promoting it to a publisher and Alison for your personal gain. After all these years, nothing seems to have changed with you, has it?"

"Is that what you think is happening here?"

"Yep, sure do, and I'm putting a stop to it right now. You will not put anything into the film that is not in the book. Understand?"

"Okay, let me clue you in on a few things. I did not reconnect with Kyle behind your back. How in the hell would I have known he hadn't told you about us talking online? Hell, you looked straight at me during the viewing at the funeral home when you walked past me, and I spoke to you.

"As for my so-called book, yeah, I thought about writing one. I might have even mentioned it in the abstract to Kyle, but I'm not a novelist, and I'm not interested in becoming one. I love being a screenwriter. When Kyle told me you were writing a book, I was in total support of the idea and talked him through his concerns over it. I assured him you were the perfect person to write it because you would do it with the compassion needed to tell his dad's story.

"The reason I talked to a few friends, who happened to be a publisher and two actors, is because it's a good book. I can recommend it to people until I'm blue in the face, but if it were a piece of crap, no one would have paid attention. All I did was recommend your book to some friends. Shoot me." I throw my arms up in the air in frustration.

Keegan stares back at me, saying nothing, and we share an awkward silence.

Finally, she breaks it by saying, "So, you weren't trying to manipulate Kyle?"

"No, I wasn't. And, as for our past, I screwed up. I loved you and Kyle. The whole commitment thing and having an instant family scared the living shit out of me, so I sabotaged things between us. It's just that simple. It wasn't until I met Madeline that I got my act together."

"Are you happy?"

"Yeah, I'm happy. How about you?"

"Unbelievably happy," she says with her face breaking out into a full smile.

"So, getting back to the movie. Alison doesn't want anything added to the script that isn't in the book. Are you satisfied now?"

"Yeah, I'm satisfied."

"Is it okay for Kyle and me to continue talking?"

She nods. "Yeah, it's okay."

"Keegan, the next time, just come talk to me. I'm not the unreasonable dick that you think I am."

"Okay."

"Promise?"

"Yeah, I promise."

"So, are we good?"

"Yeah, we're good for the time being."

"Who knows? You and I might end up being friends by the time all of this is over," I tell her.

"I wouldn't count on it. That ship sailed a long time ago," Keegan throws back at me.

"Never say never." I grin back at her.

25

Keegan

On the Fourth of July, Marcy and I are poolside at my parents', watching Roger and Jack play with Aaron in the shallow end of the pool. It seems like it was only yesterday when I was holding my godchild in my arms after he was born, and now, he's five years old.

Roger is showing Aaron how to hold his breath to put his face underwater. Marcy and I bust out laughing, watching Aaron splash both Roger and Jack in the process. Sean and Kyle are tubing out on the lake with my dad and Seth while Annie is inside, helping Mom with the food. Jack's parents and Joyce are sitting on the other side of the pool, lost in conversation.

I can't help but notice how much my extended family has grown, transitioning into the one here today.

As we continue to watch the fun in the pool, I ask Marcy, "God, I can't believe how big Aaron is getting. Where has the time gone?"

"Yeah, I know. Before we know it, Aaron will be graduating from high school. I could barely make it through his preschool graduation."

Suddenly, a wave of nausea comes over me, causing me to blurt out, "Excuse me." I run inside to the bathroom to throw up.

I make it to the toilet just in time.

As I kneel on the floor with my head in the bowl, Marcy bursts in, asking, "Are you all right? Do you want me to get Jack?"

I feel her take my hair and hold it back as I heave one last time. "No. I must have eaten something bad. I wonder how long that dip has been out."

"I got it right out of the fridge when I came out to the pool. Maybe fifteen minutes, tops. I don't think it's the dip," Marcy answers.

"Well, maybe I'm coming down with a stomach bug. I haven't been feeling good for the past couple of days. You'd better keep Aaron away from me."

Once I get back to my feet, I desperately search through the medicine cabinet, trying to find something to settle my stomach.

"Or maybe you could be pregnant," Marcy offers.

I brush her off by saying, "That's not even funny, and no, I'm not pregnant. I haven't missed any periods, Ms. Smart-Ass."

I don't bother to mention that my last period was a couple of days late and shorter than usual. I don't need Marcy to start teasing me about being premenopausal.

When I come back out, everyone is getting their food and finding a place at the huge picnic table on my parents' deck. I grab a ginger ale and take a seat next to Jack.

"You're not eating? Everything okay?" Jack asks with a concerned look.

"Yeah, my stomach is just a little upset. No biggie," I respond back. "I really would like to leave as soon as you and the boys are done eating. I think I'm coming down with a stomach bug, and I should probably keep my distance from everyone."

Jack places his hand on my forehand. "It doesn't feel like you have a fever. Do you want to leave now? I'm sure your mom would understand."

"No, I'm fine. I just don't want to be here for any longer than we have to."

The next morning at the studio, I'm rinsing out my mouth in the bathroom after throwing up again. I come out to find Marcy waiting outside the bathroom door, ready to pounce.

"So, we're getting sick again, huh?"

"No, *we're* not getting sick." I point my finger between the two of us. "I'm getting sick," I snap back at her.

"I think you're pregnant," she states matter-of-factly.

"God, Marcy, get off the pregnancy kick. I'm not pregnant. I just had my period. Stop bugging me about it."

Marcy starts quizzing me, "Was it a regular period?"

"It was a little lighter than usual, but I had one."

"You know, some women have what they think is a period, but it's not. Just take an over-the-counter pregnancy test, so you know for sure. With all the seizure meds that you've been on since your brain surgery, it might be the smart thing to do," Marcy tells me.

"Seriously? Okay, I'll tell you what. On Friday, I go for my yearly. If I bring a note back from the doctor saying I'm not pregnant, will you then get off my back?"

"All I'm saying is, if it looks like a duck and quacks like a duck, there's a damn good chance it is a duck!"

"Don't you have some work to do? I've got to get out of here. I still have to stop at the store to get something for dinner."

"And pick up a pregnancy test while you're there!" Marcy shouts to me.

I leave in a huff out the back of the studio. The mere thought of being pregnant makes me queasy again.

Walking down the aisle of feminine products, I pass the home pregnancy test kits.

Me pregnant? Yeah, right!

I find myself walking back to the kits and reading the label of one. Then, I pitch it into the cart, knowing Marcy will continue to hound me until I can prove she's wrong.

Once home, I put all the groceries away and head upstairs to the bathroom. I take the test out of the plastic grocery bag and place its contents on the vanity counter. Stalling, I read the instructions over and over again. My nerves get the best of me, and all of a sudden, I need to pee badly.

"All right already," I mutter under my breath to myself.

Carefully following the instructions, I pee on the applicator and set it on a piece of tissue. Waiting, I intently watch it, and the next three minutes seem like three hours.

There, before my eyes, appears *YES +*.

What? It should read NO! I'm in my forties. I can't be pregnant.

Not wanting Jack to find the use applicator, I gather up everything from the pregnancy test in the plastic grocery bag to take with me before leaving the bathroom. I drop the bag on the bed when I see my laptop charging in the bedroom. Sitting on the bed, I decide to explore websites on the Internet to research what the odds are for this happening to a woman my age.

Quickly, I type in the search bar, *Women getting pregnant in their forties.*

A list of numerous links comes up with some referring to in vitro fertilization. Most agree that the chances of a natural pregnancy drop to about twenty percent for a woman of my age.

Damn it!

It's my fault. I didn't think it was a big deal if I was a little late in scheduling my appointment for my birth control shot and yearly exam.

My hand drops down to my stomach, imagining the life Jack and I have created. Gradually, the horror over my discovery begins to fade as nervous excitement starts to emerge in its place.

Now, the million-dollar question is, how is Jack going to take the news of becoming a dad at his age?

When the baby is twenty, we'll be in our sixties. I start envisioning someone pushing me around in a wheelchair, occasionally stopping to wipe the drool from my chin.

When I hear Jack downstairs, I hurriedly pick up the plastic bag laying beside me on the bed and stuff it in the top drawer of my dresser, like a five-year-old hiding something from her parents.

Jack enters the bedroom just as I shut the drawer.

I jump when he says, "Hey, you look flush. Are you still not feeling good?"

"No. I'm fine. I've been running around all afternoon."

"Are you sure?"

"Yeah, I'm sure," I try to say convincingly.

"How were things down at the studio today?" Jack asks.

For some unknown reason, I decide to respond with a story to try to gauge Jack's possible reaction to the news of becoming a dad again.

"There's a woman down at the studio who's the same age as me, and she just found out she's pregnant. Can you imagine that? I mean, she'll be in her sixties when her kid is in college."

"I can think of a lot worse things happening to someone. Hey, do I have time for a run before dinner?"

I nod. "Sure. Go ahead. There's plenty of time."

After changing into his running gear, he leaves the room.

I flop down on the bed, lying on my back, and Kirby hops up and lies down next to me, placing his chin on my stomach.

He looks at me with his dark brown eyes, as if to ask, *So, what are you going to do now?*

Smiling, I scratch Kirby behind his ears, and I quietly say, "We're having a baby."

Kirby wags his tail, as if he understands and is happy about the news I just told him.

26

Jack

Out of the blue, Keegan suggests we head to the beach for a long weekend. As I load up my Jeep for the trip, I notice Keegan is a little on edge this morning.

She has seemed a little distracted the last couple of days. I think it's her doctor's appointment today. Ever since her surgery, she has been hypersensitive of every ache or illness, fearing another meningioma could be developing.

I slam shut the back hatch of the Jeep after everything is loaded and walk back into the townhouse to tell Keegan. I find her inside, waiting, with a playful smile and the infamous green scarf dangling from her fingers.

Keegan repeats what I've said to her in the past, "Do you trust me? I mean, really trust me to take full control of the day?"

I'm not sure how those words affected Keegan when I said them, but they are a huge turn-on for me.

"Yeah, I trust you. What do you have in mind?" I ask, giving her my sexiest grin.

"Oh, you have no idea what's in store for you today, babe. Are you game?"

"Yeah, bring it on. I can handle anything you can dish out," I arrogantly counter back.

She cracks up, laughing. "Yeah, I'll be the judge of that one. Your world is about to be rocked to the max."

Keegan ties the scarf around my head, double-checks to make sure I can't see anything, and then leads me out to the garage.

Not wanting to take the packed Jeep to her appointment, the plan was to return afterward for Kirby and switch vehicles to head to the beach.

We settle in Keegan's Jeep, and she backs out of the garage with me in the passenger seat, not having a hint as to where we are going. About ten minutes later, she parks the car and helps me out of it. She guides me through a door, and the familiar smell of sandalwood gives it away that we are at the tattoo parlor.

Keegan removes the scarf and then points to the counter at a mock-up of a tattoo. Confused, I look at her for an explanation.

"Well, what do you think?" she asks.

"Is this it? Did you blindfold me to come down here to look at a drawing for another damn tattoo for you? You said you were going to rock my world."

I hear one of the tattoo artists let out a deep-throated chuckle as he stands behind the counter. I flash him a look that makes him stop immediately.

Keegan then giggles. "Babe, if only you knew what is about to happen to you. Now, look at the design carefully. I want your opinion of it."

I look down at a drawing of a grouping of five shamrocks of different sizes. There are two larger shamrocks in the center with a smaller one on each side of them. One of the bigger shamrocks has a flower, as if it's in bloom. I also notice there is a smaller shamrock raised just a bit between the two larger ones. There are decorative swirls throughout the artwork, connecting it all into one cohesive design.

Knowing that all of Keegan's tattoos memorialize significant events in her life, I look at her and ask, "What does this mean?"

She smiles with tears welling in her eyes. "It represents our family and will be placed here, at the base of my neck." She gestures with one hand to the area where the ink will be located on her body.

"Are you getting it now?"

She whispers, "Not today. Probably sometime this winter."

"I'm sorry. I still don't understand. Why are we here today if you're not getting it done until winter? And how do five shamrocks represent our family? Is one of them Kirby?"

Keegan shakes her head with a tear streaming down her face. "The largest one represents you, I'm the one in bloom, the smaller one next to you is Sean, and this one beside me represents Kyle."

I point to the smallest shamrock between the two larger ones. "Then, who is this?"

"We haven't named that one yet," is all she says.

It all clicks into place with me.

At first, I'm speechless.

Then, I turn to her. "Are you…you're pregnant?"

Keegan nods her head as she asks barely above a whisper, "Are you okay with us having a baby?"

"Oh, hell yeah! Really? We're having a baby? Seriously?"

Now laughing, she answers, "Yes, we're having a baby. Are you ready to take me to my first doctor's appointment?"

I take her in my arms. "God, do you have any idea how much I love you right now?"

"Yeah, because I feel the same way. Did I live up to my promise of rocking your world?"

"You have no idea." I lean down to kiss her.

The few people who are in the tattoo parlor congratulate us as we leave.

"We have to make a quick stop at the studio. I have something to show Marcy." Keegan winks at me.

A few minutes later, we walk into the studio.

Marcy shouts out to us from across the room, "Morning, Gradys! What brings you guys here this morning?"

I watch as Keegan says nothing while she walks up to Marcy, only to pull something out of her front pocket to show to her.

Marcy starts jumping up and down, screaming, "I knew it! I knew it! Congratulations!" Marcy then pulls Keegan into a bear hug.

Before leaving, Keegan swears Marcy to secrecy since we haven't told the boys or our parents yet.

During the first ten minutes of Keegan's appointment, we find out her age and the anti-seizure medications classify her as a high-risk pregnancy. This means Keegan has a higher risk for developing complications that could threaten the health or life of the baby or herself. Our obstetrician, Dr. Bowers, explains in great detail what we could be facing. We walked into his office with a spring in our step with so much hope for the future, only to leave with my arm around Keegan in a feeble attempt to comfort her.

"Where to now? Do you still want to go to the beach?" I ask her.

"I want my mom," she cries into my chest as I hold her in our SUV.

As we walk in the Fitzgeralds' home, Sandy and Mitch look up at us from the kitchen island and see the devastation on Keegan's face.

Sandy is the first to reach Keegan, embracing her while asking, "Honey, what happened?"

Keegan cries on her mother's shoulder. "I'm pregnant!"

Sandy laughs. "Oh, sweetie. Everything will be okay."

By now, Mitch is standing beside Sandy and rubbing Keegan's back. "Princess, congratulations!"

Keegan pulls away while wiping the tears from her cheeks with the backs of her hands. "There could be something wrong with the baby because of my age and seizure meds."

"Princess, come sit down and explain what this is all about." Mitch motions for us to have a seat in the family room.

Sandy holds Keegan as I explain, "At Keegan's age, there is a higher risk of losing the baby through a miscarriage or stillbirth. Her seizure meds also complicate things. The dosage will be reduced to the lowest effective level, or she could even end up being taken off of them entirely. But doing that puts her at a higher risk of having a seizure. Even if she carries full-term, the combination of her age and meds could cause problems for the baby."

"Mom, I'm scared," Keegan cries into her mom's arms.

"I know, baby," Sandy says to help calm Keegan.

Mitch adds, "Princess, you've got to have faith."

"But, Daddy, what if…" Keegan can't finish her question.

"Princess, you've got to take this one day at a time," Mitch tells her.

I say nothing as I think back to Keegan's car accident, watching them do CPR as they unloaded her from the ambulance because she had gone into cardiac arrest after having a seizure en route to the hospital. The thought of that happening again is one of the biggest fears I live with every day of my life.

I'm jarred back to the here and now when I hear Keegan ask, "Jack?"

"I'm sorry. What?"

"Do you still think we should go to the beach?"

Before I can answer, Sandy says, "I think that's exactly what you should do. Getting away from here for a few days will do a world of good for the both of you."

Still distracted by my thoughts, I tell Keegan, "It's up to you. Whatever you want to do is fine with me."

"I still want to go."

"Then, I guess we'd better get going," I answer back.

As we stand at the front door, ready to leave, Sandy hugs Keegan one last time.

Mitch gives me a firm pat on the back, saying, "Take good care of my little girl."

"Yes, sir. I always do," I reassure him.

As we pull out of the Fitzgeralds' drive, I tentatively ask Keegan, "Is it okay if we stop by my parents' on the way down to the beach and tell them?"

Keegan only nods in response as she gazes out the window.

When we pull into the garage, Keegan goes inside the townhouse to get Kirby, and I double-check the already packed Jeep to make sure we have everything before rolling out.

It's only a matter of minutes before Keegan returns with Kirby, and we're on the road, driving to my parents'.

Occasionally, I glance over at Keegan and watch her interact with Kirby. It's almost as though Kirby senses something is wrong as he snuggles in Keegan's lap while she unconsciously strokes his fur, getting further lost in her thoughts.

A little over an hour later, we pull into my parents' driveway.

As we walk in through the back door, Mom takes one look at us and can tell something is wrong.

She calls for Dad and then asks, "What is it? What happened?"

Dad enters the room before I can answer. "Hey, guys, what a nice surprise." He then sees our expressions and asks, "What's going on?"

I answer, "Keegan's pregnant."

My parents look confused.

Dad continues to question us, "Why such a look of gloom? That's great news! Isn't it?"

"Let's go out to the sunroom, and I'll explain everything."

The bay view from this room usually takes center stage, but today, no one seems to notice it.

I start sharing details of Keegan's doctor's appointment with my parents the same way that I did earlier with the Fitzgeralds.

Mom gets up and sits beside Keegan, taking her hand. "I'm so sorry. I can only imagine how worried you must be."

Dad looks over to me and says, "Come on, Jack. Let's take a walk."

When we step out to the backyard, I look out toward the bay, holding back my tears.

As Dad stands beside me, he puts an arm around my shoulders in comfort. "It's okay, son. Let it out."

"What do I do, Dad?"

"There's nothing you can do other than to be strong for Keegan and show the love you have for her more than you ever have before, son."

27

Keegan

I look out the window with little registering with me as we drive through the small towns of Maryland's Eastern Shore in silence on our way to the beach. Usually, we would stop along the way at our favorite produce stands to pick up fresh vegetables and fruit. I'm too distracted by today's events to even care about food right now.

I think back to when Marcy and Roger told me they were expecting Aaron and their happiness. It was also the day she feared I was going to kill her for setting up a page for me on a dating website, but that was how I met Jack. I feel a small smile come across my face as I think about the texts between Jack and me before we met for the first time at my favorite coffee shop. My smile fades as thoughts return to the precious life that Jack and I have created.

In all the day's doom and gloom, the good news that the heartbeat was strong and the fetus seemed okay during the transvaginal ultrasound today got lost somewhere along the way.

I look over to suggest to Jack that maybe we need to focus on the positive instead of the negative that might or might not happen. Jack's wearing that frown of his where he's so deep in thought that his brows are drawn in close together, separated in the center by a large wrinkle. There's no reaching him when he's like this. I'll wait to have this conversation until we're at the beach, surrounded by the soothing surf of the bay.

I've come to the reality that, no matter what happens, I love this new little life I'm carrying, and I accept all that is facing us. Dad was right when he told me to keep the faith. I'm going to do all that is humanly possible to give this baby the best chance at life, and I'll leave the rest in God's hands.

I must have dozed off because I Jack saying, "Keegan, wake up. We're almost there."

When I open my eyes, I see we're turning onto the street where our beach getaway sits. As Jack pulls underneath the house, between the wooden stilts that protect it from storm surges, I smile when I see the Beach Shack sign hanging from the deck above.

I hop out of the vehicle with Kirby on his leash and blurt out, "Jack, I'm taking Kirby for a walk."

"I think we need to talk."

"No, I'm done talking."

"Wait a second, Keegan. What if you have a seizure and go into cardiac arrest again?" Jack asks.

"Babe, we can't live our lives, fearing all the what-ifs out there. Today, we saw our baby and heard the heartbeat for the first time. The doctor said everything looked okay. I'm focusing on the good news and not all the other stuff. You coming with Kirby and me?"

"No. Go ahead while I unpack the car."

A half hour later, I enter the house and grab Kirby's bowl to get him some fresh water. I look out the small window over the kitchen sink that overlooks our little private beach out back. I see Jack sitting in the sand with his arms propped up by his bent knees, his head hanging down in between them. I put the water bowl down for Kirby and then go outside to join Jack.

"You do know that everything is going to be all right, right?" I say reassuringly, sitting down next to him.

"How can you be so sure?"

"I don't know. Call it my woman's intuition. I just feel it in my bones."

"Why does this kind of shit keep happening to us? Haven't we been through enough? Keegan, I can't lose you. As much as I want this baby, the thought of you having another seizure and possibly going into cardiac arrest again scares the living shit out of me."

"Jack, it's going to be okay. I went into cardiac arrest only once. That didn't happen during my other seizures. I promise to take care of myself by taking my vitamins, eating properly, and exercising. The doctor is going to monitor me closely, too. Trust me, it's all going to be okay."

Jack says nothing for a moment, letting my words sink in. "You've had more than one seizure?"

"Yeah, after we broke up, I had two more. It was all my fault for not taking my meds the way I was supposed to."

Jack suddenly becomes agitated and asks, "Why didn't anybody tell me?"

"Tell you what?"

"About the seizures. Why didn't anyone call me when you had them?"

Confused by his sudden change in demeanor, I reply, "They happened after we broke up. Why are you getting so upset?"

"Because you're just like Chelsey, keeping shit from me. Damn it, Keegan!" He stands up and starts brushing the sand off of himself. "I don't think I'll ever forget them doing CPR while rolling you into the ER. The years we were apart was the worst fucking time of my life. Now, I find out you were having seizures, and I wasn't even important enough to be called?"

Standing up, I sarcastically snap back, "Well, maybe if you had sent me a card or even one damn flower to show that you gave three shits about me…" I regret my hateful words to him as soon as they are out of my mouth.

"I guess you're never going to let me off the fucking hook for that," Jack says. "You know what? I'm going for a run."

"Jack, I'm sorry. Please come back," I call out, only to be ignored by him.

As I watch him jog off down the beach, I debate on whether to go after him. Maybe it's best I give him time to blow off some steam. I'll just wait here at the house until he returns.

Over an hour passes by, and Jack still hasn't come back from his run. I keep going out on the deck to see if there is any sign of him.

I hop into the car and drive around the area in hopes of finding him.

He's nowhere to be found.

Where could he be?

I return home, hoping to find him there, waiting for me.

He's not there.

Grabbing a quilt from the couch, I decide to wait for him out on the porch bed swing.

Kirby jumps up on the swing with me as I get comfy. The slow sway of it moving back and forth soon rocks me to sleep.

A noise wakes me up. I check my phone and see almost three hours have passed.

I then hear another noise.

Jack mutters, "Damn it!"

I get up and go to the direction of the sound at the end of the deck and see Jack stumbling up the stairs. He's been drinking. A lot.

As he reaches the top step, I cross my arms, and like some old housewife, I ask, "Where have you been?"

"Running, thinking, drinking. Why?" Jack replies back in a nasty tone.

"I was worried about you."

He brushes by me and says over his shoulder, "Yeah? Were you? How does it feel to be worried about someone you love? Not knowing if they're all right? Kind of sucks, doesn't it?"

I follow behind him. "Jack, I'm not fighting with you. God, you stink! Go take a shower."

He stumbles his way back to our bedroom, occasionally finding the need to hold on to the wall to help guide him.

I follow him into the bathroom and turn on the shower as he begins to strip out of his clothes. I pick up his clothing piece by piece as they drop to the bathroom floor. For a few moments, as he stands motionless in the shower while the water beats down on him, I watch him, making sure he's okay before leaving the room.

Before laying his clothes on a chair in the corner of the bedroom, I pull his keys and wallet out of the pocket of his shorts along with a napkin that has some writing on it. I can't help but notice a girl's name and phone number scribbled on the napkin. I look at it a little closer and read the message.

Thank you.
We had fun tonight.
Give us a call if you want to get together to play pool again.
Jill

What the hell is this?

Jack comes back out into the bedroom with a towel wrapped around his waist. The shower seems to have sobered him up a little.

I hold the napkin up to his face for him to read. "I'm glad to see you were having fun this evening while I was home, worried sick about you."

I then ball the napkin up in a wad and throw it at him before I walk out of the bedroom.

I need air, so I escape to the deck.

A few moments later, I hear Jack come outside.

"It's not what it looks like."

Quickly, I turn to face him. "It never is. I'm going to bed. Good night."

The next morning, I wake up with Jack nowhere to be found. My guess is, he's gone for his morning run. It's just as well because I'm not in the mood to rehash last night with him.

Standing at the coffee pot, waiting for it to finish brewing, I hear the screen door of the porch squeak and assume it's Jack returning from his run.

He comes into the kitchen and asks, "Keegan, can you step outside for a moment?"

I follow him out to the porch to find an attractive blonde in her twenties standing there.

Jack introduces us, "Keegan, this is Jill. Jill, this is my wife, Keegan."

"You're right. She is beautiful. You should have heard your husband going on about you last night. By the way, I'm sorry about my note. I never gave it a thought as to how it might sound when I wrote it. I got mad at Tom— that's my boyfriend—and he left the bar. Your husband came to my rescue when some guy started bothering me. It wasn't long after that when Tom had cooled off and came back for me. The three of us ended up playing some pool. I guess we all had a little too much to drink. Sorry."

"Thanks for coming by to explain." Rudely, I turn my back on Jill and go back inside, leaving Jack with his new pool buddy on the back porch.

A few minutes later, Jack comes into the kitchen as I drop a bagel in the toaster.

"I'm sorry about last night. On the way back home, my run took me by the bar. I went in to get a beer and lost track of time while playing pool with Jill and Tom. I never even knew Jill stuck that damn napkin in my pocket."

"What do you want from me, Jack? Yesterday started out as a day full of promise with the news of us having a baby. We went to the doctor and heard all the horrible things that could happen during my pregnancy. Then, you threw all your bullshit from a past relationship with Chelsey in my face along with trying to make me feel guilty about things that had happened after we broke up. I get that you're still mad at Chelsey for what she did, but how dare you say I'm like her. I made damn sure you were the first one to know about the baby. What should have been one of the happiest times of our lives turned into a pile of grade-A shit.

"To top it off, you decided to disappear to play pool with Barbie at some local bar while I was sitting here, wondering what the hell happened to you. You need to grow up and accept that there are times when you just have to suck it up, buttercup, and you play the hand that's been dealt. Now, if you'll excuse me, I'm taking Kirby for his walk."

"Keegan, we need to talk about the baby."

Nobody has uttered the words *termination* or *abortion*, but it feels as if those words are lurking out there on the edge of where the light ends and darkness begins.

The closest it came to being spoken out loud was during the doctor's consultation when he said, "If you should continue with the pregnancy…"

At the time, neither Jack nor I acknowledged his comment because we were in no state of mind to have that discussion. But I know my husband all too well. I know he hears the doctor's words over and over in his head while envisioning paramedics doing CPR on me.

In that split second, I decide drastic times call for drastic measures. "So, what other choice do we have, Jack? Do you want me to get rid of this baby? If that's what you want, here's the phone."

I grab my cell phone off the counter and push it into his chest as I walk by him to leave. "You make the damn arrangements. Come on, Kirby. Let's go for walkies."

When Kirby and I return, Jack is sitting out on the deck, staring at the phone in his hands.

"So, did you take care of things?" I snap at him.

He shakes his head, stands, and takes me in his arms. "I'm sorry. I want this baby more than anything. I just don't want to lose you."

"Jack, when will you get it through that thick skull of yours that I'm going to be all right?"

"You promise to grow old with me and raise our children together?"

"I promise."

Later that night, as we make love, Jack is treating me as though I am a fragile doll that might shatter at any moment.

Increasingly becoming frustrated with his tenderness and my need for more, I manage to wrap my legs around him and demand, "For God's sake, stop playing around!"

Jack pauses for a minute, and a perplexed look comes over his face. "But you heard the—"

"Don't you even think about finishing that sentence, Mister. More than ever, I need to feel all of you tonight. I'm not going to break. Now, show me how much you love me."

He wastes no time in making sure that I feel every bit of his desire.

Afterward, lying satisfied in Jack's arms, I decide it's time to share one last thought with him regarding my pregnancy, and I brace myself for his reaction.

I speak quietly into the darkness of our bedroom, "Jack, I need you to promise me something with no argument."

"Sorry, I can't do that, babe," he responds with a resolute tone in his voice.

"It's important to me. Promise me you will do what I'm about to ask," I plead.

Jack suddenly throws the covers back and gets up from our bed. He grabs his sweat shorts off the chair and hastily pulls them up before walking out of the bedroom.

I get up, not bothering to cover up, to find Jack. He's standing outside on the screened-in porch. I put on his sweatshirt that's hanging on a hook by the door before going outside to him.

Before I can get a single word out, Jack turns to me, pointing his finger. "Don't even go there. After everything that's happened today, I don't want to hear what you want me to promise you."

"You have no idea what I'm going to say," I respond defiantly.

"Yeah, I do. You want me to make some stupid promise in case something happens to you. I can feel it in my gut. I might not know what it is, but I'm pretty sure it's something I can't do."

"That's not fair. At least hear what I have to say!"

He stares at me with a defensive stance. "What? Like I did before your surgery? I know you. I know how that brain of yours works. You have been lying in our bed, thinking of the worst-case scenario, and you expect me to promise you something I'm incapable of doing."

"Jack, you have to do this for me. It's important," I beg once more.

"God, why do you always do this to me?" He plops down on the bed swing, dropping his head down with his elbows on his knees.

I kneel down in front of him to lift his chin up, so he looks at me. "Please promise me, you'll save the baby if, for some reason, I become incapacitated during the pregnancy and I'm no longer capable of making decisions."

Jack jumps up, walking away, "Christ, I knew it! How can I make a promise like that?"

"It's important. After doing everything possible to have this baby, I don't want to lose it in an attempt to save me. I need to know that you'll do this."

"Well, Keegan, I can't." Jack leaves the screened-in deck in a huff and jogs down the steps to the beach.

As I watch him, I wonder if I've pushed him too far this time.

Tired, I decide to turn in for the night and give Jack the space he needs to sort things out.

Right as I start to doze off, I feel Jack slip into bed behind me and slide up close next to me, wrapping his arms around my waist while placing his hand on my stomach.

Jack then whispers into my ear the words I've heard so many times before, "From this day forward, know that I will always remain true and honest to you. I promise that you and our children will always be my first priority in life. I will be by yours and our children's sides through the good times and, more importantly, the bad through sickness and health. And, above all, I will always respect, love, and cherish you until we are parted by death. This is my solemn vow to you."

The next morning, I wake up to the sound of both Jack and Kirby snoring. I decide to get up and catch up on my emails.

After getting a cup of coffee, I set up shop on the screened-in porch with my laptop. As my computer comes on, I watch the seagulls gracefully swoop down while others scavenge the beach for food.

There are several emails waiting for me in my inbox. One is from Alex with more scenes of the movie attached for my review.

> *Keegan,*
>
> *I wanted to give you a heads-up that one of the scenes is the night Will gets shot. It's pretty intense.*
>
> *Alex*

Appreciative of the warning, I stare at the zip file icon sitting underneath his name, debating if I should read it now or wait until after we get back home.

I decide to bite the bullet and click on the file to open it. I pull up the scene that Alex referenced in his email and read it first.

The dialogue takes me back to that night when my dad's phone call interrupted Jack's and my picnic celebrating my recovery from surgery. Alex has captured the devastation I felt that night, but something is missing.

I have just closed my laptop from reading the script when Jack comes outside.

"Morning," he greets me with a kiss. Then, he takes a seat beside me at the table.

"Good morning."

"What are you doing up so early?" Jack asks.

"You and Kirby were snoring up a storm in the bedroom, so I went ahead and got up."

"Sorry. How's the baby doing?"

"She's good." I smile back at him.

"She?"

"Yep. She. I've decided there is way too much testosterone in our family, so it's going to be a girl."

"You know what? I'm good with that. Having a mini you running around would be cool. Have you named her, too?" He chuckles.

"I have a few names in mind, but I do have a favorite one. I'll tell you what. If it's a girl, I'll pick her first name, and you can choose the middle one. If the baby is a boy, you get to choose the first name, and I'll pick the second. Deal?" I extend my hand out to him.

"Sounds fair to me." Jack shakes my hand in agreement. "So, how do you feel about the name Cyrus?"

Ignoring Jack's pick for a boy's name, I rub my belly. "As I was saying, we're having a girl, and her name is Molly."

The biggest grin spreads across Jack's face. "Molly, it is." He nods his head toward my computer. "So, anything earth-shattering happening in the world that I should know about?"

"No. Alex sent me some scenes to review. One of them is the night Will died."

"You okay?" Jack asks with concern.

"Yeah, I'm fine. Alex's writing has given me a new perspective on things. I owe him an apology though."

"For what?"

"I told him that, if it wasn't in the book, it couldn't be in the movie. In the book, it's more about my feelings after hearing that he was dead. The movie shows the shooting through my viewpoint from conversations I had with others. It just doesn't work for me."

"Maybe it's Alex's writing," Jack offers.

"No, that's not it. Alex needs more to work with than what's in the book. He needs a firsthand account from Brittany. She should be the one helping him with this part, not me."

"Why don't you take a break and deal with it later? Let's go down to the beach."

"Sounds perfect."

I have found the old standby of flat ginger ale with a few saltine crackers helps ease morning sickness. Our new routine is Jack serving my breakfast combo in bed before leaving for work in the morning.

Jack has also been reading everything he can get his hands on about high-risk pregnancies and the effects of seizure meds on a fetus. On the contrary, I've chosen not to read any of it. Some might think I'm being naive or foolish, but at times, I find that ignorance is bliss for me. I'd rather consume myself with worries about what color to paint the nursery instead of getting bogged down with fretting over things that might never happen. I've decided to let my doctor keep me informed of those matters on a need-to-know basis.

I contact Alex after we return home from the beach, and he agrees with me regarding the scene of the shooting and Will's death.

At first, Brittany is hesitant to meet with Alex to relive the details of that horrible evening. Aiden is also less than enthusiastic over the idea of it. Eventually, Brittany reluctantly agrees to meet under the condition that, if she feels either her or Jace's identities will be at risk of being discovered, then the meeting will end.

This afternoon, Alex and I are meeting with Aiden and Brittany, hoping to get what we need for the movie. Jack insisted on coming with me because of what had happened the last time when we came here to discuss the book.

As we enter the building where Aiden works, I see Alex in the lobby, and it occurs to me that he has never met Jack.

Awkwardly, I introduce them, "Um, Alex, this is my husband, Jack. Jack, this is Alex."

Although they politely shake hands, acknowledging one another, I can see them sizing each other up.

We no sooner enter the room where Aiden and Brittany are waiting when I unexpectedly stop walking, causing Jack to bump into me.

I hold up my index finger. "Excuse us for a second. I need to speak to Jack privately. We'll only be a minute."

I pull Jack back out into the hallway.

"What's going on?" he asks, confused by my actions.

"Is it okay to tell them I'm pregnant, or do you want to wait until after the first trimester before telling anyone outside of the family?"

Jack considers my question for a moment. "Well, if we don't want to live in fear of the what-ifs, then I say, why not?"

Smiling at him, I reply, "My sentiments exactly! Have I told you how much I love you today?"

"Hmm, I'm not sure. You'd better tell me just in case you haven't." Jack chuckles as I wrap my arms around his neck and kiss him.

"Molly and I love you beyond the stars and back, Mr. Grady."

He says nothing at first and then chokes out, "I love my two girls, too."

We walk back in, arm in arm, wearing the silliest grins on our faces.

Jack motions to me. "Go ahead, and tell them the news."

"We're pregnant!"

At first, everyone stares in shock, and then they burst out with congratulations and questions. After they settle down from hearing our news, we move on to the business at hand.

I'm glad Jack is here with me because I had no idea how in-depth Alex's probe for details was going to be.

Since Alex has access to an eyewitness account of the shooting, he not only cares about dialogue, but he also makes sure he has accurate placement of furniture and the movement of everyone who was there. It's the first time I'm hearing the details of that night. At times, the intense emotions filling the room are more than I can handle.

Aiden tells Alex, "I want to check the final script to make sure nothing reveals either of our identities."

"I promise. In fact, there is no reason we can't change the location of the story in the movie. It might be better for everyone if we did that," Alex offers.

I speak up, "No. The location is already in the book. The change would only cause questions. By sticking to the book, there's less chance of that happening."

Everyone agrees.

I feel sorry for Brittany. I try my best to show my support during her emotional account of that night. At one point, I suggest we take a break, so she can have a chance to regroup before continuing.

During the break, Jack asks, "How are you doing?"

"I'm fine. I can't imagine how hard it is for Brittany to relive that night in such detail. We should have done this in several smaller sessions instead of one big one."

"Maybe she needs to do it this way to be able to move on," Jack says thoughtfully.

An hour later, Alex announces, "I think I have everything now. Thank you, Brittany. I know this has been hard for you today. Once I finish writing it, would you be willing to read the scene for final approval?"

She answers, "Yes, as long as you promise to do Will proud."

"I promise."

When we get ready to leave, Alex walks over to Brittany and pulls her into a warm embrace before walking out of the conference room. I couldn't hear what he whispered in her ear, but I see the tears welling up in her eyes from his words.

28

Jack

Annie and Seth are coming over for dinner tonight, so we can tell them about the baby. We also invited Marcy and Roger, too, thinking it would help put Annie at ease.

Everyone stands around the kitchen island, catching up with each other with drinks in hand while enjoying the assortment of appetizers that Keegan prepared.

It doesn't take long for Seth to notice that Keegan doesn't have an alcoholic drink like everyone else. He starts questioning her, "Hey, what's up with you being a teetotaler tonight?"

Marcy chimes in with a smirk, "Yeah, Keegan, where's the Black and Tan?"

With a death glare, Keegan sends a nonverbal message to Marcy to shut her up, and Seth sees it.

"Okay. I know that look you flashed over at Marcy. What's going on?"

I immediately jump in, "Well, we asked you over to share some news. If all goes well, it seems that somewhere around February 18, we're going to have a baby."

Annie's shock is visible.

Seth stares in amazement at us, saying under his breath, "Well, I'll be damned." He reaches over to Keegan, pulling her into a hug. "Congratulations! I'm really happy for you guys."

He looks over to Annie, as we all do, for her reaction to the news.

Annie raises her glass to Keegan, as if giving a toast, and sarcastically comments, "Congratulations! I guess, since there's now more than one of us that Jack Grady has knocked up, I should welcome you to the club!"

Seth quickly responds, "Annie! Don't!"

She jerks her head to him. "Don't what? Speak a little truth? Or would you rather I stand here politely and smile, while he"—she motions over to me—"dumps another load of crap for Sean to deal with?" Looking back over at me, Annie continues, "When are you planning on sharing your happy news with *our* son?"

Memories of how I proposed to Keegan and Annie's hurt feelings come flooding back. I have unintentionally broken my promise of not blindsiding her with unexpected news. She wasn't prepared or ready to hear this, and having an audience watching only makes matters worse for her.

"I'm sorry, Annie. I didn't think—" I start to say when she interrupts me.

"You're damn right you didn't think. What in the hell do you expect from me? I came over here this evening, thinking I was finally being accepted into this little group, only to be ambushed again by your damn shit. Tell me, exactly where does our son fit into this new happy little family of yours?"

I'm not only stunned by her outburst, but I'm also not sure how to defuse the situation.

"What? Cat got your tongue?" Annie asks.

Again, Seth tries to step in. "Annie, let it go. You and Jack can sort this out later in private at a more appropriate time."

Turning to Seth, she says, "No, Jack needs to hear this." Then, looking back at me, she resumes her rant, "Since the age of five, Sean's world has been nothing but a series of adjustments. He took any little crumb of precious time you graciously threw in his direction, so he could have you in his life. Our family was back together for three years after you and Keegan split up. It was just like it used to be with you coming over all the time. Then, Keegan showed up on your front doorstep one night, and off you went, running back to her. Once again, Sean finds himself in a place not of his choosing, where he is forced to share you with others. He never complains and does what he's told just to please you. Now, he has to compete with a baby for his father's affection. How is he supposed to do that, especially at his age?"

Taking a deep breath in an attempt to calm down, Annie turns to Keegan. "I'm sorry, Keegan. Please try to understand where I'm coming from."

Keegan reaches over and touches Annie's hand. "I get it, Annie. I totally get it. What can we do?"

"I don't know. I guess…just be sensitive to Sean's feelings and see the world through his eyes for a few minutes. Kyle was an easy adjustment because he was the cooler, older kid to look up to, but a baby is a whole different story."

As Keegan allows herself to get sucked into Annie's little temper tantrum, I'm still reeling from her words.

I decide it's now my turn. "No, Annie. You're not going to lay me out like that in front of everyone without hearing my side of things. How dare you act like I never take Sean's feelings into consideration. He's one of my first thoughts when I wake up and the last when I go to sleep. Compete? Hell no, he's not going to compete with a baby, no more than any other child his age does when a new sibling enters the world. Sean will play the role of a big brother and be a damn good one. Don't you dare try to play the guilt card on me! Just like everything else in our past, we'll figure this out together. I was planning on telling him this weekend. Do you have a problem with that?"

Annie shakes her head. "No."

"Do you want to be there when I tell Sean?"

Surprised by my question, she replies, "Yeah, that would be good. Is that okay with you, Keegan?"

"I think it's perfect. Why don't you, Seth, and Sean plan to come up to our lake house on Saturday? That way, Sean will always remember it as a fun day when he found out about his new baby sister."

Marcy screeches out, "Sister?"

"Yep, a sister, and her name is Molly." Keegan sharply nods her head, as if to put an exclamation point at the end of her statement.

We all look at her and bust out laughing.

Later that night, Keegan and I lie in bed in each other's arms, saying nothing and enjoying the quiet.

"Penny for your thoughts," Keegan says to me with her head on my chest.

"Not sure they're even worth a penny," I answer back.

She props herself up on one elbow, causing her hair to cascade down, so it lightly brushes against her breast. Since Kyle is working at a soccer camp back at school this month, we have gone back to the habit of sleeping in the nude. My body starts to respond as I look at her.

"Jack, I have to give Annie props for standing up to us tonight about the baby and Sean. That was a pretty gutsy thing she did. Maybe it's because I got divorced when Kyle was around the same age as Sean, but I identified with what she was saying. We need to stop doing this kind of stuff to her and be a little bit more sensitive to her and Sean."

"Wait a second. I thought that's what tonight was all about along with all of our past heart-to-hearts with her."

"No, it's been our MO to make decisions and think, as long as we told Annie or Will about them, everything would be right with the universe. Her words of seeing the world through Sean's eyes struck home with me. I think we're both guilty of just seeing it through our eyes and expecting everyone to fall in line behind us.

"Think about it. In February, our family will be unique with none of our children having the same parentage. They will be half-siblings. We need to be sensitive to that for this blended family to work. It means—God, I can't believe I'm saying this—that, sometimes, we might need to include Annie and Seth in on family celebrations. You know, like birthday parties and things like that."

Lying there, listening to her, I can't help but see how far we've come as a couple in such a short time.

I roll Keegan over to her back with our bodies perfectly in line with each other. I begin to gently kiss Keegan, starting with her full lips and moving up to the tip of her button nose. I get lost in Keegan's sea-blue eyes when I ask, "How did I get to be such a lucky man?"

She giggles softly. "No, I'm the lucky one, and you're not allowed to argue with me because I'm pregnant."

"Oh, so we're playing the old pregnancy card, are we?"

"For as long as I can get away with it."

I drop my head to kiss her breast. They are getting fuller as each day passes. Knowing how sensitive they have become, I tenderly take one in my hand and play with her nipple. She begins to arch her back in response. I continue with my foreplay until Keegan becomes frustrated with need and begs me to make love to her. It isn't long after that when our intense orgasms shatter us.

As we spoon later, with my arms holding her tight, I whisper in her ear, "How about we agree to be the luckiest couple in the world? Deal?"

She pulls my arms tighter around herself and snuggles into her pillow to fall asleep. "Deal."

29

Keegan

Nervously, I look at the clock and see only five minutes have passed since the last time I checked the time. Another two hours to wait until my doctor's appointment today when I'll get the results of my nuchal translucency scan—more commonly referred to as an NT scan—and blood work. I am going to go crazy if I sit here any longer and count down the minutes until it's time for Jack to pick me up. Grabbing Kirby's leash, I decide going for a walk will be an excellent way to kill time.

As Kirby makes his routine stops at the mailboxes along the way, I can't help but think about how different this pregnancy is from what I experienced with Kyle. There was never any fear of seizures, my medications, or even my age threatening to harm him. Yes, there are risks with most pregnancies, but now, there are added ones, making the odds even higher that our child could be born with special needs. No matter how much I try to avoid reading or thinking about the issues that could occur, I have a mental checklist in my head of each hurdle or test we overcome, inching closer to delivering a healthy baby.

Kirby and I casually stroll through the neighborhood's streets that eventually lead us to a playground full of children playing with parents standing guard. As Kirby investigates one of the many fence posts surrounding the park, the cutest little girl who appears to have Down syndrome catches my attention. A woman who I assume is her mother is pushing her on the swing as they both laugh from their fun. I can't stop myself from placing my hand on my stomach, wondering if that'll be Molly and me in a few years.

I tug on the leash and tell Kirby, "Come on, buddy. We need to head back, so I can get ready before Daddy gets home."

Kirby gives me one of his looks, as though he understands every word I said, and starts to walk in the direction of home.

Jack is waiting for me when I walk through the back door of the townhouse with Kirby.

Surprised to see Jack here so early, I reach down to unhook Kirby's leash and comment, "You're early."

"I thought we could grab a quick bite before your doctor's appointment," he responds back.

Not quite believing him, I ask, "Okay, now, tell me the real reason you're here."

Looking as if he was caught with his hands in the cookie jar, he says, "All right. I called a few times to see how you were holding up, and there was no answer. I came home to see if everything was okay."

I smile at him. "I took Kirby for a walk."

"Yeah, I see. Where's your phone?"

I look over at the kitchen counter and point. "Over there."

"Why didn't you have it with you?"

"I forgot it."

"Keegan, you can't—"

I interrupt, "I went for a walk and forgot to take my phone. I'm sorry. It's going to be a very long six months if you come searching for me every time I don't answer my phone."

"I know. But what if something had happened during your walk?"

Shaking my head, I tell him, "Jack, you can't act like this, or I'll go crazy."

"I'm sorry. Just try to remember to take your phone with you, okay?"

I nod. "As long as you promise not to call out a search party if I forget it again."

He hangs his head and mumbles, "I promise."

Relieved to learn that the NT scan and blood work are normal, I check another milestone off a list that seems to be endless. Over the years, I have forgotten all the stages there are to pregnancy.

The morning sickness and fatigue have passed, only to be replaced with leg cramps and heartburn. I must admit, my leg cramps have turned into some interesting massage therapy sessions from Jack.

Thankfully, I'm starting to get surges of energy that I take full advantage of when they happen. I'm also now sporting a sweet baby bump that Jack finds incredibly sexy until I remind him that it's his daughter. My ever-changing body shape is making it impossible to hide my condition from others.

Although it's too early to find out the gender, we still refer to the baby as Molly. Jack has decided on the name Bea for her middle name and now calls her his little sweet pea, Molly Bea. The nickname is catching on to the point that I fear our daughter might grow up to hate her name. I try hard to only use Molly, but I find myself sometimes letting Jack's version slip out.

Of course, all of this is meaningless if Molly is a boy. Jack still insists the name will be Cyrus if we have a boy. I'm kind of digging the name, and I like the idea of having a little Cy running around the house.

In all the excitement of the baby, the screenplay has taken a backseat in my life and become a little anticlimactic for me. Alex rewrote the scenes of the night Will died, and I've chosen tonight to read it since Jack and Sean are having a boys' night out.

As I read Alex's words, my grief becomes all-consuming while I mourn Will's death once more. I also grieve for Brittany's loss of finally being with the only man she has ever loved, only to lose him so tragically.

As I walk out of the bathroom with a tissue, blowing my nose, I hear Jack come through the kitchen's back door. I can't get to him fast enough, needing to feel his arms around me.

"Babe, what's wrong?"

"Please, no words, just hold me."

I take his hand, lead him upstairs to our bed, and silently strip him out of his clothes. Once in bed, I take charge of the most intense and intimate night of lovemaking we've ever had. I can't seem to get enough of him, knowing how fleeting time can be in this life.

Kyle decided he wanted to visit his father's grave before leaving for school today and invited me to go with him.

Standing there, in front of the gravestone, in reverent silence, Kyle asks, "Mom, do you think the day will come when we'll stop coming here?"

Kyle's question surprises me.

"Why do you ask?"

"I don't know. It feels as though we're all at a junction in our lives where we're moving on to new things. Me, in college, and you, pregnant and married to Jack. It's as if we no longer need to live in the past anymore," he answers.

"I don't feel as though we're living in the past. We're remembering your dad."

"But this isn't Dad. I know his remains are here, but he was so much more than this-this stone and plot of grass. He was fun and made me laugh. Coming here seems only to bring back the pain of losing him."

Now questioning my decision of making these visits to the gravesite, I apologize, "I'm sorry. I thought you wanted to come here. If I had known…"

"It's okay, Mom. I think I did need to come in the beginning. Now, I'd rather visit him through my memories than a grave. Would it upset you if I didn't come so often?"

"I get it. You do whatever feels right in your heart."

"Thanks for understanding. I love you, Mom."

"I love you, too. How about I give you a few minutes to say good-bye?"

"Thanks."

As I watch Kyle from the car, he stands, looking at his father's gravestone while wiping away a few tears. My heart is bursting with love for this incredible young man. I know Will is looking down, beaming with pride, too.

When we return home, Kyle packs the Mustang with stuff for his dorm and is ready to roll out. Jack said his good-byes to him this morning before leaving for work. I give him a kiss and hug, promising him I will be up midweek for his first home soccer game of the season since his school is only an hour's drive away.

As I walk back into the townhouse, I become acutely aware of the deafening silence and the feeling of emptiness.

I rub my belly, saying under my breath, "It won't be long before you're here, Molly Bea, filling this house with noise."

The following weekend, Jack and I decide to take advantage of the beautiful day by spending it relaxing poolside at my parents'. Mom and Dad walk down to join us, which is unusual. More often than not, they don't feel the need to entertain us when we come over. Instead, they go about their day-to-day routine while we selfishly kick back and relax.

They summon the two of us over to the patio table shaded by a vibrant multicolored striped umbrella. As we join them, I see an exchange of nervous glances between the two of them, and I grab Jack's hand to brace myself for the possibility of bad news. I pray silently, begging God to please let them both be all right so that they can be a part of their new grandbaby's life.

Dad begins, "Um, we have some news to share with you that might be a little difficult for you to hear. We wanted to tell you personally instead of you hearing it from someone else."

I squeeze Jack's hand harder as I keep repeating in my head, *Please, God, don't let the word* cancer *come out of Daddy's mouth.*

Jack clears his throat. "Mitch, please just tell us, so we can deal with it. Keegan is about to cut off all the circulation in my hand."

Dad chuckles. "Relax, Keegan. Your mom and I are okay. We're at the age where we want to travel and enjoy retirement. What I'm trying to say is, we're downsizing and selling the house."

The prayer inside my head quickly changes as I heave out a heavy sigh and release Jack's hand. *Thank you, sweet Jesus!*

Then, it registers that my parents are selling the home that I love as Jack shakes his hand, trying to get its circulation flowing again.

My emotional prego hormones take over. "What? Sell this place? You can't! I mean, no! What about the *dock*? That's *my* dock! *Our* dock!" I tell them. "You can't sell this place," I cry out while pushing my chair back to seek out the comfort of my safe haven.

A few minutes later, I feel Jack walk up from behind, and he wraps his arms around me as I cry quietly.

"Shh, babe. It's going to be okay."

"They can't do this to me. I come here to sort things out in my head. I need to bring Molly here next summer." I turn in Jack's arms and cry into his chest.

"Shh, I have an idea. You need to calm down, so we can talk about it."

"Okay, but first, you need to know something," I tell him.

"What?"

"We're moving," I announce while sniffling and wiping my tears on his shirt.

"We are? And where exactly are we moving to?" he asks with a grin.

"Here. We're buying this house and moving here. I don't care how much it costs. I'll sell both the townhouse and lake house for us to be able to afford it. We're moving here. Nobody is taking our dock away from us."

"Funny thing about how great minds think alike. I was going to suggest the same thing. So, I guess the next thing is, how do we negotiate with your father on this?"

"Oh, leave that to Daddy's little princess," I say, looking up at him with a wicked grin.

"For some strange reason, I'm feeling sorry for Mitch right now. Go easy on him, baby," Jack says through his laughter.

I giggle. "It will be like taking candy from a baby."

Dad isn't the pushover I thought he would be in his negotiations with his favorite pregnant daughter, but we come to a fair price and terms. Jack and I will put the lake house up for sale and wait until after the move to sell the townhouse. We'll be able to take our time and move in after the baby arrives. It'll also give my parents time to purge what they won't need at their new place. I'm also buying the boat. The day will come when I will want to get a different one, but today isn't that day.

On the way home, Jack says, "You know, with the baby coming, this might not be the best time for us to move."

"What are you trying to say?" I ask.

"Let me handle getting the lake house sold. I'll hire Annie to take care of getting your parents' house ready for the move. You know, like painting or any other thing we might want to do to it before moving in. She's an interior designer, and she does this kind of stuff for a living. Consider it my baby gift to you."

"No."

"Come on, sweetheart. Please at least think about it."

I remain quiet for a second or two and then say, "There. I thought about it. My answer is still no."

"Why?"

Counting points off on each finger, I explain, "Number one, it's Annie. Number two, it's going to be our home, not Annie's. Number three, it's Annie."

"Seriously? You change like the weather when it comes to her. Where's the person who said how we needed to include Annie and Seth in our lives?"

"In our lives with Sean, like on special occasions. It's our home for me to make special for us and not your ex-girlfriend, who is also the mother of your son! You seem to forget that it's only been a couple of years since the two of you were playing house together."

"We weren't playing house, goddamn it! Stop making it sound like more than what it was!"

"Were you not over there every night? Did you not hook up with her? Did she not think you were going to propose to her? What is it that Marcy says? If it looks like a duck and quacks like a duck, it must be a duck!"

"God, pregnancy has made you wacky. You're willing to risk the baby and your health over this shit?"

By now, we're pulling into the garage, and I'm coming to a slow boil. "I'll tell you what, Jack. Since it seems so important for you to include Annie, why don't the two of you just take care of everything? That way, you can play house together again!"

I slam the car door and stomp toward the townhouse. When I open the back door, Kirby bolts out to do his business. I close the door behind me, not caring that Jack's arms are full of beach bags and towels from today's trip over to my parents'.

I continue upstairs until reaching our master bath and start to draw a bubble bath to soothe away my anger. Taking off my clothes, I slip into the warm bubbles, tilting my head back against the edge of the tub with my eyes closed. I listen to Jack come up the stairs to our bedroom, eventually leaning up against the doorframe of the bathroom. I can feel him watching me, but I continue to play possum and refuse to acknowledge his presence.

Finally, he kneels down and orders, "Sit up."

Once I sit up, he starts massaging my shoulders.

Damn it! How am I going to stay mad at him when he does something sweet like this after all the crap I just said?

"Keegan, what the hell was that all about?"

"Who knows? Me being a hormonal mess or being fat and insecure? Take your pick. Would you like to join me?" I scoot further up in the tub to make room for Jack to sit behind me.

He answers by removing his clothes and climbing in. Stretching his legs out on either side of mine, he pulls me back against his chest and then cups water in his hands, spilling it down over my shoulders and chest. I feel his erection against my back and know he's also having a hard time staying mad, too.

Jack wraps his arms around me, slowly rubbing my belly with one hand while caressing my breast with the other. He nuzzles my neck and starts kissing me from my ear down to my shoulder. "You can take being fat off the list. Right now, you are the most desirable woman I have ever seen."

My body responds as his one hand travels from my baby bump to down between my thighs as he continues to fondle my breast. He whispers in my ear, "I love watching you come undone when I do this to you."

"Please." The word escapes me.

"Please what? Tell me."

"Please—ah, God, don't stop."

"Is this what you want?"

I get lost in the pleasure that my orgasm brings, forgetting our argument and all the silliness connected to it. Turning around to face Jack, I straddle him, and neither of us cares about the water splashing out of the tub and onto the bathroom floor as we make love.

30

Jack

As I walk out to my Jeep to pick up Keegan at the studio for her doctor's appointment, I can't help but think about how this warm fall day with all the dry leaves provides the perfect conditions for a wood fire.

At eighteen weeks, I can't believe we're almost halfway through Keegan's pregnancy. The good news is the doctor has had little concerns with all tests and blood work coming back within normal ranges.

Our pending move—with the assistance of her parents and my sister-in-law, Liz—has been relatively hassle-free. Surprisingly enough, Marcy and Roger decided to buy the lake house, making it an easy sale, like the Fitzgeralds' home to us.

Mitch and Sandy did hire Annie to decorate their new place. Sandy admitted to needing assistance in downsizing and not getting hung up on keeping things that were no longer necessary or that wouldn't fit in their new condo.

I pull up into a parking space not far from the front door of the studio. Before I can turn off the car, I see Keegan making her way toward me. God, she's beautiful with her rounded belly carrying our baby. Today, we are going to find out the sex of the baby—or as Keegan puts it, get confirmation that it's a girl.

The door opens, and she slips in the front seat and leans over to give me the sweetest kiss. "Hi, baby. Ready to go see Molly?"

"Or Cy," I remind her.

She nods and laughs. "Or Cy. By the way, I've come up with a middle name for Cyrus."

"You have? Well, don't keep me in suspense. What is it going to be? Cyrus…"

"Hamilton!"

I laugh while trying out the name, "Cyrus Hamilton Grady. You know, I like it. I was joking around about the whole Cyrus thing, but now, I think it's a cool name!"

"It's not one you'll hear every day. I believe it has a literary ring to it. I can see it printed across the dust cover of a Pulitzer Prize–winning novel."

"And what about Molly Bea Grady? What do you see for her?"

"Oh, our Molly Bea is going to be a great artist, like her mama!"

Smiling over at Keegan, I tell her, "You've got their futures all mapped out, huh?"

"*Their* futures? Babe, there is only one baby in here, but Cy and Molly would be cute names for twins!"

"Bite your tongue, woman!"

After checking in at the imaging center's front desk, we follow a nurse down the hall to one of the rooms used for ultrasounds.

We anxiously sit there as the technician spreads the clear gel over Keegan's stomach while asking, "Do you want to know the baby's sex?"

Keegan speaks up, "Absolutely!"

It seems as though it's an eternity with the technician moving the ultrasound transducer to different locations, at times pressing down on Keegan's stomach and clicking. The technician asks Keegan, "Have you been feeling the baby move?"

"I have, but Jack hasn't. Every time I place his hand on my stomach, Molly stops kicking. I think she's playing hide-and-seek with her daddy."

The technician laughs. "Molly, huh? Well, let's see if I can confirm that. Oh, she's real cooperative today. Yep, it's definitely a Molly."

Keegan's tears start as the technician gives us our first look at our daughter, Molly Bea Grady. We hold tightly to each other's hands as features are being pointed out to us while we look in amazement at the screen.

"Since you're considered high-risk, you'll have a 3D ultrasound, too. You will be able to see a clearer picture of Molly during that one. When's your next appointment with Dr. Bowers?"

"Two o'clock this afternoon. When I scheduled the ultrasound, it was my understanding that there would be no problem with getting the report to Dr. Bowers in time for my appointment."

"I'll send it right over to them."

We leave the imaging center with our first baby pictures of our daughter in hand.

Later in the afternoon, while waiting in the exam room, Keegan and I are lost in conversation about seeing Molly for the first time when our obstetrician, Dr. Bowers, enters.

"So, I see it's a girl."

Keegan laughs. "Yes, it is. It appears Molly has no problem with showing off her girlie parts."

He proceeds through the motions of Keegan's routine examination that have become customary to us, saying little to nothing as he makes notations in her chart along the way. He excuses himself from the room, only to return a few minutes later with another piece of paper in his hand that he places in her folder.

I begin to carefully watch the doctor, sensing something is off with him today.

Keegan must pick up on the same vibes because she suddenly becomes quiet. "What's wrong?" she asks.

Dr. Bowers answers, "Keegan, as I explained when your pregnancy was confirmed, there could be possible complications due to your age, one of them being preeclampsia. It becomes even more complicated with your history of seizures."

"But I haven't had a seizure in years."

The doctor explains, "Keegan, your craniotomy makes you a candidate for more seizures and the reason for being on seizure meds. Your blood pressure is a little higher than I would like to see it, and your feet are showing signs of some slight swelling. The good news is, there are no elevated levels of protein in your urine. By having you come in weekly now, we can closely monitor you to prevent issues like this from becoming bigger ones."

"Bigger ones? Like what?" I ask.

"Like keeping Keegan from going into premature labor. The closer we can get to thirty-seven weeks when the baby is considered full-term, the better. So, this is what we're going to do," Dr. Bowers says.

He lays out a plan that includes me taking and documenting Keegan's blood pressure every day. She's to bring the log of blood pressure readings to each of her visits. Keegan is not happy when she hears the doctor ban salt from her diet. Although Keegan is taking naps during the day, she is now on mandatory bed rest in the afternoon for a couple of hours each day.

The joy we felt earlier from seeing Molly for the first time has dissipated with a dark cloud of the returning what-ifs hanging over our heads.

As we walk out of the doctor's office, Keegan says, "Take me over to the house."

I take that as code for, *Take me to the dock.*

Although it'd probably be best to get Keegan home and off her feet, I do as she asked.

After I turn off the ignition, Keegan looks toward the house and says, "It's an awfully big house for the two of us."

I get out of the car and walk around to the passenger door to help Keegan out.

"What do you mean, the two of us? There will be five of us living here," I say once she's out of the car.

"Come on, Jack. Think about it. Kyle is never going to live in this house other than the occasional weekend when he comes home from college. Sean is in middle school, coming over a few nights during the week, and he's only a few years away from graduating from high school. If something should happen…" Keegan doesn't finish her thought.

Taking her in my arms, pulling her close into my chest, I kiss her on top of her head. "Babe, everything is going to be fine. Dr. Bowers is keeping a close eye on things. Our baby girl is going to make the same kind of happy memories that you did while growing up in this house."

"You promise?" Keegan asks as she looks up at me.

"Promise. Now, let's go inside and decide what we want to do before moving in."

Once in the house, we enter the kitchen to find a couple of boxes on the island. One has Keegan's name, and the other has mine with a note lying on the counter between them.

> *Dear Keegan and Jack,*
>
> *Welcome to your new home.*
>
> *In these boxes are some special moments in this house that we feel should stay with you. Cherish and build upon them by making new memories with your family.*
>
> *All our love and best wishes during this special time in your life,*
>
> *Mom and Dad*

We each open the box with our name and find framed black-and-white candid photos of us.

In Keegan's box are pictures of her growing up on the lake. There is one of her down on the dock after her surgery with her ball cap, gazing out over the water.

In my box, there are pictures of us on the dock, talking and holding each other. One is from our wedding day on the front porch with me caressing Keegan's face as we are intently looking into each other's eyes.

We look at each other in astonishment at the thoughtful gifts.

As if her mom has ESP and knew we were here, she calls Keegan on her phone.

"Hi, Mom. We're over at the house. The pictures are beautiful. Thank you so much. The ultrasound? Yes, it's Molly." Her smile fades. "Mom, I need to tell you something. My blood pressure is higher than it should be, and I'm starting to show signs of preeclampsia. The good news is, there were no elevated protein levels in my urine.

Yeah, I know." She looks at me as she listens to her mom go on for quite some time. "Yeah, I know. I will. I promise. Okay, we can talk later. Okay, Mom. Will do. Love you, too." She hangs up and smiles at me.

"What was that all about?" I ask.

"You know, one of her pep talks that she's great at giving when I get bad news. She also said something else that will probably make you happy."

"What's that?"

"How great Annie is and that I should let you hire her." Keegan shrugs.

"And?"

"And I'll think about it, but I'm not promising anything," she tells me.

I start to stare her down, leaning against the counter with my arms folded across my chest. After several seconds of staring at each other without either saying a word, Keegan blinks first and looks away.

"Okay, go ahead and call her." She then points her finger at me. "But I want to go on record and say that I'm doing this under protest. I'm not happy about it at all!"

I pull her into my arms to kiss her forehead, as if she were an obedient child. "Good girl. I'm just glad Sandy could talk some sense into you."

After walking through the house, we decide to change the layout of the downstairs to make room for a master bedroom and bath. Now, we have no choice but to hire Annie to design the space and see if our ideas are doable. I make a call to her and arrange a time for us to meet to discuss the project.

I tell Keegan when I get off the phone, "Annie can come over here on Monday evening. I'm going to meet her here after work and show her our ideas."

"Excuse me?"

"What?"

"I'm sure you meant to say *we* are going to meet her here Monday evening and show her our ideas."

"No. I will meet Annie here while you stay home and rest."

"Annie's fired."

"What do you mean, Annie's fired?"

"Either I'm included every step of the way, or we wait until after the baby is born so that I can be involved. We're only talking maybe a five- to six-month delay in getting started, which would have us moving in maybe by the end of next year."

"You're kidding me, right?"

"We either do this my way or not at all!"

"Fine. *We* will meet Annie here on Monday evening, but let me make one thing clear. When this place becomes a construction zone, you will not be over here, taking a chance of getting hurt."

"We'll cross that bridge when we get to it."

I decide not to argue any further about it. "Come on. It's been a long day. Let's go home. Do you want to stop and pick up something for dinner?"

"No. We have some of that leftover casserole from last night," Keegan replies.

When I slide behind the driver's seat after helping Keegan into the car, I find she's on her phone again.

"Okay, we can stop by for a few minutes," she says before ending the call.

"Now, what's going on?" I ask.

"Seth wants us to stop by the coffee shop on the way home."

"Come on, Keegan. You need to get home. Call him back and see if we can make it tomorrow," I try to reason with her.

"No. I could tell in Seth's voice that something big is going on. He knows we can only stay for a few minutes."

Walking into the shop, we see Seth in the corner booth, nervously tapping his left foot as he waves us over.

Sliding into the booth after Keegan, I ask, "Hey, what's up?"

"Um, I want to let you two know that, um…I'm going to ask Annie this weekend to marry me. Jack, I know how you feel about things, and I promise—"

I interrupt him, holding up my hand, "Seth, it's okay. I'm cool with it. Congratulations!"

Seth looks over at Keegan for her reaction to the news. She is looking down at her hands, trying hard not to make eye contact with him.

"Well? Say something, Keegan," Seth tells her.

She looks up at him. "Seth, please don't do this. You don't know what she's capable of doing."

"Are you kidding me? After all this time, you still don't get it, do you?" he asks.

"Seth, have you forgotten how she lied about Jack and tried to keep me away from him? Who does shit like that?"

"Keegan, she was in a bad place back then. That wasn't Annie but someone who was hurting and trying to get her family back. Jack knows the real Annie. Tell her, Jack. Go ahead and tell Keegan what Annie is really like."

Keegan glares at me, and says, "Yeah, Jack, by all means, tell me."

Shit!

Talk about being caught between a rock and a hard place, especially after our conversations about hiring her.

I carefully start to step through the minefield before me. "Um, well…" Looking over to Seth and seeing his look of desperation for me to come to his rescue, I hesitantly continue, "Seth's right about Annie trying to get her family back."

When I see the hurt in Keegan's eyes, I look down at the table. "Before meeting you, I went out on a couple of dates after breaking up with Annie, but they never amounted to anything. She figured it would be the same with you and that I would eventually come back home to her and Sean. It wasn't so much that she was in love with me but that she wanted to keep her family together. Annie got scared when you and I got serious. She was afraid that I would become an absentee dad.

"I guess, because I understood why she did all that stuff to us, I always gave her the benefit of the doubt. Annie has always been there for me, even after you and I broke up." Then, like a coward, I add, "Sorry, I need to go use the restroom."

While throwing some cold water on my face, I silently berate myself for saying all that to Keegan. I return to the booth and find Keegan staring out the window with a distant look, as though she is daydreaming.

Seth immediately starts to talk before I can figure out what happened in my absence, "So, you're cool with me marrying Annie and becoming Sean's stepdad, Jack?"

Reaching over, I shake his hand. "Yeah, I'm good with all of it. When do you plan on doing it?"

"I'm still figuring out the details on how I'm going to ask them."

"Them?" I ask in surprise.

"Yeah. I think Sean should be there when I do the deed."

"Got to say, that's a classy move. Wish I had thought of it."

"Well, I've got things to do and plan. Thanks for meeting me on such short notice," Seth says as he stands up to leave.

After Seth leaves, Keegan softly asks, "Can we go home now?"

"Sure." I stand to assist her with sliding out of the booth.

The whole way home, Keegan says nothing. Once back at our townhouse, she goes straight upstairs to bed without a single word to me. I'm at a loss as to what to do.

I decide to go upstairs to check on her. She has taken off her clothes and is only wearing her Irisheyes football jersey. I love how it hugs the curves of her expectant belly. I kick off my shoes while stripping done to my boxers and climb into bed, close behind her. She acknowledges me by taking my hands in hers, holding them on top of her stomach.

I can no longer take her silence and ask, "Can we talk? I'm sorry if what I said about Annie hurt or upset you."

"I'm okay. Don't worry about it."

"Come on, Keegan. Talk to me. This silent treatment is worse than just battling it out."

"Is that how you see our disagreements? As battles?"

"Well, you've got to admit, sometimes, they do turn into a battle of wills."

She turns, facing me, her eyes glassy from the tears she's fighting back.

I put my finger under her chin to raise it up, so she's looking at me. "Hey, tell me what's going on in that head of yours."

"When you left for the restroom, I was ready to tear into you until Seth said something that stopped me."

"What was that?"

"He told me that you were only answering his question honestly. That one of Annie's qualities was being there for the people she cared about, especially when they were hurting. The reality of everything hit me as to how close we came to this moment—right here, right now in this bed—not happening."

"Babe, maybe we needed to go through all of that to get to where we are today."

"But what if something like that happens to us again? What if something goes drastically wrong with my pregnancy? Are you and I going to be able to handle it?"

"Have you forgotten the promises we made to each other on our wedding day? Remember what I promised?" I ask.

"Yeah, I remember. You promised to stay with me through both the good and bad times."

I then tell her, "And you promised to be my beacon of light when I'm struggling to find my way. I'm counting on you to keep your end of the bargain."

31

Keegan

I'm leaving my thirty-one-week doctor's appointment today, knowing the pregnancy is progressing nicely. My fears of a premature delivery subside a little more as I check each week off of the calendar.

Holidays serve as other little milestones for me. I found out about my pregnancy shortly after Fourth of July. Since then, Labor Day, Halloween, Veterans Day, and Thanksgiving have passed by. Thankfully, the upcoming Christmas holidays will be relatively quiet and hassle-free. Jack and I agree there will be limited decorating and no entertaining at our home. I've been doing most of my shopping from the comfort of my bed with Jack and Mom picking up a few odds and ends for me during their travels. Since my parents have moved to a smaller home, the family dinner will be at Ryan and Liz's house this year. My brother has wanted to do this for years and is more than happy with the change of tradition.

By carefully following the doctor's orders, I've been able to manage my blood pressure and weight. I've been diligent to schedule my days so as not to overdo, and I lounge in bed for a couple of hours during the afternoon. At times, I feel like a beached whale, causing me to become frustrated with my current sedentary lifestyle. Whenever I find myself start to whine, I stop because it's a small price to pay to ensure Molly is born healthy.

On the way home from the doctor's office today, I decide to stop by my parents'—I mean, *our* house to meet with Annie and see the progress on the renovations. I'm glad Jack and Mom convinced me to hire Annie to oversee the remodel.

At first, I was worried about how my parents were going to handle all the changes to my childhood home. Surprisingly enough, they were thrilled and excited when they saw the beautiful virtual tour of each room that Annie had produced. In fact, Mom and Dad even made a few suggestions that we hadn't thought of and have included in the plans.

We've even managed to have a few laughs along the way, like the day when we were determining with Annie which pieces of furniture would go to a local consignment shop for sale.

Annie pointed to the recliner and asked, "Consignment shop?"

Both Jack and I shouted a resounding, "No!"

The recliner will have a place of honor in the lower-level man cave along with Jack's fire and sports memorabilia. One of the guys on the construction crew let it slip that Jack was having an unsightly metal support pole in his room be covered in brass to replicate a firehouse pole. Traditionally, these types of supports are hidden by drywall columns. I informed Jack that I knew what he was up to and that there would be no pole dancing in either of our futures. He just grinned at me, not saying a word, before he walked away.

Parking next to a construction van in our driveway, I think back to our first meeting here with Annie to discuss our plans a couple of days after Seth had proposed to her.

The moment Jack and I turned into our long drive that day, we saw a huge banner stretching across the front porch banister with the words, *She said yes!* Behind the banner was Seth dipping Annie back, giving her an over-the-top kiss, while she held up her left hand to show off her ring. It was obvious they were mocking Jack's post on social media of us announcing our engagement after he proposed to me.

I walk inside to see how the renovation is coming along, and I am impressed by how fast the house is coming together. It looks entirely different from the home that I grew up in with a few walls gone to accommodate the new layout. I see Annie talking to the foreman in the kitchen, and she motions me back.

"Keegan! You have perfect timing," she tells me as I approach them.

She proceeds to explain a final decision is needed for the backsplash and countertops along with the hardware for the new kitchen cabinets. We already narrowed it down to three options with Jack leaving the final decision up to me. I love all three choices, which makes it difficult for me to pick one. Looking at them one more time on a temporary table made of plywood and sawhorses, I study each one again. All are beautiful, but there is one I think is particularly stunning. It will give the space a clean, fresh, timeless feel to it. Annie agrees with my choice, as it is her favorite, too. When I am ready to leave, Annie walks me out to my car.

"Annie, everything looks fantastic. I'm glad we decided to do all of this before Molly is born. You're doing an amazing job," I commend her.

"Thanks, Keegan. I'm glad you're letting me do this for you and Jack."

"Me, too."

As I leave the house, I find myself in a particularly good mood today. Thanks to Annie, the house will soon be ready for us to move in. I'm slowly inching my way to my due date with no major issues. The screenplay is finished, and the movie is now in preproduction.

From the garage, I walk into our townhouse and suddenly feel exhausted. Kirby follows me upstairs to the bedroom where I slip on my Irisheyes football jersey, and the two of us get comfy in bed.

I'm startled awake when Jack's arms wrap around me as he snuggles up behind me.

I turn my head toward him. "What time is it?"

"Shh, go back to sleep. It's only two o'clock. I didn't hear from you after your doctor's appointment, and I took off the afternoon to check on you," he whispers in my ear.

"Oh, babe, I'm sorry. I stopped by the house. I was tired and forgot to call. Molly and I are fine. I didn't mean to worry you," I tell him, turning in his arms to face him.

"I know. I checked on the way home to see if you were at the house, and Annie told me you were fine. Now, go back to sleep." He holds me close with him being in only his boxers.

Snuggling up to him and feeling his hardness against me, I begin to ache for him to make love to me. I start giving him featherlight kisses up his chest and to his neck.

"What do you think you're doing? You need your rest," he tells me.

"I need you," I answer back.

It isn't long until he is lovingly kissing me, but then the doorbell rings.

Jack stops and looks up at the clock. "Who in the hell is that? Stay here while I get rid of them."

He quickly pulls on a pair of sweats and a tee, and then he goes downstairs to answer the front door. I lie in bed and can hear hushed voices downstairs.

Jack comes back up to the bedroom door and says, "Sweetheart, you need to get up. Your parents are downstairs."

"My parents? Why?" I ask.

"Just get dressed, and come downstairs," he says in a far-too-serious tone for my liking.

"Jack, you're scaring me."

"Everything is okay. Your parents will explain." He walks over to my side of the bed, leans over, and kisses me. Then, he leaves to return to my parents.

It takes only a few minutes for me to throw on some clothes and join my parents, who are waiting for me in the TV room with Jack. I feel a nervous tension as I enter the room and see the looks of apprehension on the faces of Mom, Dad, and Jack.

Not bothering with niceties, immediately, I ask, "What's going on?"

Dad begins by saying, "Keegan, princess, come sit down. Everything is going to be okay. The last thing we need is you getting upset."

Dad is treating me like he did during my breakdown after Will's death. I look to Jack and see the worry in his eyes, too.

"Dad, I'm fine. Just tell me." I remain standing, wrapping my arms around Molly and myself in a feeble attempt to protect us.

Jack comes to my side, putting his arm around me and pulling me tight against him.

"Princess, the other day, I went in for my annual physical. The doctor didn't like the sound of things when he listened to the main artery in my neck and referred me to a specialist."

I interrupt, "A specialist? What kind of specialist?"

He continues, "A vascular specialist. There's a partial blockage in my left carotid artery."

My hand flies to my mouth as I gasp. The thought of my father being sick is incomprehensible to me. In my eyes, he's invincible. He's my superhero.

"Now, everything is going to be okay. It was caught in plenty of time before causing any problems. I'm going in for a carotid endarterectomy."

"What's that?" I ask.

"They make an incision here in my neck"—he indicates the location with his finger—"and surgically open up the artery to remove the plaque and the diseased portion."

"When?"

"Tomorrow," he says calmly.

I look over at Mom and see her trying to hide her concern to downplay the seriousness of it all.

"Mom, are you okay?" I ask.

She nods. "Of course, I was shocked to hear the news, but after talking to the doctor today, I'm feeling much better about things."

By now, my eyes can no longer hold the tears, and they begin rolling down my face. "Jack?"

"It'll be okay, babe," he consoles me.

I sit down beside my dad, wrap my arms around his waist, and cuddle up next to him, like I did when I was a little girl. "You're going to be okay. It's all going to be okay, right?"

He returns my hug and chokes out, "Yeah, princess, I'm going to be fine. I've got a brand-new baby granddaughter who will need me to teach her how to put a worm on a fishing hook."

I giggle. "Yeah, you sure do because I don't bait hooks."

I call Kyle, and Dad talks to him. Dad insists that Kyle stay at school, promising that someone will update him throughout the day.

After Mom and Dad leave, Jack takes me upstairs and draws a bubble bath for the two of us. As we settle into the bubbly, warm water, I heave out a heavy sigh, lying back against his chest, as the bath soothes away my frayed nerves.

"How is it that you always know what I need?" I ask him.

He shrugs. "I don't know. I guess, at the end of the day, all we need is each other."

I look over my shoulder, up at him. "Thank you."

"For what?" He looks down at me.

"For loving me."

He lets out a deep chuckle. "Babe, you have no idea how easy it is to do that. How's our baby girl doing?" he asks, putting his hand on my belly, hoping to feel her move.

Molly doesn't disappoint and gives a hard kick for her daddy.

"Whoa! She's a little feisty this afternoon!"

I laugh. "Yeah, I think she's getting anxious to meet us." Looking down at my belly, I tell her, "You need to stay put for a little while longer, baby girl."

"Not to ruin the moment, but the weather report is calling for ice tonight, and there is no way I'm letting you drive in it. I've already called in, and I have taken the next two days off. Since Ryan and Liz are taking your parents to the hospital, why don't we plan on staying home until your dad is done with the procedure and taken to recovery? That way, you can get your rest and then see him the minute he can have visitors."

"Normally, I would argue and insist on being there all day, but you're right; there's no way I'd last. Yeah, that sounds like a good plan. I'll call him in the morning to-to"—once more, the emotions of today catch up with me as tears gather in my eyes—"tell him I love him." I sniffle.

Jack holds me close. "Hey, don't worry. Everything is going to be okay. Your dad will come through this with flying colors and will be his old self by the time Christmas rolls around and our sweet pea, Molly Bea, makes her grand entrance."

Little do we both know how much our lives are going to change during the next twenty-four hours.

32

Jack

Exactly as predicted, we wake up to a winter wonderland of sparkling ice coating the trees and roads. Wasting no time, Keegan calls Sandy to find out how they are getting to the hospital.

"Hi, Mom. Are you guys okay? That's good. Yeah, let me talk to Dad. Hi, Dad. I know. Yeah, I'm good. We're not coming to the hospital until you're out of surgery and the roads are safe to travel. Yeah, we'll be careful. Okay. I love you, too."

I signal to Keegan to let me talk to her dad before hanging up.

"Dad, hold on. Jack wants to speak to you." She hands the phone to me.

"Hey, Mitch. How are you doing? Ryan's there, too? Good. Yeah. Yes, sir. I'll be sure to drive carefully. We'll see you later. Okay. Bye."

I hand Keegan's phone back to her while saying, "That was a smart move for them to stay at the hotel across from the hospital last night. I'm glad Ryan is with them."

"Yeah, you know Dad, always thinking ahead."

After I finish salting our walkways, I go upstairs and crawl back in bed with Keegan.

She shrieks, "Oh my God, you're cold. Stay away from me."

I continue to tease her by placing my cold hands on her. "Aw, come on, help warm me up."

She jumps out of bed and grabs her robe.

I laugh. "Come back to bed. I was only joking around."

Keegan, halfway scolding me, says, "Thanks to you, I need to get some hot chocolate. Do you want some, too?"

Smiling at her, I answer, "Yeah, spending the morning drinking hot chocolate in bed with you sounds like a great way to warm up. Thanks."

The morning drags on as I try to distract Keegan from worrying about her dad by making small talk about the house and Molly.

At one point, she says, "I know what you're doing, and thank you, but one of these days, everything is not going to be okay with my parents or yours. We need to accept that and not take our time with them for granted."

I nod in agreement. "You're right, but everything is going to be okay today, babe."

I decide to call my mom and dad to bring them up to speed on Mitch along with Keegan's last doctor's visit, and I promise to call them back later today. I end our conversation by giving them both my love.

Mitch's surgery was scheduled for eight thirty this morning and was supposed to last a couple of hours. By eleven o'clock, Keegan is up, pacing around the townhouse, not understanding why her mother hasn't called. I try to explain all the possible delays that could have happened, but she is in no mood to listen.

With the combination of the sun coming out and the roads being treated with salt, the ice soon melts, making it possible for us to start thinking about going to the hospital.

The phone rings with the news we've been waiting for all morning that all went well and that Mitch is now in recovery. We each let out a sigh of relief and go about the business of getting ready to leave for the hospital.

Slowly, we inch around the parking deck that is connected to the hospital, looking for a space to park the car. Finally, I find one that is not far from the elevator, making it a short walk for Keegan.

As Keegan and I walk toward the elevator, we excitedly talk about her dad and laugh without noticing where we're walking. Within seconds, Keegan begins to slip. Fortunately, I am able to catch her, keeping her from falling all the way to the ground.

Once Keegan is steady on her feet, I ask anxiously, "Babe, are you okay?"

"Yeah, I'm good. Boy, that was a close call. You would have needed a crane to get me back up if I had gone all the way down."

As I check her out, I ask, "Are you sure you're okay?"

"I'm fine."

"Okay, just checking. What the hell did you slip on?" I ask, looking at the floor of the garage.

"I don't know. I guess some water. You know, with this big-ass belly of mine, I can't see my feet anymore, much less where I'm walking!"

We both break out laughing and continue to head inside the hospital to see Mitch.

We find her mom and Ryan sitting patiently, waiting to go back to recovery to see her dad. We timed it perfectly because a nurse is just entering the room to take everyone back to Mitch. I decide to stay in the waiting room, so there aren't so many people back in recovery at one time. It isn't long afterward when Mitch is taken up to ICU for the night, and then he will be in a regular room tomorrow. If all goes as expected, he will be released in a couple of days.

We've been at the hospital for a little over an hour, and Keegan is beginning to look drained from the day's stress.

Mitch suggests to her, "Hey, princess, you seem tired. Why don't you go home and get some rest?"

Keegan nods in agreement. "Okay, but first, I need to use a bathroom. All I seem to do these days is pee." She giggles.

When Keegan returns, she has a strange look on her face. She quickly picks up her coat, walks over to the bed, and gives Mitch a kiss. "I love you, Daddy. We'll see you later."

We walk out to the hall, and Keegan takes me to the side. "Jack, I'm bleeding."

"What do you mean, you're bleeding? A lot?" I ask nervously.

"No, it's more like spotting. Do you think we should go to the doctor's office or find someone here to check me out?"

"Call Bowers's office and see what they want you to do. I'll go tell your mom."

Keegan grabs my arm as she pulls her phone out of her purse with the other hand. "No, not yet. Let's see what Dr. Bowers says first."

As luck would have it, Keegan's obstetrician is currently on call at the hospital. She is instructed to meet him on the maternity floor.

Dr. Bowers is waiting for us as we exit the elevator and has a nurse with him to take us to a room.

During his exam of Keegan, the doctor asks, "Did you fall or possibly run into anything with your stomach?"

Keegan answers, "I slipped a little while walking into the hospital earlier today, but I caught myself."

"That might have done it," Dr. Bowers replies.

"Done what?" I ask.

"A placenta abruption is the cause of the bleeding," Dr. Bowers replies. Then, looking at Keegan, he continues, "I'm admitting you to the hospital, Keegan, on full bed rest and observation. There is a chance the bleeding will stop on its own."

"What about the baby? Is Molly okay?" Keegan asks.

"Yes, Molly is doing fine. Her vitals are good. If the bleeding increases or Molly's status changes, we will go ahead and deliver her."

Alarmed by this news, Keegan says, "But I'm just starting my thirty-second week. It's too soon."

"Keegan, a placenta abruption is irreversible. You were already at high risk for developing one due to your age. Since you're not experiencing any pain with the abruption, we might be able to stop the bleeding and delay delivery by putting you on full bed rest. Each day we can put off having you go into labor, the better. If it turns out we need to deliver sooner than later, the survival rate is excellent for a baby at thirty-two-weeks. It's good that you're here in the hospital should your condition suddenly deteriorate."

After hearing this news, we decide I should go upstairs and tell her family. Before I leave, Keegan asks for her phone to call Marcy.

Everyone is surprised to see me walking back into Mitch's room.

I guess the look on my face gives me away because Sandy immediately jumps up from her chair and asks, "Jack, what happened?"

"Everything is okay. When Keegan was in the bathroom, she noticed some bleeding. Fortunately, Dr. Bowers was on call and met us upstairs in maternity. They've decided to admit her and put her on bed rest to try to stop the bleeding. We just wanted to let you all know what was going on. Hey, I need to get back upstairs to be with Keegan. I'll keep you posted."

"I'm going with you," Sandy says as she grabs her purse.

"No. Stay here with Mitch. I'll let you know if anything changes. I promise."

When I return to Keegan's room, I find that all hell is breaking loose. She's doubled over in pain, crying, with nurses scurrying around, tending to her. Once I get closer to the bed, I see blood.

It registers with me that Dr. Bowers is now in the room.

He says, "Notify delivery that I need an OR, stat." He then takes me out in the hallway. "Jack, I have to deliver the baby."

"I can be there, right?" I ask.

As they wheel Keegan out of the room past us, he answers, "Normally, we would get you in some scrubs and allow you to be there, but under the circumstances, you need to wait in the waiting room. I'm sorry, but I've got to go."

And, like that, both Keegan and the doctor disappear through some doors at the end of the hospital corridor. I didn't get to reassure her that everything was going to be okay. There were no exchanges of *I love you*. I lean back against the wall and slide down into a sitting squat with my forearms resting on my knees as I look down at the floor, feeling lost.

A nurse walks up to me. "Mr. Grady, are you okay?"

I stand back up with tears in my eyes, trying to compose myself. "Yeah, I'm okay."

She offers, "Let me take you to the waiting room."

I nod and follow her down the hallway.

Before she leaves the waiting room, the nurse explains the procedure to me and how the doctor will come here to talk to me afterward.

This isn't the way it was supposed to happen. I should be with Keegan to witness the birth of our daughter. I should be the one to cut the umbilical cord. I should be there to hear Molly cry as she takes her first breath.

I pull out my phone and start making calls—first to Sandy, then Kyle, and finally, my mom. Before I finish my call to Mom, I see Ryan and Sandy walking down the hall toward me.

As soon as I disconnect from Mom, Sandy hugs me, and says, "Keegan and Molly are in good hands."

My emotions become too much for me to handle as I tearfully tell her, "There was so much blood. I'm scared."

Sandy continues to console me, "I know. We just have to believe in our hearts that everything is going to be all right."

Ryan stands in the hall outside of the waiting room, updating Liz, as I sit beside Sandy, who is holding my hand. I focus on the door, trying to will the doctor to return and say that my daughter and wife are doing well.

Please, God, I beg you to let them both be okay.

I start remembering my time together with Keegan— from our first date up to the last time we made love. The night I felt Molly kick for the first time while holding Keegan in bed. The sonogram pictures we have on our refrigerator door, proudly on display for all to see.

We did everything right, only to have all of it be put in jeopardy by a stupid little bit of water on a parking deck floor.

It seems like I've been sitting here forever, waiting for news. Any news. The unknown is killing me. I continue to stare at the door.

Waiting.

Wishing.

Hoping.

Praying.

I see Dr. Bowers coming down the corridor toward the waiting room. I can tell from the grave expression on his face that something went wrong.

All I've been wanting is for him to return to talk to me, and now, I'm not sure if I'm strong enough to hear what he has to say.

33

Keegan

Feeling confused and a little groggy, I wake up, unsure of my surroundings. My hand goes to my stomach, and then the memories flood back—the pain and seeing Jack standing in my room, looking lost, as they wheeled me out to deliver Molly without him. After that, I don't remember anything else. I don't remember Jack cutting the umbilical cord or me lovingly kissing my new baby girl or counting her fingers and toes to make sure there was ten of each.

Why don't I remember doing any of that?

I hear the door open and see the outline of Jack's figure, backlit by the light from the hallway. He steps fully into the room and says, "Welcome back. You've been coming in and out of it for a while."

"Molly…" I stop, not sure of what to ask.

Jack takes a seat in the chair beside my bed. "She's in the NICU. I'll explain everything in a second. First, how are you feeling?"

My throat is dry, feeling like sandpaper when I swallow. "Thirsty. Confused."

Jack stands to pull my hospital bed tray table up closer to me. Sitting on it is a Styrofoam cup that I assume is full of water.

He lifts the cup and straw to my mouth. "Here, take a sip of this."

The water is cold, and it soothes the scratchiness of my throat.

I can tell from Jack's expression that something is wrong. I wince as I try to pull myself up further in the bed. I make little progress between my weakness and the pain from my incision.

"Jack, I'm fine. Please tell me," I plead.

Jack sits back down in the chair. He reaches over and takes my hand into his. "You started to hemorrhage and began convulsing when they delivered Molly. They couldn't stop your bleeding and"—Jack focuses on my hand as he tenderly starts stroking the top of it—"they had to do a hysterectomy to stop the bleeding."

My only concern right now is Molly.

"But what about Molly? Is she all right?"

"Yeah, so far, so good. Our little girl weighs three pounds and ten ounces. The doctor said her weight is within the normal range for thirty-two weeks. The biggest concerns are her breathing and gaining weight. Since Molly isn't sucking yet, they had to insert a feeding tube down her nose. It looks like Molly will be in the NICU for a few weeks if she doesn't develop any complications."

"Such as?"

"Molly's lungs are still developing, and there is also a risk of infection, like pneumonia." Jack then quickly adds, "We just need to take this one day at a time." He drops his head on the bed and starts to cry while still holding on to my hand. "God, I thought I had lost you both."

I reach over with my free hand and run my fingers through his hair. "I'm okay. I have to see Molly. Please, Jack, tell them I have to see my baby girl."

Jack lifts his head, and he wipes the tears from his face. "You've lost a lot of blood. I'm not sure if they will let you. I'll see what I can do." A small grin comes across his face. "In the meantime, I took some pictures of her until you can get to the NICU."

Jack holds his phone up to me. I gasp at the things hooked up to Molly as she lies in an incubator. My heart aches over the need to hold her.

"Jack, I've got to see her. Please make them understand," I beg once more.

"I will. Right now, you need to rest. You had major surgery."

A nurse enters the room. "So, how are we doing?"

"Terrible," I snap at her. "*We* want to see our baby."

"All in due time. First, I need to check your vitals," the nurse replies in a condescending, dismissive way.

I know then that I have to do whatever it takes to convince her I am in good enough shape to visit the NICU. I lie quietly in bed while she checks my blood pressure, temperature, and my incision, and then she runs through her seemingly endless list of questions.

After she finishes, I ask, "So, can I see Molly?"

"We'll need to check with the doctor."

The nurse's constant use of the word *we* is becoming both irritating and annoying.

Just when I am about to lose my patience, Jack speaks up, "That would be great. I'm sure you can understand how anxious Keegan is to see her daughter for the first time." Then, he gives the nurse his sexiest smile that visually flusters her.

"I'll see what I can do." She smiles back at Jack with reddening cheeks.

After she leaves the room, I suspiciously eye Jack and ask, "So, what was that all about?"

"You get a lot more bees with honey." He winks at me.

I correct Jack, "I believe the saying is, *You catch more flies with honey than vinegar.*"

He shrugs. "Whatever."

"All I know is, if someone doesn't take me down to the NICU soon, I'll get up and go down there by myself."

Jack laughs. "I don't think you're going anyplace on your own for a while." His voice changes to a softer tone as he tries to reason with me. "I know you want to see Molly. I felt the same way, but they know what's best, and you need to listen."

"Have you talked to Kyle?" I ask.

"Yeah. Kyle's upset that he can't be here because of finals. I sent him pictures of his new baby sister. He said to call him as soon as you felt up to it. Sean was here earlier to see Molly. He's pretty stoked about being a big brother."

Suddenly, I feel exhausted, and my eyes start to get heavy. I'm unable to stop yawning.

Jack says, "Hey, I'm going to go back down to the NICU while you get some more rest."

"Don't go. Stay. How's Daddy?"

"He's doing good. He's out of ICU and in a private room. Your mom has already wheeled him down to see Molly."

I smile and then fade off to sleep.

Finally, I've been given the okay to see Molly. I can barely contain my excitement as Jack carefully wheels me down the hospital corridor to the NICU.

"Jack, you're going too slow," I complain to him.

"Calm down. We're almost there. It's just around this corner."

As we turn the corner, I see the doors to the NICU up ahead.

When we enter, a nurse greets Jack, "Hello, Mr. Grady. I assume this is Molly's mom."

I smile at her and nod.

The nurse then introduces herself, "Hi, I'm Kelly. There's a sweet little girl who is waiting to meet you."

Kelly hands a sterile gown to Jack and then one to me to put on.

I start to stand, but Kelly stops me. "No, please sit still. Just put your arms through the armholes here, and then we can tie it at the back. That way, you don't have to get up."

Once our gowns are on, Jack begins to wheel me back through the unit. I notice a couple of babies lying in their incubators with an assortment of wires connected to them. I watch one mother hold her baby against her chest. With a blanket draped over them, she rocks back and forth in a rocking chair. She acknowledges me with a smile, knowing the common bond that we share.

As we approach Molly's incubator, I'm overwhelmed with emotions the moment I see her. She looks so small and fragile, lying there. She's wearing a pink knit cap that fully covers her head, coming down almost to her eyes. Kelly lowers the unit as Jack maneuvers the wheelchair closer. Next to the incubator, I notice a monitor on a pole with other gadgets attached, tracking Molly's vitals. Peering back in the unit, I become fascinated with watching her chest rise and fall with each little breath. Molly then quivers, as if she has a chill.

"Is she cold?" I ask Kelly.

"No. Molly's muscles are still developing, and that's normal movement at thirty-two weeks. The incubator is keeping her nice and warm. When she's able to maintain her body temperature, we'll move her into an open bassinet."

Kelly picks up a bottle with some clear liquid from the table beside the incubator and squirts some of it into my hands. "This is hand sanitizer. Always be sure to use some before touching Molly."

"I can touch her?" I ask in amazement.

"Yes, it's important for you to have contact with her. She needs to feel the touch of her mommy."

I lean forward, not caring that it's causing my stitches to pull on my incision. I insert my hand through one of the hatches of the incubator. "Hey, my little sweet pea, Molly Bea. It's Mommy. I'm so happy to see you. I love you, my sweet baby girl."

I tenderly stroke her little fingers as I mentally count them one by one in my head. I giggle as Molly wraps her little fingers around mine.

As Jack pulls a chair up next to me, he says, "I already did a count. They're all there. Ten fingers and ten toes."

I laugh, looking over at Jack and then back at Molly. "Your daddy is making fun of Mommy."

Without warning, my joy is snatched away when an alarm on Molly's monitor starts to sound. I look up to see Kelly and another nurse rushing toward us. In a panic, I look back down and see Molly's chest is no longer moving, and she is lying perfectly still.

God, no! Please don't take my baby away from me. Dear Lord, I beg you to let my baby girl start breathing again.

34

Two Years Later
Jack

On this gray wintery day, only a couple of weeks before Christmas, I enter the kitchen and find Keegan standing at the sink, daydreaming, while looking out the window at the dock. It's not unusual to find her like this when the house is empty and quiet. She's unaware that I'm watching as her hand goes to her stomach.

Coming up from behind her, I wrap my arms around her, startling her. "Hey, how's my favorite wife doing?"

"Good. Everything is under control. Most of the food is ready. The table is set in the dining room. I'm just waiting on the roast to finish. Did you remember to pick up the flowers?"

"Yes, I did. I left them in the garage where it's cold. When is everyone supposed to get here?" I ask.

"I told them around two."

Keegan's melancholy mood starts to worry me.

"Hey, what's wrong?" I ask, turning her around in my arms to face me.

She snuggles into my chest. "Nothing. Absolutely nothing. I love you."

I hold Keegan tighter and kiss the top of her head. "I love you, too, babe."

Our moment is interrupted by Keegan's cell phone chirping on the counter.

"Sometimes, your ringtone can be a real mood killer," I jokingly tell her.

She apologetically looks up at me. "I'm sorry."

Keegan sees it's Alex calling and answers as I get a can of soda from the fridge.

"Hi, Alex. How are you?"

The last time we saw him was at a private screening of *Ultimate Cost* that Alison Kennedy and Keith Steele hosted in Baltimore for the cast and crew of the movie. It was one thing to read Keegan's words in the book, but it was a whole different thing to see them brought to life on the big screen.

I hear Keegan ask, "What news?" Then, I see her break out in her happy dance while shaking her hand at me to get my attention. "That many? Wow! That's wonderful. Congratulations!"

I have no idea what is going on from the scene taking place in front of me other than it must be good news.

Then, Keegan's next words take me by surprise. "She's flying us out to attend the ceremony? When is it? Okay. Please tell Alison and Keith thank you. That is very generous of her. Again, congratulations, Alex. I'm so happy for all of you."

Keegan ends the call.

"What was that all about?" I ask.

Smiling back at me like the Cheshire Cat, she says, "Oh my God! *Ultimate Cost* has been nominated for five Golden Globes." She begins ticking them off on her fingers. "Alex for Best Screenplay, Alison for Best Director, Keith for Best Actor, the movie's soundtrack for

Best Original Score, and *Ultimate Cost* for Best Motion Picture. Can you believe that?"

"I told you from the very beginning that it would be a blockbuster!" I laugh. "And, to think, all of it is because of your book."

"And Alex's script along with Keith's acting and Alison's directing," Keegan adds.

I walk over to Keegan and take her back into my arms to pick up from where we were so rudely interrupted by the phone.

"We have certainly lived a lifetime in a few short years."

Keegan smiles. "Any regrets?"

"Hell no!"

Keegan then asks, "Who would have thought when we exchanged our wedding vows down at the dock that we would end up living here, in this house, raising our family?"

"Not me, that's for damn sure. When I walked in here a few minutes ago, you looked as if you were in another world, gazing out the window. What were you thinking about?"

"Two years ago, back in the NICU, when Molly stopped breathing in front of our eyes. I don't think I will ever forget that."

Keegan's comment takes me back to that horrible moment when we sat in the NICU, watching helplessly, as our daughter lay in her incubator, not breathing, with alarms sounding off all around us. All my years as a firefighter had not been enough to prepare me to witness what I thought was the death of our child. Little did either of us know at the time that apnea was not an uncommon occurrence with preemies. Thankfully, the nurses were able to get her breathing again within seconds. Molly was one of the lucky babies in the NICU who had few problems and was able to come home after a thirty-two-day stay in the hospital.

Keegan snaps me out of my thoughts by asking, "Hey, the roast should be ready to come out in about an hour. Why don't you come join me in the shower while we have the house to ourselves?"

"I like the way you think." I smile and wink back at her.

35

Keegan

I stand in front of the mirror, naked, waiting for the water to reach the right temp. I notice the scar from my cesarean and drag my index finger over it.

Jack walks up behind me and lifts my hair off the back of my neck, exposing the tattoo of shamrocks that represents our family. He softly kisses it as his other arm comes around me and slowly finds its way to the apex of my thighs. My hair falls back in place as his free hand travels around me to caress my breast. I lean back against him as he continues to fondle me. I become aroused, wanting more.

Jack then stops his foreplay and pulls me into the shower with him. The spray of water beats down on us as he pushes me against the tiled wall and passionately kisses me as he makes love to me. A rush of emotions comes over me as my orgasm shoots through me.

As we towel off afterward, I look out into the bedroom and see the time on the bedside clock. "Jeez, I've got to get moving. Your parents are going to be here soon. I want to make sure the flowers are out on the table."

Giving Jack a quick kiss before hurrying out of the bathroom, I go into our walk-in closet to find the outfit I plan on wearing today. Once dressed and ready for our guests, I head out of the bedroom, leaving Jack behind as he gets ready for the party.

I'm setting the last of the jars of sweet peas on the main table when the front door opens.

The cutest little voice yells, "Mommy!"

I answer back, "I'm in here, sweet pea!"

I hear the patter of little footsteps as Molly runs down the hallway to me. Every day, I give thanks for this precious little girl standing here in front of me, who fills my heart with so much love and joy.

I watch Jack sneak up behind Molly, and he scoops her up into his arms as she squeals with laughter.

"I've missed my little sweet pea, Molly Bea. I need to get a little nibble of her!"

Pat and John Grady walk up behind Jack, laughing, hands full of all the paraphernalia an almost two-year-old requires to take on a sleepover to Grandma and Grandpa's.

The house soon fills with family and friends to celebrate Molly's upcoming birthday on Tuesday.

I stand at the sink, loading the dishwasher, as the people we love enjoy our home and each other. I pause to watch Molly show Mom and Dad her latest masterpiece of scribbles that she created with her new set of crayons. As I admire her artwork from afar, I overhear Seth and Jack give Sean a hard time about a girl in school. Annie scolds them for their teasing. I glance out the window and see Kyle standing down at the dock with his girlfriend. It takes me back to when his father, Will, and I used to do the same thing at that age. I wonder if Mom stood here and watched us, too.

While everyone enjoys a slice of cake after singing "Happy Birthday" to Molly, I announce *Ultimate Cost*'s numerous Golden Globe nominations. We are then upstaged by Brittany and Aiden announcing their engagement, and Joyce proudly beams at the two of them.

As I clean up the kitchen, Marcy walks up with a handful of dirty paper plates and sees the garbage can is full. "Where do you want me to put these?"

"Just set them down on the counter. Jack is gathering up all the garbage to take it out." I stop what I'm doing to look over at Marcy. "Did you ever think we could be this happy?"

"Without a doubt," she says before walking away.

Later that night, after everyone has left to go home, Jack happily carries our partied-out daughter upstairs to bed. I let Kirby out for the last time of the evening. Kirby is starting to feel his age and has been moving slower these days. He eventually finishes his business and doesn't even bother with the neighbor's cat lurking in the yard.

Once back inside, I head to the bedroom to get ready for bed. Jack enters our room as I walk out of the bathroom in my faded Irisheyes jersey. Kirby sits on the floor at the foot of the bed, pathetically looking at Jack for assistance because he doesn't have the energy to jump up onto the bed tonight.

"Hey, buddy, do you need some help?" Jack asks as he lifts Kirby up to the bed. He then says to me, "That little munchkin of yours got two stories out of me tonight!"

"She has you wrapped around her little finger." I laugh as I crawl under the covers.

"Yeah, just like her mommy does!" Jack replies over his shoulder as he walks into the bathroom.

A few minutes later, Jack joins me in bed, taking me into his arms, and he gives me the sweetest of all kisses. "Do you have any idea how much I love you?"

"Just as much as I love you. Beyond the stars and back."

Epilogue

Jack

Stretched out across the bed, watching the Golden Globes on the TV in our hotel suite, I couldn't be prouder of Keegan and her accomplishments. I always knew she was a talented, amazing woman, but this was far more than I could have ever dreamed for her.

When the camera goes to the table where the cast of *Ultimate Cost* is sitting, I catch a glimpse of Keegan and Kyle. I can't help but notice that Alex Parker is sitting next to Keegan, holding her hand. She's still as beautiful as the day we met for the first time in the coffee shop.

As I watch her book's movie take center stage, my thoughts go back to the night at the restaurant when we had a disagreement over her married name, eventually leading her to the idea to write a book. It has taken us on a ride that neither of us envisioned, ending here with us waiting to hear if her book's movie wins tonight.

Ready for bed in her pajamas, Molly is quietly playing with her toys nearby on the floor. She decides to climb onto the bed, refusing any help from me, with her favorite stuffed animal in hand.

Once settled next to me, she looks at the TV, and says "Mommy!"

I point to the TV. "There's Kyle, too."

It only takes a few minutes for Molly to become bored, and she drifts off to sleep as I continue to watch the show.

Keegan

When the graphic for the Best Screenplay appears on the stage screen, Alex holds both Madeline's and my hands as we wait for the announcement of the winner.

After the presenter runs through the list of nominees, Alex's grip becomes tighter as we hear the words we've been waiting for, "And the Golden Globe for the Best Screenplay goes to…"

It seems as if time moves in slow motion as the presenter breaks the seal of the envelope and smiles.

Then, he announces, "Alex Parker, for *Ultimate Cost*!"

The film's theme music plays as the crowd erupts in applause, and we all stand at our table, congratulating Alex on his win. Alex takes Madeline in his arms and kisses her. He turns to give me a hug, followed by shaking Kyle's hand. As Alex makes his way to the stage, he grabs my hand and pulls me along to go with him. Knowing this show is being broadcast to millions of viewers, I decide not to make a scene, and I go willingly. As I stand a few steps behind him, Alex accepts his award before stepping in front of the microphone to make his acceptance speech.

He then pulls me beside him and starts to speak, "If it weren't for this incredible woman, Keegan Grady, and her bravery to write such a phenomenal book, this evening wouldn't have been possible for me."

Alex's words cause me to blush as I beam with pride at his accomplishment.

Alex continues by thanking others on his long list, including Alison and Keith. He then finishes his short speech by saying, "And to my wife, Madeline, thank you for loving me and for believing in me during a time in my life when I didn't. Your love inspires me every day, and it's why I'm here today, accepting this award. I love you with all my heart." He then raises the statue in the air and ends with, "Thank you all."

After Alex finishes speaking, a young starlet and the presenter escort us backstage where winners are photographed and interviewed. Even all these years after my surgery, there are still times I become overly stimulated by bright lights and chaos.

There is only one place I want to be, and it isn't here. I let Alex know that I'm ready to leave, and he makes arrangements for a car as I pull out my phone to text Kyle about my change in plans.

> *Me: I'm going back to the hotel.*

> *Kyle: Are you okay?*

> *Me: Yeah, just tired. Have fun with Alex and Madeline at the parties tonight.*

> *Kyle: I'll see you tomorrow.*

Alison and Keith arranged for a suite at one of Hollywood's luxurious hotels for Jack, Molly, and me while Kyle decided to stay with Alex and Madeline at their house. Alison also had an assortment of couture gowns made available to me from some of her favorite designers. I chose an understated one that was breathtakingly beautiful in its simplicity.

Jack felt that Kyle should be the one to escort me tonight while he stayed with Molly in the suite. The real truth was, Jack would rather stay with his little sweet pea than dress up in a tux and deal with the hype of the red carpet.

By the time I reach the limo Alex arranged to take me back to the hotel, Kyle texts, saying that Alison won Best Director. As my driver navigates the busy streets of Beverly Hills, my phone pings again, signaling another incoming text.

> *Kyle: Keith just won Best Actor. This place is going crazy!*

Kyle also attached a picture of Keith accepting his award onstage.

The limo is now stuck in traffic, keeping me from Jack, who is the only person I want to be with to celebrate this exciting news.

Finally, the limo pulls under the portico of the hotel where we're staying. The doorman opens the door for me to climb out.

I receive another message from Kyle as I enter the elegant lobby that only contains a video of the presentation for Best Motion Picture. I stop in the middle of the lobby and play it.

"And the Golden Globe for Best Motion Picture goes to *Ultimate Cost.*"

As my eyes become teary, I do a fist pump, exclaiming out loud, "Yes!"

I hurry over to the bank of elevators to catch the next one up to our suite.

It's deathly quiet when I enter and walk across the beautiful sitting room to the door of the master bedroom that is slightly cracked open. I gently push it open, and there, asleep in the bed, are Jack and Molly.

Jack is sprawled out on his back with his head facing me while Molly is on the other side, curled up in a ball, holding her favorite stuffed dog. As I stand, watching them sleep, Jack's eyes crack open, as if he senses my presence. As he focuses on me, I bring my finger to my lips, signaling for him not to make a sound, and then I point to Molly. Jack carefully removes himself from the bed. We exit the bedroom, and he closes the door behind us.

I turn to Jack. "Oh my God! Have you heard?"

He grins at me. "*Ultimate Cost* won more than Best Screenplay?"

"We didn't win Best Original Score, but"—I start bouncing up and down with excitement—"Alison won Best Director, Keith won Best Actor, and *Ultimate Cost* won Best Motion Picture!" I squeal to him.

Jack takes me in his arms and kisses me. "Congratulations. By the way, I saw the hottest woman on TV tonight."

"I could have died when Alex dragged me up onstage."

"I wanted to kill that son of a bitch for molesting your hand half the night."

"Jack!"

"Hey, it was hard to watch with my sweet pea next to me, asking who that man was holding Mommy's hand. God, I'm only human."

Chuckling, I tell him, "While I was standing up on the stage with him, the only place I wanted to be was here with you."

"I love you," Jack says to me as he kisses me once more.

"I love you beyond the stars and back."

I snuggle into Jack's chest, enjoying the feel and smell of him enveloping me. After my failed marriages to Will, I fought hard to become an independent woman, not needing to share my life with anyone. The whole time, the joke was on me. It's here, in the arms of this man, where my real happiness lies.

Acknowledgments

Once again, I'm sending kudos out to two amazing women who contributed to this book—Sarah Hansen of Okay Creations for another beautiful book cover, and Jovana Shirley of Unforeseen Editing for her editing, proofreading, and formatting talents. I am blessed to have these two ladies working with me on my books.

To my beta readers, Lois and Rebecca—Thank you, ladies, for your blunt and honest insights. I love our conversations about the characters and story.

On a more personal note, thank you to my family—My husband, Mike, for the love and support he gives each day on this journey My son, Michael, the photographer who works magic with the headshots he takes of me. My daughter, Kate, for encouraging me to write my first book, *Enduring You.*

Lastly, thank you to my readers. Your kind words of support mean so much to me. I couldn't do this without you.

About the Author

S.T. Heller was born and raised in Maryland. She now lives on a lake in southern Pennsylvania with her husband and dog. Retired from a local school system, she has two children and five grandchildren. Along with enjoying fun times on the lake with family and friends, her other pastimes include quilting and making pottery. She loves the sound of her grandchildren's laughter, daydreaming on a  beach by the water's edge, getting lost in a good book, and floating on the lake at sunset.

The first book of The Dock Series, *Enduring You*, is the start of Keegan and Jack's story. The next book in this series, *Regarding You*, picks up their story at their twenty-fifth wedding anniversary.

Please follow S.T. Heller at www.shellerauthor.com.

42660461R00201

Made in the USA
Middletown, DE
18 April 2017